# REBECCA ROOK

Her last chance may end her life.

# FALSE HAVEN

*For my own Uncle Rick.*

I miss you every day.

# ***False Haven*** **Soundtrack**

The *False Haven* Playlist is available on **Spotify**.

1. "Run from Me" by Timber Timbre.

2. "The Only Thing Worth Fighting For" by Lera Lynn.

3. "Brother Run Fast" by KALEO.

4. "Hypothermic" by Goodnight, Texas.

5. "The Curse" by Agnes Obel.

6. "In the Woods Somewhere" by Hozier.

7. "Seven Devils" by Florence + The Machine.

8. "Don't Know Who I Am" by Rebecca Roubion.

9. "Crazy" by Daniela Andrade.

10. "It Knows Me" by Avi Kaplan.

11. "Meet Me in the Woods" by Lord Huron.

12. "Fight Like Gods" by Chelsea Wolfe.

13. "House of the Rising Sun" by River Matthews.

14. "Dodged a Bullet" by Greg Laswell.

15. "Stand by Me" by Tracy Chapman.

# FALSE HAVEN

# Contents

## PROLOGUE

The worst part of these meetings was the smell.

The room reeked of body odor poorly masked by overpowering cologne, unwashed hair, and nicotine gum. Vivienne breathed in shallow, careful bursts, trying not to taste the air.

Metal folding chairs formed a tight circle of tired eyes and haggard faces that Viv still found jarring on people her own age. The fluorescent light further bleached the color from skin. It reminded Viv of Grafton Stake. Of *them*. She shifted, cold discomfort seeping through the hard seat into her body.

"Vivienne?"

She glanced at the facilitator, a nice enough woman named Alice who appeared to be in her forties with bottle blonde hair and a faint unibrow. *Nice but persistent.* "Yes?"

The other woman gestured to the group of teenagers and young adults. "You haven't had an opportunity to share yet. Would you like to go tonight?"

Viv froze. "Um, maybe not."

Alice frowned. "You'll need to do it at some point. That's how these meetings work."

Viv knew how Narcotics Anonymous meetings operated. Everyone shared, eventually. Viv didn't object to the sharing. She only worried that they wouldn't believe her. Who would? "I'm not ready, I think."

"No?" Alice kept her tone neutral, free of judgment. Viv appreciated that.

Nearby, a young man (Jake? Jackson? Viv couldn't recall.) snorted.

Viv glared at him. He stared back, a disdainful sneer across his face. His eyes were much older than his face. Viv knew her own eyes had a similar quality. "What?" She challenged him.

"Just get it over with," Jake or Jackson retorted. "Whatever it is, this thing you think is so bad, we've all heard it or seen it or done it." He motioned around the tight circle. Viv saw a few heads nod in agreement. "You ain't going to shock no one in this room." He leaned deeper in his chair and shook his head in disgust.

Alice prompted again. "Well, Viv? Is tonight your night?"

Viv studied her knees without seeing them. She thought about the asylum, about Uncle Rick and Helen. About Cat and Joel. About *them*. Viv rubbed her hands together and she could almost feel the loose dirt, the viscous slick of her own blood, under her nails and between her fingers. A chill chased across her scalp and trickled down her neck.

Viv scrutinized the group. They wouldn't believe her. So, why not? What did she have to lose?

"Sure." Viv offered a grim, tight smile. "I'll share."

## CHAPTER ONE

The Greyhound breathed cold, sterile air on the near comatose passengers. Vivienne folded further into her seat, her forehead resting against the window despite the chill. She traced a single drop of rain across the fogged pane with a fingertip. Her backpack rested in the seat beside her, a sentinel against the few others that remained on the tall and narrow bus. After a moment, the raindrop flicked away, and Viv dropped her hand. She resettled her black hood atop her head.

The bus had shed more and more passengers as the vehicle wended its way south along I-5, until only Viv and three others remained. The bus driver, a weary but capable woman in her fifties, switched on the PA system.

"Hard Luck, Oregon, in five minutes."

The PA switched off with a sizzle.

That was her stop. Viv forced herself away from the bus wall and gathered her phone, earbuds, and wallet into a tidy pile before tossing them into her pack. She watched the trees and the underbrush along the road thin, becoming less dense, less green, as signs of human habitation took over. Billboards stood stark against a dark gray sky and promised great grub at Honey's Diner or a cozy stay at the Hard Luck Motel. As the Greyhound sliced through the outskirts of town, a worn wooden sign welcomed newcomers to Hard Luck, Oregon, established in 1898. The bus slowed, coming to a stop in front of the foretold Honey's Diner.

The PA switched on again. "We have arrived in Hard Luck, Oregon. If this is your stop, please gather all of your belongings before leaving the bus. Greyhound is not responsible for lost or stolen items."

Viv joined the short line to get off the bus. Outside, the rain-laden air was damp against her skin. She smelled exhaust, and the cold tainted air stung her nostrils. Viv pulled her hoodie tighter around her body. She watched a mother and a daughter with matching dark rims around their eyes wrestle four enormous suitcases off the bus, struggling to move them onto the nearby sidewalks. Viv eyed the pair. Grief and envy snaked through her. *They look exhausted. But at least they have each other.*

Once they stepped away, Vivienne ducked into the carriage hold and grabbed her large, navy hiker's backpack. She waved off the bus driver's attempt at assistance and shrugged the pack onto her shoulders, holding the smaller backpack in her hands.

Viv felt her phone vibrate and glanced at the screen.

A text from her uncle: *At Honey's Diner. I grabbed a booth.*

Viv took in the restaurant in front of her. Well, she wouldn't have far to walk.

The diner was busy. A line of people trailed out the door and into the parking lot, which housed trucks, Suburbans, and motorcycles. Viv stepped inside, dodging the line and the irate glares cast her way. She searched for her uncle, inhaling the scents of deep-fried foods and coffee.

He sat in a booth by a window, chatting with a man seated nearby. They sported similar outfits: jeans and work boots, with plaid flannel over a worn T-shirt and a baseball cap over thinning hair that had seen thicker days. Viv trudged through the aisles, dodging a harried waitress with a stained apron and ugly sneakers. Stopping in front of her uncle's table, she waited for a pause in the good-natured conversation. After a moment, the stranger in the next booth cast her a sideways, skeptical glance.

Viv knew what he saw: a rail-thin teenager with long brown hair and black eyes, in a black hoodie and blacker jeans, decent work boots — a gift from her uncle — and weighed down by an incongruous hiker's backpack so full it strained at the seams. Silent and dark, she stood out like an inkblot in the colorful noise that echoed through the diner.

She waited.

Without turning to Viv, Rick spoke. "Tell Honey I'll have the number two."

"I don't know who Honey is, Uncle Rick," Viv replied.

Her uncle stilled with recognition. His eyes twinkled as he stood up to hug Viv. She returned the hug with a tight embrace of her own. Not a tall man, Rick seemed even shorter than she remembered. His auburn hair, a family trait on her mother's side, had faded in his middle age, but his enthusiastic manner of conversation, punctuated by wild hand gestures and boisterous laughter, remained the same. Viv remembered how his often bawdy sense of humor had offended her father. Her mother had enjoyed his silliness, though. Viv remembered the pranks Rick pulled in the hospital to cheer her mother up during treatment: rude noises made by balloons and machines, snakes that sprung from a can... Her mother would chuckle until she started to cough. Then her father would frown at Viv and Rick until they fell quiet.

*I haven't seen Rick since the funeral*, Viv realized. *It's been a year.*

Rick stepped back. "Good to see you, kiddo. Sit down, sit down."

Viv tucked the hiker's backpack into the booth, then slid herself onto the bench seat opposite her uncle. The tabletop was sticky with soap residue. She winced to herself. *I hope it's soap.* The waitress with the ugly shoes came to collect their orders — a Rueben sandwich and a burger — before Rick leaned across the table.

"How was the ride down?"

Viv shrugged. "It was quiet, for the Greyhound."

"No trouble at all?"

Viv shook her head. "No. Cold, smelly. It could have been worse."

"Did your father see you off?"

"He dropped me off at the station."

Rick frowned at his hands on the table. "Well, how is he?"

Viv rolled her eyes. "Like you care."

Uncle Rick chuckled. "We're not besties, but we both love you."

"You can admit it, he's kind of an asshole."

"Hey." Uncle Rick's voice sharpened with disapproval. "Be respectful. He's still your father."

Viv stared down at the tabletop, her teeth grinding together. Her dentist had wanted her to wear a nightguard. Viv hadn't cared enough to tell her father; that was the least of her problems.

"Vivienne." Her uncle gentled his tone. "I'm sorry to be short with you. You both lost your mother, and I feel for him. It's not easy."

Viv looked up. "You mean, it's not easy to lose your wife and gain a loser for a kid."

His lips firmed into a thin line. "That's not what I meant. At all. I'm just saying the man means well."

"I got a Reuben and a burger here." The waitress and the sandwiches had arrived.

Grateful for a distraction, Viv dug into her burger. They ate in silence. Viv was pleasantly shocked by how good the food was. *Or maybe I'm just hungry.* She hadn't expected much from Hard Luck, Oregon.

As the food dwindled away, the tension returned. Viv fiddled with a French fry.

Rick broke the silence. "You ready for this, kiddo?"

Viv studied him. Worry marred his face, and his thick auburn brows pleated with concern. His beard had so much silver that he had a roan rather than rust coloring.

*He deserves the honest answer.* "Probably not."

He let loose a gravelly laugh. "That's comforting."

Viv gave a half-smile. "How did you even find this program, anyways?"

Her uncle sipped from his coffee mug before answering. "Working for the Bureau of Land Management, I encounter a lot of third-party contractors and nonprofits tied to land conservation and stewardship." A pause for another sip of coffee. "Your program is loosely based on the Civilian Conservation Corps from the 1930s, part of the whole New Deal environmental initiatives. But it's different because it focuses on helping kids get back on track, expunge their records, and the like." He focused on Viv, his tone hard. "From what your father shared with me, this program is your only chance. Don't waste it."

Viv dropped her French fry onto the plate as a tremor shook her hand. She leaned back against the booth seat, grateful for its solidity. She thought about her nights in the juvenile center in Portland, only weeks ago. After the first night on the thin, hard mattress, she simply didn't sleep. She couldn't relax. She didn't trust any of the others in the ward. Viv had napped during the day, but that was hit or miss. The concrete walls, tile floors, and metal bars across the windows had wrapped around her like an unwanted quilt. The very air had tasted of astringent cleaners, body odor, and somehow, anger.

Then there were the other girls. One of them, a large girl with unnaturally yellowed hair and teeth, had pinned Viv to the wall and breathed foul imprecations into her ear while choking her with a single hand. The ward guard had been slow to intervene, irritated by the extra fuss rather than concerned for Vivienne.

She hadn't stopped shaking that day.

Viv had almost sobbed with gratitude when her father picked her up a week later.

He hadn't noticed anything unusual. But then, he never did these days. *Not since the funeral.*

Viv refocused on her uncle. "I only have to get through these six weeks, right? Then I get to go home?" She cleared her throat. "I don't go back to the detention center?"

She saw sadness seep into her uncle's gaze, like he could see inside her head. "This program is literally a Get Out of Jail Free card. You just got to do the work, okay?"

Viv nodded.

Her uncle cleared his throat. "You want something else to eat?" he asked with forced cheerfulness. "You've got to put some meat on those bones if you're gonna do trail work."

Viv shook her head.

Her uncle checked his phone. "When do you check in with Helen Whiteaker?"

"4:00 p.m."

"We should get going then."

Uncle Rick carried her hiker's backpack as they walked to the Bureau of Land Management office and commented on the limited points of interest in the small town. Many of the buildings along Main Street were decorated in the Wild West tradition, with false balconies on the second floor and signs inscribed with Ye Olde West typeset. They strolled down the old-fashioned walkway, covered in wooden beams fixed together in a snug fit. A large billboard of a miner with a pan of gold rose above the main drag of shops and stores; the town's main street doubled as the freeway that wove through it. The overall result was a calculated attempt to cash in on the nostalgia for the town's historic appeal.

*A tourist trap*. Aside from the tourism angle, the town seemed to have one of each establishment: one diner, one general store, one hardware store, one gas station.

Viv shivered. The day had grown chilly.

"Wait." Rick's sudden command interrupted her thoughts. "Your sponsor. For NA. They know you're here?"

"She knows. We text and talk when we need to."

Rick seemed doubtful. "And that will work for you?"

Viv shrugged. "It will have to, won't it?"

Rick lapsed into silence, worry and skepticism veined across his face. Viv studied him with a sideways glance, and her heart sank within her chest. *He doesn't trust me. Not anymore.* She swallowed hard the sadness that tickled up her throat.

Fog had settled on the mountains surrounding the town, cloaking the green with gray. Just past the post office, Viv saw the Bureau of Land Management office. Reminiscent of a log cabin, the building was obviously built to retain the rustic Old West aesthetic, with a low roof and log walls. Only the small metal overhang that projected over the glass double doors modernized the structure. The American and State of Oregon flags flew at top mast, rising from a manicured lawn.

They paused before the double doors.

Her uncle scrutinized her. "If you need anything, you call me."

Viv nodded. "Sure."

Uncle Rick dropped her backpack, then wrapped Viv in another hug. He smelled of Reuben sandwiches, coffee, and soap, and his beard was soft against her forehead. Viv leaned into him, grateful for the warmth. He felt like home. She hadn't felt that sense since her mother had passed.

"You're gonna be fine." His voice was gruff as he released her. *He sounds like he's trying to convince himself.*

Viv didn't respond.

Time would tell, wouldn't it?

## CHAPTER TWO

Viv stepped into a small lobby.

A woman dressed in a neat Bureau of Land Management uniform, her blonde hair in a pristine braid, peered up from her small desk and computer as Viv approached. "Can I help you?"

Viv fumbled to pull the registration paperwork out of her backpack. "I'm here to meet with Helen Whiteaker."

The smile on the older woman's face froze, then dimmed. "Oh, you're one of those kids. You'll find Helen and the others in the first conference room. That way." The woman pointed down a hallway, then refocused on her computer, dismissing Viv.

*One of those kids?* A flare of frustration, chased by shame, rocked through her. She ground her teeth. *Yeah, I guess I am. Asshole.* Viv hefted her backpack with more force than necessary, then walked down the hallway on polished floors. She found the room and stepped inside, then paused.

Five faces looked up at her entrance: two girls and three guys. They sat around a conference table in office chairs that were sleek, professional, and out of place in the rustic lodge. An open box of cheap pastries rested at the center of the table, surrounded by water bottles, sodas, and napkins. A pile of hiker's backpacks rested in the corner of the room. Viv cast the others a quick glance, then placed her pack next to the pile. She picked a chair at the end of the table, closest to the door.

Viv found five pairs of eyes studying her. She felt grubby after a long day on public transportation and tried not to squirm under the scrutiny.

"What's your name?" one of the girls demanded.

"Viv." She didn't inquire about their names. None of them were there to make friends.

The girl who had demanded Viv's name opened her mouth to say more but was interrupted by the arrival of a woman in her thirties with thin black hair pulled into a low ponytail, nut-brown skin, and a stocky, muscular build. The woman walked with authority and purpose, her shoulders back and her head upright, and when she came to a stop at the head of the conference table, she cast an assessing gaze over Viv.

"You must be Vivienne." It wasn't a question.

Viv nodded.

"Welcome." The woman didn't smile. "I'm Helen Whiteaker, and I run this program. You will report to me for the duration of your time here." Helen's dark eyes held a steel promise of order.

Viv found herself sitting up a bit straighter.

Helen swept a glance around the room. "We're all here, so let's start." She then eyed the pastries in the center of the table. "I'd eat those if I were you. Our meals over the next six weeks won't be spectacular."

One of the boys reached for a Danish.

This seemed to satisfy Helen. "Welcome to the Conservation Corps for Teens. Let's discuss what you're here to work on for the next six weeks. At the direction of the Bureau of Land Management and the local county council, we'll be providing the grunt labor for the demolition and cleanup of Grafton Stake, a local institution with several old buildings. We will also build a trail system, campsites, and recreational day sites around the area. The goal of our work is to help create a park-like setting for a future campground and visitor's center."

Helen paused. "Does anyone have any questions?"

No one responded. The boy with the Danish ate loudly, without closing his mouth. Viv winced at the sight, then glanced away. The squelching noise turned her stomach.

Helen eyed Danish Boy with a flicker of amusement in her eyes before continuing. "We have a tight schedule and will need to work fast. We work eight hours a day, every Monday through Friday, with lunches and breaks. Weekends will be spent at the campsite, or in town for short durations."

Helen paused again and gazed around the conference room with her eyebrows raised. When no one said anything, she sighed. "I'm going to be blunt: Most of you are obligated to be here."

Viv felt the impact of the words like a dash of cold water across the face. She saw the others react, too, shifting uncomfortably in their seats or staring at the floor or the ceiling.

Helen stared at the table. "For various legal and privacy reasons, I do not know the specifics of why you are here, but I will not tolerate any insubordination or disruption on my team. If you misbehave, I will ship you home without a second chance. This is a job. You will be paid a stipend at the end of the six weeks or a prorated amount for the time you've spent in this program. I expect professional behavior from each of you, towards me and towards each other. That means no sex, no drugs, no shit talking, and no fights."

The conference room was still. Viv's stomach roiled with anxiety. She almost admired how efficiently Helen had asserted control over the group.

"Really?" Helen cast a skeptical glance around the room. "No questions at all?"

"Are we allowed to have fun?" A sullen question from the girl who had demanded Viv's name.

"That depends on you," Helen replied without missing a beat. "If you all do your jobs well, comply with the rules, and don't cause trouble, we will have excursions on the weekends. We are surrounded by an abundance of natural wonders, many of which we can visit if all goes well."

One of the guys scoffed. "Field trips for good behavior?"

Helen didn't bat an eye. "Yep."

"Um, where are we staying?" A timid question from the third young woman.

Helen nodded. "You will stay at a campsite at Grafton Stake. Sleeping accommodations are basic. You will be issued a sleeping bag, pad, and pillow, and you will sleep in tents, separated by gender." Helen paused, glancing through her paperwork. "I have no indication that anyone on this team is trans or nonbinary, but if you are, you will stay in the tent that best reflects your gender or wherever you feel safest." Helen raised her eyes to them. "Tonight is an exception, however. We're staying in the motel due to a delivery delay with our supplies. After our briefing, we'll head over there and settle in for the night."

A car backfired in the parking lot and Viv flinched.

Helen surveyed them. "I think that's enough for now. Let's do a quick round of introductions, complete the paperwork, and head over to the motel."

"Will we have to do ice breakers?" The angry girl spoke with sharp sarcasm.. "Trust falls?"

Helen stared the younger woman down with a flinty smile on her face. "This isn't summer camp. We're not here to braid each other's hair and to confide our darkest secrets." She shifted her focus back to the table at large. "Tell everyone what you want to be called and anything else you want to share. That's it."

Viv almost smiled. *I think I like her. Maybe.*

The timid young woman seated next to the snarky one started first. "I'm Morgan. I'm from Eugene."

Viv eyed Morgan's mousy brown hair and bright blue gaze, which jumped from person to person within the room in nervous motions. Under their collective gazes, Morgan fidgeted with her hands and her hair and her clothes, which were made from hemp material and darned with multi-colored patches. The young woman wore impractical sandals, her feet a pale blue-white from the air conditioning inside the lodge. She seemed young for her age and out of place in this room. *So why is she here?*

The snarky one went next. "I'm Cat." She glared around the room. Adorned with thick black hair, dark brown eyes, and tan skin, she was beautiful, with a slender neck and unblemished skin. Her clothes, though suitable for hard work in a forest, were high-end brands from popular recreational chains. She also wore a self-assured confidence and the air of expectation that people would pay attention to her. Her polished surface nagged at Viv. Why would someone that coiffed and put together be stuck in the woods of rural Oregon?

Danish Boy spoke, dragging Viv's attention from Cat. "I'm Zane. I'm from Klamath Falls." He shrugged. Viv could tell that Zane was tall, with a long torso and longer legs that folded beneath the conference table. He had light brown skin covered with facial stubble and thick brown hair. "I'm not sure what else to say."

"Thank you, Zane." Helen nodded. "Who's next?"

The scoffer, a young man with tan skin, spoke up. "I'm Devlin. You can call me Dev. Portland." He spoke in a quiet voice and clasped his hands in his lap. He had a button nose under a strong brow, his curls were shaved tight against his head, and he had trouble making eye contact with anyone. A cheap, scratched watch rested on his right wrist, seemingly out of place with his expensive clothes, clean hiking boots, and a citrine stud in his right earlobe.

The last boy spoke without prompting. "I'm Joel." His deep voice cut through the quiet of the room. Viv studied him. He was tense, visibly unhappy, but he held himself still. Black hair and dark eyes on a pale face watched the room with a careful gaze. Motorcycle boots, jeans, and a dark Henley completed the standoffish vibe.

After a long silence, Viv realized that they were all staring at her. Waiting.

Cat smirked at her. Devlin and Morgan offered encouraging smiles, and Viv wondered why these two sweet people were in this room of angry misfits.

"I'm Viv."

Helen straightened. "Thank you for the introductions. Let's finish your paperwork, then head to the motel."

The motel was...decrepit.

The cabins were small wooden structures with tin roofs that seemed like a good wind would blow them over. They reminded Viv of garden sheds sold at home improvement stores. A gravel path led up to each cabin, lined with twin rows of poorly tended pansies on either side. A large neon sign glowed bright in the twilight with the letters D and M burnt out so the name read *Har Luck otel*.

"Good lord," Devlin muttered.

"Classy," she heard Cat snark from behind her.

"Maybe it's better on the inside?" Morgan said.

Viv snorted to herself. *Optimist.*

Helen led them to the main office, a humble room with sparse and worn rattan furniture. The reception desk had deep scratches across the wooden surface; the walls were painted an unexpected and garish pale pink. A small, grey metal rack stood to the left of the reception desk and held a few well-worn brochures that advertised local tourist attractions. *See THE Demolition Derby of 2011!* exclaimed one.

A worn nameplate rested on the desk and identified the man standing behind it as Mr. McCully. He was rail-thin, except for a small belly that protruded over his slacks. A ring of thin brown-gray hair circled his balding skull. His dark eyes were sharp as he assessed the group with a discerning glance. He then turned to Helen.

"You Helen Whiteaker?" he queried.

"Yes." Helen pulled out a sheaf of paperwork from a satchel and handed it to the man. "We're staying tonight, maybe tomorrow, too."

The man accepted the paperwork, then pushed the registrar across the desk and placed a pen next to it. "Sign everyone in. Here are the keys." He laid several sets of keys on the counter, then turned away without another word.

After signing her name, Viv left the main office with trepidation. Helen had sorted Viv and Morgan into Cabin 3, and the underwhelming exteriors didn't promise much. Once inside, Viv paused in surprise. *Huh. Better than I expected.* Two full beds bisected the room, each covered with worn blue duvets and flat pillows. The carpet was a dark brown shag, and two wooden dressers, a shade lighter than the carpet, stood along the wall opposite from the beds. A small TV graced the table next to the restroom.

"It's not too bad," Morgan said.

"It could be worse," Viv agreed.

Viv moved into the room and claimed the bed closest to the door. Ever since her stay in the detention center, she liked having an exit nearby. Morgan struggled with her blue backpack, hefting it over the doorway. Once inside, Viv unpacked just enough clothing for the next day and pulled out her phone charger.

Morgan yawned, stretching her arms out. "I'm going to take a shower."

"Okay." As the bathroom door closed, Viv pulled out her phone and thumbed open her messaging app.

*Made it.*

A few seconds passed. Then the typing bubbles popped up, followed by a text: *Is it terrible?*

Viv snorted to herself. *Yes and no.*

*So that means yes.* Her sponsor at NA, Olivia, had always been able to see through Viv's bullshit.

*It's not awful.*

A pause from Olivia. *Yeah. You all right, though?*

Viv assessed the modest motel room with the worn furniture and ragged carpet. She could hear Morgan in the bathroom, making an inordinate amount of noise for one person in a small space. The room was cold and smelled of damp, moldy laundry. She thought of the strictly neutral decor in her father's house, grays and beiges in the carpet and the couch and the drapes. He had redecorated just after the funeral, over Viv's protests. After that confrontation, she had broken a window in a shopfront.

Viv sighed. Crummy as it was, at least the motel wasn't the detention center and it wasn't her father's home. She typed a final text.

*I'll be fine.*

## CHAPTER THREE

A door slammed outside the motel cabin.

Viv jerked awake. The motor of a nearby car turned over and rumbled to life before fading away. Outside, she could hear the faint sounds of the highway traffic from the main street of Hard Luck. In a bleary motion, Viv grabbed for her phone on the nightstand.

6:17 a.m.  Almost an hour before she had to get up.

*Ugh.*

Viv turned over, her limbs constrained by the sleeping bag. She hadn't slept well. Unfamiliar surroundings, nerves, and Morgan's robust snores kept her up. After inspecting the beds last night, Viv had elected to spread her sleeping bag on top of the comforter. She didn't trust Mr. McCully to wash the linens often or well.

Viv checked her phone once more. 6:21 a.m. *I might as well get up.*

She dressed in the dark to avoid waking Morgan. Viv didn't want company or conversation. She slipped out the cabin door and cast a glance around the motel grounds. They didn't appear any more attractive than they had last night: sun-bleached plastic chairs, half dead flowers, a closed pool with an aquatic forest growing within. She found a smoking area and walked over.

Viv tapped out a cigarette, then lit it. She inhaled the first drag and sighed to herself. She felt the unease of a sleepless night begin to unknot from her shoulders. She took another drag, smoke streaming from her nostrils and mouth into the chilled air. Viv hadn't smoked before her mother's death. Afterwards, the cigarettes helped her focus, to stay calm, and gave her something to do with her hands.

"Mind if I join you?" a voice interrupted her third inhale.

Viv turned around. Devlin had stepped up, pulling out his own pack and a metal lighter.

Irritation flared through Viv like the flame out of his lighter. But she only nodded.

After his first exhale, he spoke. "You're up early."

Viv shrugged. "Couldn't sleep."

"Neither could I. Zane snores like a demon," Devlin volunteered. He heaved a deep sigh. "There's something wrong with that guy's face."

Viv choked on an inhale from sudden mirth. She met Devlin's eyes through the smoke, and they grinned at each other. A small warmth stole through her despite her earlier irritation. "Morgan snores, too," she admitted.

Devlin exhaled again. "Bummer."

They smoked a first, then a second cigarette in companionable silence. Viv studied the mountains around them. They hemmed in Hard Luck from every direction. The sun seeped over the east mountain range and stained the dawn sky in oranges and pinks. The town and the west mountain range was draped in a thin, wispy fog. Honey's Diner was two blocks away, and cars pulled into and away from the lot with frequent regularity. Another line of customers filed out the door. After some time, Viv checked her phone again. 7:01 a.m.

She ground out the second cigarette. "When are we supposed to meet up with Helen?"

Devlin had started towards the cabin. "Now," he called back to Viv.

With a final glance at the sunrise, Viv trailed after Devlin. In the parking lot, the others had already gathered around Helen, who handed out warm breakfast sandwiches and cups of coffee or chocolate from the open entrance of a short, rundown white bus. Cat and Morgan huddled together, as though to share warmth. Zane and Joel gave each other a wide berth, shoulders hunched against the chilly air. Devlin stood next to Viv.

"Nice of you to join us," Helen said. She handed a sandwich and a coffee to Viv.

Viv cast a sharp glance at the older woman, searching for any hidden meaning to the words. But Helen's face was impassive so Viv relaxed and accepted the offerings. The coffee was fresh and warmed her from within.

"Good morning," Helen began. She ran a ginger eye over the motley assortment of cabins behind the group, then grimaced. "I assume you all slept as well as I did."

Devlin and Zane nodded.

Morgan giggled.

Cat heaved a dramatic and irate sigh.

Viv bit into her sandwich.

"Here's our plan for today." Helen drained the remainder of her large coffee in a single gulp. "We're driving out to Grafton Stake to look over the property. I'll show you where we're working, where we'll store our equipment, and where we're going to set up camp." Helen held up her phone, then waggled it back and forth. "I got the notice that our camping gear has been delivered, so tonight will be our first night on site."

"You mean we won't stay here tonight?" Devlin asked. He waved a hand at the motel behind them.

"Yes."

He heaved a sigh. "Thank god," he muttered. Next to him, Joel snorted.

Helen's eyes crinkled at the corners and she appeared to swallow a grin. "Get your gear and put it in the bus. I'll check us out of the motel, then we'll drive out to the property."

Everyone was on the bus in under ten minutes. It seemed that no one had wanted to linger at the Har Luck otel, with the lackadaisical manager and unkempt cabins. Being one of the last onto the bus, Viv glanced through the cramped vehicle. The limited space on the bench seats were taken up by people or gear. She would have to sit in the front seat and next to Joel, just behind the driver's seat.

She sat down and edged her body towards the aisle, careful not to touch him. The bench seat squeaked in protest and the smell of mold wafted up.

He sniffed. "You reek of smoke."

*Asshole.* "Yep." She stared at him.

Joel glared at her, then out the window. Viv could hear him grind his teeth.

Viv turned to stare out the front of the bus. *Great start. Making friends already.*

Taking a road that led east out of Hard Luck, Helen drove the white bus onto a two-lane highway that was in decent enough condition, but empty of other vehicles. A dense evergreen forest lined both sides of the road while a thin mist obscured the road in front and behind the bus. Dark green and light gray dominated the landscape, with the odd splash of color from rocks or berry bushes peeking through the underbrush.

Viv tried to remember the last time she had been in the wilderness. *Elementary school, maybe?* Certainly not middle school. And her mother had gotten too sick for outdoor activities by the time Viv had reached high school. Viv remembered that her father had checked them into a yurt at a well-maintained campsite in northeastern Oregon. He hadn't wanted to sleep on the ground, and Viv recalled her mother's gentle teasing over his fastidiousness. They had only stayed for a weekend during that summer. She remembered the taste of roasted hot dogs and sweet s'mores and the smell of campfire smoke and insect repellent. Her mother had smiled like a sunrise the whole trip.

*It won't be like that this time. This isn't a camping trip.* She winced, feeling an ache in her chest like she had swallowed something wrong. She missed her mother so much.

Helen continued to drive up the highway, which had turned narrower and then started to wind in twists and turns. Viv checked the clock on the dashboard; Helen had been driving for almost forty-five minutes. A faint unease stole up her spine and spread up to her throat. Viv hadn't realized how remote the worksite would be, how far away from civilization. She shook herself. *Silly. You're being silly.*

Helen drove for another twenty minutes before she turned left onto a wide single lane gravel road that led deeper into the woods. The other passengers on the bus had fallen quiet during the drive but now sat up straight and peered through the windows. Careful not to encroach on Joel's space, Viv peered through the window to her right. The trees blurred together, and it all looked the same to her: dark velvet green, interspersed with lighter shades. She wondered how anyone could find their way through the forest.

After a few minutes, Helen turned off into a wide gravel parking lot. Two large trucks were there, both bearing the name of what Viv assumed was a construction company. A tan dumpster rested at the far edge of the lot. Helen put the bus into park alongside one of the trucks.

"Finally," Viv heard Cat mutter from the back of the bus.

"We're here," Helen called out. "Get out, stretch your legs."

Viv was the first off the bus. She glanced around at the parking lot. The gravel was new, or at least not as muddy as the road had been. *I don't see any buildings.* She turned to Helen, but Joel beat her to the question.

"This is where we're working?" he asked, doubt clear in his voice.

Helen nodded, then pointed to a small opening in the underbrush across the parking lot from where they stood. "We have to walk up to the property. It's only a few minutes," Helen reassured him.

Viv eyed the faint trail with misgiving. *This won't be fun.*

"We have to hike to the property?" Cat demanded, her voice rising with each word.

Helen simply stared at Cat. "Yes."

Cat glared at Helen, then at the muddy ground. Viv noticed that Morgan edged away from Cat. *She doesn't like confrontation*, Viv realized.

"Leave your gear in the bus for now," Helen continued. "I want to show you around, then we'll get the campsite set up. Grab a jacket and a hat. It will likely rain on us."

Helen led them to the small opening in the evergreen underbrush across the parking lot and up the trail. Viv picked her way up the mud and gravel trail, grateful for her new hiking boots. Branches leaned onto the trail and pulled on hats and clothing; blackberry brambles snatched at them as they struggled through. Viv felt moisture on her neck and reached up to touch, puzzled. Her fingers came away with a faint smear of blood. Something had scratched her.

About five minutes into the trail, they stepped into a large pasture. The transition was abrupt from the bushes they'd been struggling though. Viv peered up from grimacing at her muddy boots, then stopped. And stared.

No one would ever guess what lay in the woods an hour east of Hard Luck, Oregon, Viv reflected.

Across the pasture stood five old buildings, constructed out of a combination of brick, stone, and wood, each of them in a state of disarray and destruction. Three of the structures were long and single-story barns that ran parallel to each other, clearly meant to house livestock. These barns were mostly still upright, though Viv could see broken boards and large gaps in the sides of the barns even from where she stood.

The other two structures were laid apart from the barns and appeared to be residences of some sort. The smaller of the two was still somewhat large: a two-story home made of cobblestone and wood with a wide porch in front. The large windows lacked glass and gave off an unsettling resemblance to empty eye sockets. The door to the home was either hung open or completely gone; Viv couldn't tell.

The last building puzzled Viv the most. A tall, three-story building with cobblestone and mortar graced by a slanted copper roof with a patina glaze of blue-green rust. Viv noted that some of the roof panels were missing. *Stolen,* she thought. Copper was valuable and could be sold for a tidy profit. Atop the copper roof was a weathervane with a large, rusted bird — *an eagle?* Viv wondered — with outspread wings. This building was easily the tallest of the five and soared over the others. It seemed to be the most well-constructed, too. Fewer gaps and holes lined the exterior walls of the structure. Small, slitted vertical windows marched up the walls of each floor across the front of the building. Large, wooden double doors with ornate carvings served as an entrance.

Viv stared. She hadn't expected anything like this. What *was* this place?

It seemed that others shared her surprise.

"What the hell?" Viv heard Zane mutter. She glanced over at him and noted with surprise that Joel stood next to her. He met her gaze with a cool, dismissive glance, and Viv almost rolled her eyes until she saw him clench his jaw. He wasn't as calm as he wished to appear, Viv realized. A trickle of relief dripped through her. *At least I'm not the only one who thinks something is... off.*

"Yeah, what he said," Morgan said. She turned to Helen. "What is this place?"

Helen smiled. "Welcome to Grafton Stake. Or homestead. The county council in Hard Luck hasn't decided what to call it yet."

"Who cares what it's called?" Devlin snorted. "What *is* this place?"

Helen nodded. "Fair enough. The Grafton Stake was originally a homestead and a mining claim in the nineteenth century. In later years, it became a farm and a dairy operation, which accounts for the barns and this pasture. There are a few more pastures beyond that corner, too." Helen pointed to a copse on the opposite end of the pasture. "A river, a tributary of the Rogue River, runs through the property, to the west." Helen pointed again.

"So...what exactly are we supposed to do here?" Confusion colored Joel's query. It was the first time Viv had heard him speak without disdain.

Cat snorted from the back of their small group. "I'm not shoveling cow shit."

Devlin looked faintly ill at that notion. Viv watched him tug at each of his neatly buttoned flannel sleeves and adjust his shirt collar, then sigh.

Helen focused on Joel's question. "County council wants to turn this place into a campsite and a visitor's center to bring in tourism. Ye Olde Farming and Mining Days, you know? So our job for the next six weeks is to lay a thorough trail system throughout the property, build campsites, and to clear out the debris from the buildings, to help the construction crews when they arrive to reinforce the existing structures." Helen seemed to pick up on the doubt wafting from the group. "None of what we're doing requires a specialized skillset or construction experience. We're just clearing out wooded areas and making piles of debris to haul off."

Silence fell over the group.

Viv scanned the pasture, the buildings, and realized for the first time since her trip had started that she was in for several weeks of hard physical labor. The projects Helen had just described required hours of intense activity, in muddy, damp, cold, and likely miserable conditions. Unease seeped into her like the chill of a bath gone cold. She wrapped her arms around herself, trying to warm up.

Viv snuck a glance at the others and watched Devlin and Cat exchange a worried look while Morgan shuffled closer to them, her pleated brows giving away her own concerns. Joel clenched and unclenched his jaw, the muscles jumping his neck. Zane was the only one who seemed... excited? *Yes, they understand now. This will be* hard.

Helen glanced around the group, her eyes on each of them. Viv had the sense that the older woman missed nothing and was taking their measure. "I see our gear next to the original homestead." She nodded to the smaller building. "Let's set up our campsite."

# Chapter Four

T he campsite came together with a few mishaps, one of them being Viv's.

Rain dripped through the light, persistent mist around the pasture. While her jacket kept her dry, the cold made her fingers stiff, and Viv fumbled with the large metal tent poles, dropping them with a loud clang. She winced at the noise; Devlin motioned her forward.

"Shake it off, Viv," he called. "Grab one and give me that end." He pointed.

Viv picked up the pole again but moved too fast, almost spearing Devlin in the stomach.

His eyes widened as he dodged the impromptu lance. "Um, maybe hold the tarp instead?"

Viv sighed in relief. "Yes. I can do that. Good."

The team's gear stashed next to the small house provided a wide array of camping supplies: four tents, three large and one small. Cookware and gas tanks. A large number of tarps and coils of rope. Camp chairs and much more. The large tents were sleeping quarters, separated by gender, and the cooking tent. The smaller tent was reserved for Helen, which she pitched between the other sleeping quarters. The cooking tent housed a small table, a grill, and the gas tanks, along with non-food goods. All food would be stored in the bus, Helen had informed them. Too much wildlife in the area to risk storing their food in t he tent.

When Helen assigned Joel and Cat to dig a firepit in the center of the campsite, Viv watched Joel do most of the work. Cat had made a few halfhearted digs into the ground, with a fierce scowl as she muttered under her breath. Viv turned away, a faint frown on her face. She was already tired of the other girl's complaints. The next several weeks would be uncomfortable in more ways than one

.

Inside the sleeping quarters, the white tents were large and as weather-proof as they could be. Viv set two neon blue tarps on the ground, hoping to insulate them from the damp and the cold. Each of the girls picked a different side of the four-walled tent and laid out a thick pad beneath their sleeping bags. Additional gear clustered at the head and foot of each bed. Viv surveyed the scrambled interior and knew that the tent would be a perpetual mess for the duration of the trip. It would be next to impossible to remain truly clean or tidy in this place. Both Cat and Zane had already lodged vociferous protests about the outdoor shower and portable toilets they would have to use. As a response, Helen had simply tossed them both an extra packet of cleansing wipes.

Viv had almost smiled at the twin looks of horror on their other two faces.

The first meal in the kitchen tent was a lukewarm success, a lunch composed of sandwiches with chips. Morgan seemed nervous as she prepared them, then laid them out on the table. But only Cat had looked askance at them before she selected one with grudging thanks. Everyone else was too hungry and too tired from the unaccustomed activity to complain about the simplicity of the fare. Helen had informed them that each of them would rotate cooking duties by meal over the next six weeks. When Viv discovered that she was responsible for breakfasts during this first week, she winced. She hoped everyone liked oatmeal. She was *not* an accomplished cook.

The remainder of the day was spent sorting and preparing the tools they would use for the rest of the week. Viv discovered that she, Devlin, and Morgan were assigned to the trail-breaking team, which meant that they would clear brush and create an entire trail system throughout the property. Cat, Joel, and Zane were assigned to build campsites to the south of the property, near the riverfront. All of them would take turns clearing out debris from the barns and the homes, Helen confirmed. She also reassured them that she would show them how to break trail and how to build campsites before turning them loose on their own.

Viv stifled a sigh of relief at this news. She was grateful for the guidance. Viv couldn't afford to screw up this opportunity. Between the strings her uncle pulled to get her a place on this team and the fact that the judge back home had agreed to expunge her record upon the successful completion of this program, Viv had to make it work.

She didn't have any alternatives.

The evening came on quick, with the bright starlight almost appearing alongside the twilight. Viv had wandered away from the campfire and back to the gravel parking lot to have a smoke. Though they were all underage and technically shouldn't be smoking, Helen hadn't batted an eye when some of the party had stepped away on break. The older woman had only insisted that they smoke on the gravel, away from the underbrush, and to pick up the butts. "No littering and no fires," she had stated in a calm, factual manner that Viv had come to expect from the program leader. "You're lucky that we're not in a drought area or a burn zone."

Viv tapped out a cigarette, then lit up. The first inhale and exhale felt euphoric. It had been a long day.

"I'm not following you, I swear." Viv peered up to see Devlin grinning at her through the darkness. Cat followed close on his heels, Viv noticed with an internal wince.

Viv nodded at them both in greeting, then drew again from her cigarette.

Cat clattered to a noisy stop next to Devlin. Viv watched them pull out their respective cigarettes and light up. Cat noticeably relaxed after the first inhale, and Viv realized just how tense and unhappy the other girl had been throughout the day. She felt a twinge of sympathy for the other young woman, which dissipated when she opened her mouth.

"So why are you here?" Cat stared at Viv through the twilight and the smoke.

Viv took another drag of her cigarette. She didn't answer.

Cat jerked her head at Devlin, who stared at the ground beneath him with deep discomfort. "He had a classic case of wrong time, wrong place," she continued. "But you... You look like Daddy's money and connections landed you here instead of juvie."

Viv stared at Cat, disturbed. Then anger lanced through her. How much did the other girl know? And how?

Cat smirked when Viv didn't respond. "Hit a nerve?"

Devlin shifted, the tip of his cigarette glowing and bouncing in the dark. He kept quiet, though. *Probably to avoid the sharp edges of Cat's tongue.*

"Seriously?" Cat continued. "You're not going to say anything?"

Viv ground out her cigarette, then picked it up. "Good night."

# CHAPTER FIVE

*V*iv was trapped.

*She didn't know where she was. In the darkness that enfolded and subsumed her, she sat on her haunches on cold brick with her knees tucked up against her chest. Her thin clothes didn't shelter her from the chilly air, and she shivered. Her bruised legs ached. But how did she get the bruises? Viv couldn't remember. Viv reached out to feel the walls around her and found them close. Too close. She could barely extend her arms to their full length. Viv waved her hands in front of her face but couldn't see anything. So dark. Too dark.*

*Viv tilted her head to listen: water dripped against metal somewhere nearby. She tried to take a deep, full breath.* Calm, *she told herself.* I need to be calm.

*But the dark pressed in on her, the walls too tight for her to expand her chest and fill her lungs with necessary air. She gasped, then huffed, and then couldn't stop gasping, trying to get more air into her body. Tears tracked down her nose and cheeks. She could taste the salt and the mucus dripping down her face.*

I can't breathe, I can't breathe, I can't breathe.

*Then a clear, crystalline thought emerged through the panic.*

I will die here.

*A metallic screech rent the air, and Viv flinched. A door, she realized. It was the sound of a metal door wrenched open, then slammed shut. Footsteps echoed through the darkness, growing fainter and fainter until she could hear them no more.*

*She was alone in the dark.*

The phone jangled in her ear.

Viv gasped awake, the echoes of the dream wrapped around her like climbing vines on a tree. She lay still for a moment, then took a huge lungful of air. *I can breathe. I'm safe.*

"Turn the damn alarm off," Cat grumbled from across the tent.

Morgan snored on, oblivious.

Viv reached for the phone with a hasty grab and silenced it. The sudden quiet within the tent seemed to magnify her fears from the dream. She took several deep breaths, grateful for the air and the ability to move despite the cold and the humidity within the tent. Where had that dream come from? Viv shivered despite the warmth of her sleeping bag. *It's a bad dream, Viv,* she told herself. *You're fine. Just a bad dream.*

After another minute of deep breaths, Viv decided to get up. She wouldn't be able to sleep after the nightmare; furthermore, she was scheduled to make breakfast for the crew. She had set an early alarm last night to ensure that she would get up in time for a quick smoke and to get supplies from the bus.

Viv dressed in the dark again, trying to muffle the sounds of zippers being pulled open and clothes rustling. She tucked her cigarettes in the back pocket of her Carhartts, the work pants her uncle had insisted that she get. Just outside the tent, she pulled on her already muddy hiking boots before walking down to the parking lot. The early dawn light was obscured by a bank of clouds, laden with rain. Viv had to turn on a penlight for extra light to see her way down the path.

No one else was in the parking lot when Viv broke through the brush. She lit up near the bus and stared into the trees, not really seeing them. She thought about the dream. The impenetrable darkness and the claustrophobia and the painful loneliness. She took a deep inhale, so deep that she started coughing.

A motion caught her watering eyes. Viv glanced up in time to see Joel approaching her. Sweat dampened his brow and his clothes, running shoes laced up on his feet. Steam wafted up from his wide shoulders and his mouth. The running clothes hugged a body he clearly kept in good condition, and it dawned on her that he was at least half a foot taller than her. Viv felt a flush steal across her face.

He stared at Viv, then gazed at the cigarette. He transferred his gaze back to her, his eyes filled with judgement and the corners of his mouth downturned.

"You should stop smoking."

Viv took another drag, staring at him through the smoke. "Yeah?"

Joel shook his head. "Whatever." He walked away and back towards the campsite.

Viv sighed, then ground out the cigarette. She shook off the twinge of remorse that echoed through her. *Maybe I didn't need to be rude. But I'm not here to make friends. I need to finish this and then go home.*

She started up the trail to the campsite. Time to make breakfast.

Breakfast could have been worse.

Viv wasn't sure how she could screw up oatmeal, but she almost did. Mostly, she didn't know how to attach the gas tanks to the portable burners, an important task since she wanted to boil water without having to start a fire in the pit outside. She almost gave up on the plan for oatmeal when Helen came to her rescue. The team leader stepped in and, in a gentle tone, showed Viv how to set up the portable burners safely. Once the water bubbled and boiled away, Viv set out the flavorings and toppings — syrups, nuts, berries — on the main table in a self-serve buffet. Helen did her a solid and got the coffee started. As Viv bustled around the kitchen tent, focused on normal tasks, she felt the sharp edges of the horrid dream fade from her mind.

So, breakfast could have been worse.

And despite the dramatic sighs coming from Cat's direction, everyone ate with a minimum of fuss or commentary.

After they cleaned up, Helen ushered them around the tools to outline the work for the day.

"I'm keeping all of us together for the day," she began. "I want to ensure that we're all working to the same caliber and that we all have the same knowledge to do so. First, we're going to walk through the outskirts of the new trail system and use these to mark the path." Helen held up a handful of eye-smarting, neon pink nylon strips, clearly designed to be visible from a distance. "Then we will walk down to the river and mark out the campsites. We'll discuss what features need to be present in each one and how best to use the landscape to make a good campsite." Helen paused. "Concerns or questions?"

No one said a word.

"Grab your water and your meals, plus your tools. We won't be back until this evening."

With some grumbling, the group gathered their gear. Viv was grateful again for her uncle's guidance before having come to Hard Luck. He had suggested a small daypack with a hydration canister built into it. She was able to fit everything into her daypack with ease and even offered to carry some of Morgan's stuff for her. Cat had simply sniffed at Viv before she could offer the same to the haughty young woman. Viv shook her head and fell into the line that left the campsite.

Helen set a bruising pace across the pasture, past the large three-story building and the barns, and up past the tree line. After consulting a handheld GPS unit a few times, Helen finally called the hike to a stop. Viv was grateful, trying not to gasp for breath like a beached fish in front of the others. She hadn't realized she was so out of shape. *The smoking doesn't help.* She cast a quick glance at the others and saw that most of the others were in bad shape, too. All except for Joel, who stood straight and breathed easy. He met her eyes and then smirked, as if he could tell just how crappy she felt.

*Asshole.*

"Vivienne."

At Helen's call, Viv peered up with a question in her eyes.

"Follow me and start placing the flags at every fifteen feet." Helen handed over the stack of pink flags to Viv, who accepted them in a ginger grip. "The rest of you, walk with me and tell me where the trail should go."

"How should we know?" Cat snarked. "You're the expert."

Helen didn't miss a beat. "If you have any, use your common sense. Barring that, use your eyes." Ignoring the stifled snickers from Devlin and Zane, Helen continued. "Look at the land. Where is the path of least resistance? What angles offer the best views of the surrounding area, offer the most stable footing? What areas will require draining or reinforcement?"

As Helen continued to talk, she pointed out how different types of terrain suited different trail-making techniques. Different vegetation offered barriers or structure to the new trail, ultimately contributing to the longevity of the trail and the ease of use experienced by hikers and walkers. Soon enough, Helen had the entire group engaged—well, except for Cat. Whether it was truly interesting, or the woman had invoked their competitive natures by turning the experience into a game, Viv was surprised by Helen's adept management of the disparate group. She kept quiet and trailed after them, tying off flags wherever the group decided the trail should go.

Around midday, Helen paused for lunch. They clustered around a small clearing just off where the trail would go and pulled out supplies. Lunch became a dismal affair: Morgan had made sandwiches with raw tomatoes, which had turned the bread soggy and inedible. After a single bite, Viv rewrapped the sandwich and placed it back in the daypack in quiet motions, attempting discretion to avoid hurting Morgan's feelings. The other young woman was already miserable; the others hadn't been so kind in their assessment of her culinary skills. Viv pulled out the trail mix and protein bars instead and listened to the casual commentary of the others.

"Hey, Helen," Zane spoke up around a mouthful of trail mix.

"Yeah?"

"You said we're going to take field trips, right?"

"Excursions on the weekends, yes — *if* our work during the week goes well."

Zane grinned, clearly confident about their chances of getting to go. "So where are we going this week?"

Helen chuckled. "If all goes well, we're headed to the next town over this weekend, for a Mining Days Festival."

Cat let out an irritable sigh. "Fun."

Viv had to swallow a grin, and as she looked away, she saw that Joel had to do the same. Their eyes met for a moment, sharing the unexpected camaraderie. Then Viv remembered she didn't like him, and turned to study the trees in the opposite direction, hoping to avoid a second encounter.

Helen seemed to have developed an uncanny ability to ignore Cat's sighs and sarcasm. "Yes, it could be fun. They set up a carnival, host a county fair, offer walking tours about Ye Olde Mining Days. You know, tourist stuff." Helen's watch buzzed, and she glanced at it. "Okay, five-minute mark. We need to get back to work."

Since no one had eaten the sandwiches, there wasn't much to clean up or sort. They spent the next few hours tracing the trail around the edges of the property, inching closer and closer to a river. Viv could hear the rush and the swirl of the water from a distance, and wondered how large it was. As they wended their way down the mountainside, Viv saw Helen glancing at her watch more and more often. Finally, they reached a small clearing that led to a pasture. Viv could see the rooftop of the large residence from where she stood.

Helen stopped and squinted at her watch again. "That's it for the first trail. We'll outline the others later. Since we have another hour before quitting time, I'd like to use this time to find and mark off the campsites. Let's get going."

Helen set off in a quick pace and Viv wondered if the woman came with any other speed setting than Too Fast. The rest of them fell into a hasty line, scrambling to catch up. As Viv stumbled after Cat and down the hill slope, she could hear the river more and more as they drew closer. Due to Helen's fast pace, they were soon among a series of clearings. The clearings had flat or semi-flat circles of dirt, the large trees and small bushes having already been cleared away by someone. A combination of boulders and logs created man-made barriers between the clearings, offering an artificial structure to the otherwise natural environment. Viv noticed a small dirt road ran parallel to the riverfront, with deep, muddy trenches lined with thick underbrush.

Helen led them from one prospective site to another and pointed out how to take advantage of the natural elements in each campsite. In one clearing, she suggested that the forthcoming firepit be situated towards the back of the site to take advantage of the view of the river. In another, she suggested the to-be-built tent pad, which consisted of a levelled square of sand, hemmed into a square by wooden beams, be situated away from the dirt road as to mitigate the intrusive noise from passing vehicles. There were nineteen campsites to be built, Helen told them. Each would have a firepit, a tent pad, a parking spot for vehicles, and trails that led to the river, the original homestead, and to the trail system around the property.

Glancing around at the rough outline of the campsites nestled within the clearings, Viv felt a wave of anticipatory fatigue sweep over her. *The next six weeks are going to be miserable.* She felt her shoulders sag, and she stifled a heavy sigh. The scale of what Helen wanted to accomplish in six weeks was staggering. The combination of brutal, unrelenting work and the rustic accommodations seemed suddenly overwhelming to her, who had been camping — in a yurt, with plumbing and showers nearby — exactly once. The isolation also ate away at her, like an animal gnawing on bare bones. None of the phones among the group had decent connectivity. Thus, she could only text or call her sponsor on the weekends. She didn't have access to the web or any of her social media accounts. She wrapped her arms around herself, staring at the ground in front of her.

*This will suck*, she knew.

But what were her alternatives? If she didn't complete this program, she would lose the chance to expunge her record. But more than that, she would disappoint her uncle. He had come through with a timely suggestion, and the right connections, that had made the difference between continued incarceration in juvie and a chance to redeem herself. She didn't care about what her father thought. That ship had long sailed; her father had washed his hands of her. Viv winced at that knowledge.

Morgan interrupted Viv's bleak thoughts. "Viv, what's wrong?"

"Hmm?"

Morgan's brow furrowed in concern as she stared at Viv. "Are you okay?"

Viv realized that she had been staring at the ground, arms wrapped around her torso as though in pain, with her face set in an anguished expression. *No wonder Morgan is concerned*. She dropped her arms and stood straight, wiping her face clear of emotion.

"I'm good," she replied. At Morgan's continued disbelief, Viv reiterated her false assurances. "Seriously, I'm fine." She glanced away from Morgan, hoping to signal that the topic was over, and saw that Joel and Cat watched her, too. Joel had a neutral expression on his face, though concern or something like it had darkened his gaze. Cat just sneered at her. Viv cursed inwardly. She hadn't meant to draw attention to herself.

Helen came to her inadvertent rescue.

"Congratulations on completing your first day of work." Helen offered a rare smile. "You have a choice: head back to the basecamp for the day, or we can visit the river first. What do you all want to do?"

A quick and unanimous agreement sent them to the riverfront, with Helen leading the way. They left the last of the prospective campsites, then followed a faint trail down the hill. Large sheets of rock coated in moss, hanging ferns, and a thin wisp of moist fumes formed a canyon of sorts, through which Helen led the group onto a long and wide stretch of pebbled riverbed.

Viv paused at the edge.

The river gushed silver, blue, and green streams of color with mist rising from the churning water. Slick boulders and tree branches littered the waterway and were scattered across the riverbed. Another bed of a similar size laid opposite of where Helen and the others stood. Viv was impressed. She hadn't known what to expect but thought it would be smaller, more like a creek. She cast an eye at the width of the river. *It must be thirty feet across.*

Delighted yells dragged her attention from the river and back to the group. She saw that Devlin and Zane had pulled off their boots, rolled up their pants, and waded into the river, stepping on the slick rocks with care.

Devlin gave a dramatic shiver and came to a pause. "This shit is too cold!"

Zane waded in deeper. "Wuss. You'll get used to it." He looked back at the group. "Come on, losers. Get in!"

Viv grinned at his glee. He seemed younger, and happier, in this moment.

Morgan and Helen soon followed, leaving their boots on the riverbed. To no one's surprise, Cat declined. She sat on a boulder and cast disparaging glances at the river and the people in it. Ignoring her, Viv wandered past Cat and walked alongside the water, stepping over unstable rocks and the loose scatter of beached branches.

A glitter lay upon the rocks directly ahead of Viv, casting a shine that seemed out of place in its surroundings despite the muted sunlight of the overcast day. Puzzled, Viv squinted at the unusual glint. *What could it be? What sparkles in the forest?* She walked a bit faster, curious to see what lay ahead.

Viv came to a sudden stop as she saw what is was.

Unease rippled across her shoulders.

The scene was unlike any Viv had ever seen: dozens of fish, of every type and size, lay across the riverbed—dead. The fish ranged from trout to salmon to a type of circular yet flat fish for which she didn't have a name. Fish scales glittered in the weak afternoon sunlight, the translucent skin marred by differing stages of decomposition. Viv could see maggots in several of the carcasses. Flies and other insects buzzed by, the noise almost drowned out by the rush of the nearby river.

Then the smell hit Viv, and she almost gagged, grateful that she hadn't eaten much at lunch. As Viv gaped in disbelief at the carcasses, she saw that the bodies stretched from the edge of the river to the forest's edge. Viv followed the glitter down the riverbed and saw that the carcasses continued until they disappeared beyond the bend in the river.

Viv swept her gaze from the river to the forest. *How did the fish get so far up the riverbank? What caused this?*

"What the fuck?"

Viv jumped at the low expletive, flinching at the unexpected noise. She glanced over her shoulder and saw that Joel had followed her. He stared at the dead bodies with distaste, chased by a faint horror. He held his hands at his side, clenched.

Viv shook her head. "I don't know. I just...found them like this."

Joel stepped forward, next to Viv. "It must be something in water," he offered, a frown on his face. "Right? I mean, what else could do this kind of damage?"

Viv swept an arm from the river's edge to where the forest began. "But how did they get up there? That's thirty feet away."

Joel met her gaze, and she could see the deep unease he tried to conceal. "I don't know." He glanced back at the group. "We should tell Helen, though."

Viv nodded. She backed several feet away from the fish. She didn't want to be closer to...whatever had happened than she had to be. As Joel went to tell Helen, Viv cast an uneasy glance at the fish scattered in front of her like an unholy offering. Something caught her eye, and puzzled, Viv tilted her head to get a better angle. A chill chased down her spine when she realized what she saw before her.

The carcasses formed a pattern of sorts, with larger bodies having been spaced at identical intervals to form a grid. Small fish completed the grid, laying between their larger cousins. The placement of the bodies almost seemed deliberate, man-made. To Viv, it resembled a macabre quilt made of unnatural materials. Viv shook her head, tempted to rub her eyes. *But that's impossible*, she thought. *No one would do something like this.* She stared at the carcasses, trying to unsee the pattern her eyes had picked out.

*Would they?*

## Chapter Six

The mood at the basecamp was subdued that evening.

After Joel had dragged Helen and the others to examine the carcasses along the beach, the lukewarm mood from completing the first day's work had dissipated. Viv watched her crewmates as the others reacted with a wide array of responses, from disgust to worry to unease. To Viv's surprise, Cat was the first to notice the grid pattern amongst the decaying remains and had pointed it out to the others. Viv had watched Helen's deep frown grow deeper, hard lines of puzzlement and then worry etched into her face. Helen had wasted no time ushering them back to the basecamp with multiple assurances of making inquiries about the dead fish and the water quality in the river. "In the meantime, until we know more, do not pull water from the river for boiling or showers. Use the bottled stuff only," she had warned.

No one demurred.

Dinner was a simple affair of sausages, box stuffing, and fruit. Viv was astonished to realize that she was hungry, despite the uneasy scene earlier that afternoon. Zane had dinner duty this week and didn't do too terrible a job. He even showed Morgan how to make better sandwiches for the following day's lunch. Viv had almost wanted to hug him when she saw the classic peanut butter and jelly fare Morgan had prepped.

Helen dragged a chair over to the firepit and sat between Joel and Devlin. "How is everyone feeling tonight? After the first day of work?"

An orchestra of groans and gripes answered her.

Helen grinned at the collective misery surrounding her. "This kind of work isn't easy, is it? You'll feel worse tomorrow, I promise." She chuckled. "The first week is the roughest. You have to be tough. But you all did well today. Good job."

Viv wrapped her jacket tight against her body and sank further in the camp chair, a small smile on her face. She had a sense that Helen's praise was as effusive as the older woman got. The logs within the flames snapped, then collapsed.

"What are we doing tomorrow?" Devlin asked, poking the fire with a charred stick to stoke the flames.

"I was going to split you up, have you work on different projects." Helen studied the flames before shaking her head. "But I'm going to have us work on the trails tomorrow. Just until I have an update about the water quality of the river and a possible explanation for the fish." Viv watched Helen shiver. "I haven't seen anything like that before — and I've spent much of my life in the woods. It's definitely...unusual."

Viv huddled against the cold in the parking lot, cursing herself. Smoking cigarettes had gotten her through rehab and the first months of NA. But the habit, which often required her to stand out in the cold, the rain, and whatever other weather pattern that happened by, was inconvenient at the best of times. *Maybe I should think about quitting.* She shivered again and took a hurried draw from the cigarette. Lights out was in fifteen minutes.

"Maybe you should consider quitting." A light voice uncurled in the darkness.

Viv almost dropped her cigarette. "Fuck," she gasped, her heart tripping against her ribs. Adrenaline coursed through her. "Dude. Not cool. Use a flashlight next time." She took deep breaths, trying to slow her rapid heartbeat.

A lantern flicked on.

Zane grinned at her. "Sorry," he said, not sounding terribly apologetic. *He's like a golden retriever*, Viv realized. *Happy and energetic, all the time.*

"Why are you here?" Viv finished her cigarette, then ground it out.

"Helen sent me," came the easy reply. "Lights out in ten minutes."

"I know." She gave a nod. "Let's go."

Viv turned to follow Zane up the trail— □

And a scream ripped through the night.

Viv froze. Her heartbeat thundered in her ears, a klaxon warning to flee, to run, to hide. Adrenaline pumped through her, and she trembled, her fingers dropping the cigarette remnant. *Who was that?*

Zane did not freeze. He dropped the lantern, turned, and fled back to the camp. Viv wondered if he ran track and field back home. He could move when he needed to. Viv stooped to grab the lamp, then hurried after Zane. She did not want to be alone in the parking lot after that scream. Viv plunged up the trail and towards the basecamp. She saw the others standing on their feet, arrayed around the firepit. The fire had died down to glowing embers.

No one seemed upset or injured. So where had that awful sound come from?

Viv glanced around, ignoring the doubled-over Zane, who gasped for breath. "What *was* that?"

"Cougar," Helen replied.

"A cougar?" Viv echoed, her disbelief evident in her voice.

"Yep." Helen nodded to the east of the property. "Likely up in the mountains." She turned to focus on Viv, then eyed Zane. "It's a terrible sound, isn't it?"

Viv shivered. "It sounded like a woman being attacked."

Helen grimaced. "I know. But as long as we take precautions, we should be safe. We make too much noise for most big cats."

"Should be?" Cat's grumble came through in the firelit darkness. For once, Viv had to agree. Nothing about a nearby cougar made her feel safe.

Helen cleared her throat. "All right, lights out. Time to get to sleep. Tomorrow will be another long day."

Viv awoke before her alarm the next morning, miserable and sore. Every muscle in her body ached and groaned and protested as she folded her out-of-shape and exhausted form into clean clothes to slip out of the girls' tent and down to the parking lot for a smoke before breakfast. She had somehow her hairbrush already so Viv had shoved a beanie onto her head to cover the snarls in her hair. Devlin was already there. He nodded when she joined him.

"All right?"

Viv lit up. "I guess." Smoke curled up and into the low mist that coated the parking lot.

Devlin snorted, then ran a hand through his short curls. "I slept like shit. Awful dreams."

Viv remembered the nightmare of her first night in the woods, remembered how cold and afraid she had felt, trapped alone in the darkness of that cramped hole. She remembered the awful screech of the metal door sliding shut, and shivered. "That sucks."

"Yeah."

They walked back to the camp in silence. In the half hour that followed, Viv managed to get breakfast prepared without Helen's assistance, a simple feat that still gave her a quiet thrill of pleasure. Eating her oatmeal, Viv scanned the others. Dark circles and rumpled hair marred most faces. Even Cat hadn't bothered with her light layer of makeup.

Helen was upbeat and cheerful as she emerged from her tent, boots on and layers of clothing tucked in and zipped up. "Good morning," she called out.

Viv abhorred the woman for a moment.

"Ugh." Morgan, to Viv's surprise, apparently shared her sentiments. "You're too *happy*. It's revolting."

Helen grinned at them. "It's a new day. Lots to smile about."

Zane stretched to his full height with a yawn, then grinned. "I'm ready. Let's do this!"

Viv eyed them both. *Ugh. What is wrong with those two?*

After a quick wash-up and upon securing the perishables in the bus, the group followed Helen past the homestead and the large residence, across the pastures, and up the mountainside. To Viv's amazement, Helen didn't need to consult her GPS unit before she led them to the first neon pink flag Viv had tied to a tree only yesterday morning. Helen waited for them to catch up before she issued instructions.

"Cat and Morgan, you're clearing brush and cutting down small branches." Helen pointed down the proposed trail. Several feet away, they could see the next pink flag flutter in the slight breeze. "Imagine walking through a tunnel. Clear every branch and bush that gets in the way. Zane and Devlin, start laying trail by removing sod where necessary or widening the existing trail. You want a minimum width of two feet."

Zane pointed at Cat and Morgan. "How come they get to cut branches, and we have to hack into the earth?"

Helen stared him down. "You're swapping tasks every two hours. Everyone does the work."□

Zane rocked back on his heels. "Oh," he muttered. He stared at the ground.

Helen continued as though she hadn't been interrupted. "Joel and Viv, you're with me. We're going to move logs, boulders, and any large obstacles. We will also assess whether we need to reinforce the area for stability or safety." Helen glanced around at them. "No sense dallying. Let's get to it."

The next two hours were a blur to Viv. The work was *hard*, being physically demanding and relentless. Unused to such a high degree of physical activity, she felt as though her body were a foreign vehicle that she had to operate with little instruction or preparation. So Viv stumbled along as best she could from one task to another, as she tripped over her feet, dropped tools, and bumped into people.

Helen was patient with her.

The others were not.

Her cheeks burned every time one of them glared at her. She glared back, staring them down until each of them turned away from her, either shame-faced or doubly angry. Only Joel seemed to be somewhat neutral. He had even reached out to steady Viv when she tripped over a large rock, then let go of her in a hasty motion. Viv had muttered her appreciation before giving him a wide berth.

At last, Helen called for a break. Viv gave an audible sigh of relief.

They sat on the edge of the newly dug trail and alternated between gulping water and inhaling their protein bars and trail mix. Viv couldn't believe how much her body constantly *hungered*. The nearby conversation between Cat and Devlin distracted Viv from her own preoccupation with her body's ravenous demands for more trail mix.

"You're from Portland, too?" Viv heard Devlin ask.

Cat smiled, the first real one Viv had seen from the other girl. "Yeah. In the northeast. The Mississippi neighborhood?"

"Same." Devlin sounded delighted. "Well, not Mississippi. My family is in the Albina area."

"We're practically neighbors," Cat teased.

Devlin offered Cat a brilliant smile. "Absolutely. What school did you attend?"

Cat's smile faded a bit. "I, um, attended one of the Catholic preparatory schools downtown."□

Devlin frowned at this. "Are you Catholic?"

Cat grimaced. "My parents are." She sighed.

"C'mon, gang, back at 'em," Helen called out.

Viv gave an audible groan as she stood up. Her bones creaked as she unfolded from her seat. Muscles and ligaments ground together. *I hurt everywhere.*

Helen had them sorted into the new tasks within seconds, and though Viv doubted Helen's judgement, she was given a long hoe with a double-bladed end: a rake on one side, a sod cutter on the other.

Viv held it with a ginger grip. "What do I do with this?"

Helen almost smiled. "You're on trail-making duty. Cut the sod or widen it, okay?"

"Right." Viv gazed at Joel, trepidation clear in her eyes.

He shook his head. "You will stay six feet away from me at all times. Clear?"

He was not joking.

Viv scowled at him as he walked away.

Viv worked behind Joel for the rest of the morning, careful to keep a good distance between them. While she wouldn't admit it aloud, she knew he had a point; Viv had a great deal to learn in managing the unfamiliar tools.

Soon she fell into a rhythm of sorts. She cleared away loose sod from the new trail, widened the trail, and raked the trail smooth wherever possible, tucking the earthen debris on the downward slope. Every now and then, they would pause to build drainage ditches into the trail, to prevent large puddles and washouts from happening.

The crew worked hard, harder than Viv expected if she were honest. They chattered away with one another as they completed their tasks, talking about their favorite music, films, and hobbies back home. Then Zane asked Helen about working for the Bureau of Land Management and how to get a job in the field. Viv listened to the conversations around her but didn't join in. With the fast pace and physical labor, she didn't have the energy. She did note that several of them were careful not to talk about immediate family. She understood that. Her own relationship with her father was terrible even on a good day.

Her father had lost his wife, his whole heart, the day her had mother died.

Viv had lost them both.

The chatter grew faint, and Viv realized that the crew had made rapid progress over the next two sections. She gave her portion of the trail a final rake, then stood to catch up with them.

A flicker caught her eye and turned her head.

Viv squinted up the hill, through the dense underbrush. What did she see up there? Was that a...monument? Viv cast a quick glance down the trail. No one else had noticed how far she had fallen behind. They likely wouldn't notice if she stepped away to investigate.

Her decision made, Viv scrambled up the hill towards the stone outcropping that had caught her attention, her rake-hoe-whatever held in a tight grip at her side. Less than a minute later, she came to a stop. A short, weathered black stone pyramid rose from a hewn base buried deep into the ground. Viv could see the chisel marks at the base, lined with dirt and moss. No words or dates were inscribed, only the symbol of a single open eye.

A shiver skittered across her scalp. She recognized the symbol for the evil eye.

*An obelisk,* she thought. *It's an obelisk.*

*What is an obelisk doing in the middle of the woods?*

Viv peered past the obelisk. The stone stood waist-high and before a wide, flat stretch of pasture mostly clear of trees and brush. Thick holly bushes with sharp, black-green leaves lined the edges of the pasture. Unsettled, Viv rubbed her arms. Why would a clearly man-made pasture be up here, away in the woods? So far from the homestead? Viv stepped forward to take in more — and paused.

A rectangle of the same black stone lay next to her foot, embedded in the ground and with edges coated in moss. The numbers 81469 were chiseled into the dark stone.

Viv swallowed. She took another step, then another.

Then she saw it — another stone, half buried in the dirt. Almost six feet away from the first stone plaque. The numbers were 73071.

Now knowing what to seek, she scanned the earth around her. There were more. Many more.

42198.

32777.

21374.

91868.

Viv shook her head, trying to make sense of what she saw before her. She stumbled down the length of the pasture, seeking more and more of the stone plaques wedged into the earth's sod, half visible.

Wholly terrible.

There were more than fifty plaques in the pasture, Viv realized.

She couldn't be sure, but she thought she stood upon a graveyard.

## CHAPTER SEVEN

V iv watched Helen survey the graveyard with a deep frown, hands on her hips.

After a moment, Viv spoke. "Well? It's a graveyard, isn't it?"

Helen tilted her head to better study a plaque by her foot. "It seems so," she said slowly, as if thinking aloud. "But why no names?"

Viv stared down at the same stone Helen studied. 91486. "I don't know." She glanced back to Helen. "Should we, I don't know, tell someone about this?"

Helen nodded. "We'll take an early lunch, and I'll put in a call to the Bureau of Land Management. See what they know about this - *if* they know anything."

Helen turned back to the others, where they had clustered around the obelisk with the evil eye symbol. Viv followed her, careful not to step on the black stone plaques. It felt disrespectful to do so somehow.

When Viv had raced up to Helen with the news of a possible graveyard, the others had jeered at her. Cat had scoffed, Morgan had tittered, and Devlin and Zane had exchanged a *look*. Joel had scrutinized her with open disdain and disbelief, irritated by her outrageous claims. But Viv had persisted, nagged, and cajoled, and the strength and persistence of her pleas — even in the face of open mockery — had convinced them to at least examine the pasture. Viv had led them back up the trail and chased her footsteps up to the wide clearing surrounded by the sharp, black-and-green leaves of the holly that stood sentinel. A drizzle of rain had started, coating the grass and stone alike, making the ground slick and treacherous.

The jeers and the mutters that had echoed behind Viv as she led them up the trail had stopped when they reached the obelisk. When she turned around, she saw that the others had arrived at the same conclusion she had: the eerie clearing was man-made, and the black stone plaques were gravestones.

Quiet and ashen, the others watched Helen and Viv walk back to the obelisk.

Helen glanced at all of them before she spoke. "This was an unexpected detour," she tried to joke.

The guys offered a half-smile or a forced chuckle. Morgan and Cat linked arms, heads nestled together against the light drizzle.

"We're going to take an early lunch on the trail," Helen continued. "I'll contact our BLM liaison and see what they can find for us. In the meantime, we should get back to work."

"Back to work?" Morgan echoed, puzzled. "But what about...that?" She pointed at the graveyard.

Helen shook her head. "This is unprecedented," she admitted. "I need more guidance about what this means for the entire project, and I can only get that from the authorities responsible for this property. Until then, we continue to work as best we can."

Viv shifted, uneasy. *That's it? We keep working?* She saw that the others were unsatisfied by the answer, too, if the scowls and head shakes were any indication.

Helen started down the trail, away from the graveyard.

"All right, crew. Let's move out."

Lunch was a tense affair. The sandwiches were palatable, thanks to Zane's intervention the night before, but no one seemed to have an appetite. Helen had stepped away and placed a call on the satellite phone. Viv had strained to listen but only caught snatches of the conversation. She noticed the others doing the same.

"...looks like a graveyard..."

"...I got spooked kids out here..."

"...not good, man..."

After the call, Helen had returned to the trail with a grim countenance. She hadn't offered any updates or explanations. The rest of the day passed slowly, quiet and disturbed. Hardly anyone spoke unless required to by the trail work. Whether uneasy about the unexpected graveyard or tired from the sheer volume of physical activity, the group trooped back to basecamp in low spirits.

In case the trail work wasn't hard enough, Viv and the others were required to do after-work chores, too. Maintenance, inventory, and proper storage of the tools. Prepping meals and snacks for the following day. Retrieving potable water from the bus in the parking lot. Cleaning up camp rubbish and storing it in a smell-proof container in preparation for taking the trash into town later that week. On and on, until Viv was grateful to sink into a slightly damp camp chair in front of the firepit with the humble combination of sausage, quick rice, a dinner roll, and fruit on her plate.

The others settled in. Zane and Devlin flanked her, while Joel, Cat, and Morgan sat on the other side of the fire, attempting to lean away from the smoke that rose from the wood. The rain had abated, an event for which Viv was grateful. Otherwise, they'd be crammed into the kitchen tent, with little space and even less comfort.

Helen was the last to join them. She had stepped away from the dinner preparations to take a call that had come on the satellite phone. To avoid the eager eavesdroppers, she had wandered up to the original homestead and talked with the other person for fifteen minutes. Viv had watched her out of the corner of her eye as she organized the tools they would need for tomorrow. The others watched Helen openly, as if they could divine the contents of the hushed conversation through their eyes. Only Joel had ignored the conversation, as he built the fire for the evening.

After the call ended, Helen gathered a plate from Zane and settled into her chair, the plate balanced on her knees. She took a swig of water from her canteen. Her fork raised to her mouth, she glanced up and caught the expectant eyes from the entire group.

She sighed, set the fork back on her plate. "At least let me finish dinner, okay?"

An exasperated sigh swept through the group.

They waited, but not patiently.

Zane added a log to the fire.

Devlin drummed his fingers on the arm of his camp chair.

Cat picked at the cuticles of her fingers.

Morgan snapped her gum.

Viv cracked her knuckles, earning an irate glance from Cat.

The fire gave a sudden pop. Everyone flinched.

Helen gave a sudden chuckle. "That scared me, too." She set her plate down by her feet. "All right, let me share what I know."

Viv leaned forward in her seat.

"We — or rather Viv — did find a graveyard today."

A sigh sieved out of Viv. *I was right.*

"What is a graveyard doing *here*?" Cat waved an arm in the general direction of the homestead and the larger building, the one which Devlin had started calling the Fortress.

"I'm getting to that," Helen replied in a mild tone.

Cat subsided with a scowl.

"I think I mentioned that Grafton Stake started out as a mining claim and a homestead before becoming a full farm," Helen began. "Well, according to my contact at the Bureau office, the Grafton family had a rough financial period in the late 1800s and decided to diversify their operations. They opened up a rest home of sorts for invalids and the chronically ill. The Graftons marketed this place as a haven for the disturbed or for those who were *different*, and families would send their loved ones for improved health and recovery, I guess." Helen nodded to the Fortress. "Apparently, that's where the guests resided."

Viv studied the Fortress through the campfire smoke. Twilight gave the large building soft edges and blurred lines, with the dark windows seeming like empty eye sockets scattered across the building. It gave the impression that the building watched them all, at the campsite, with manifold eyes. She turned back to Helen in time to catch Joel's question.

"Why would a rest home need a graveyard?" Joel asked in a quiet voice.

A silence fell over the campfire as all present contemplated the implications of that question.

Helen sighed. "Because it wasn't a well-run or safe rest home. The Graftons oversold their medical expertise and made all sorts of snake oil promises to lure families into sending their most vulnerable to the facility. They wanted to make money — at any cost."

The night air ate into the layers of Viv's clothing. She felt cold, a bone-deep cold she knew wasn't due to the evening chill. "They killed those people," she surmised. "All of them. In the graveyard."

Helen nodded, her face grim. "Very likely. Either through neglect or out-right abuse. There were rumors, of course. When so many people enter a rest home but never leave, people whisper. But nothing was confirmed until 1912. Apparently, a visitor found the graveyard and reported it to the sheriff." Helen grimaced. "When the sheriff and his posse arrived to inspect the place, they forced their way into the Fortress. They were appalled at the conditions they found: unkempt and unclean patients, open wounds, clear evidence of assault, starvation. The sheriff arrested several of the Graftons. The scandal made both the local and regional newspapers. The remainder of the family abandoned the property and the patients by fleeing the state. No one heard from them again. Most assume that they adopted a new name, built a new life somewhere."

No one spoke for a moment.

Viv shivered. "There are so many graves."

"Too many graves. How long did they run the place?" Joel asked.

Helen shook her head. "It's hard to know with certainty how long they were in business. You must remember that this area was so remote, so difficult to access in those times. People didn't have the ease or luxury of traveling by car." Helen winced. "Likewise, there was no or very little oversight, especially in rural areas, for businesses or medical practices. The Graftons could do what they wanted with impunity."

Viv wrapped her arms around herself and sank deeper into her chair. Emotions buffeted her body: despair at the suffering the patients had experienced. Disbelief at the cruelty of the Graftons. Horror at the loneliness experienced by the inmates. Deep disquiet crawled through her torso and tightened her chest until she couldn't take a deep breath. Viv swallowed hard, choking back her rising panic. She knew what it was like to be imprisoned. To be jailed instead of aided in her darkest moment, only to be told that incarceration was for her own good. She remembered again the sheer volume of the gravestones in the cemetery, and Viv shivered. *Those poor people.*

Cat spoke up. "So, are we continuing the project?"

Helen gave a nod. "Yes, of course."

"Really?" Cat's voice climbed into the higher register. "We're going to stay here. With the bodies. And that." She pointed at the Fortress.

Zane jeered at Cat. "What's the matter? Afraid of a few ghosties?"

"Shut up, dude," Devlin retorted. Viv noticed that Devlin had clenched his hands together, holding them in his lap.

Helen ignored the boys and replied to Cat. "Honestly, nothing about the project has changed for us. Hard Luck's county council still wants to turn this place into a campground and visitor's center. They knew about Grafton Stake's unfortunate history and have known all along. Apparently, they feel that they can focus the narrative on the region's history of homesteading and mining." Helen didn't seem entirely convinced by her own words, Viv noticed.

"That's bullshit," Cat replied in a hushed, angry tone.

"I agree that they should have disclosed the presence of the cemetery to us before we signed onto the project," Helen replied. "That was...unprofessional on their part. However, now that we have this information, each of you has a choice: if you are discomfited by the presence of the graveyard or the history of this place, and you wish to leave the program, I will drive you into Hard Luck tomorrow morning and make sure you have a bus ticket home."

A sudden silence fell over the campfire.

Viv studied the others, trying to determine who — if anyone — would leave. Devlin and Joel were unreadable. Morgan appeared two shades paler than her usual fair self. Cat seemed mutinous and scared all at once. Zane stared at the ground.

"I'll give you until tomorrow morning to make your decision," Helen said. She stood. "We should turn in soon. We may have a long day ahead of us tomorrow."

# Chapter Eight

*Viv stood at the riverfront. She glanced down and saw that she wore her city clothes — boots, hoodie, and jeans — rather than her trail clothes. She frowned. Why hadn't she worn the right clothes? What was she doing at the river's edge?*

*She glanced up and studied the river. The water rushed by, greens chasing blues with foam frosting the liquid ripples. She glanced upriver. Boulders and branches formed a dam of sorts, laden with slick wooden debris. She glanced downriver. Free from the obstruction upriver, the water gathered momentum and rushed along, forming swirls and eddies and waves in the water.*

*A glitter caught her eye. She tilted her head, squinting into the distance. Suddenly, she knew. The fish waited for her.*

*They had something to show her.*

*Dread rang alarm bells inside her head, warning her to turn away, to run, to flee. Still, she continued forward. She had to see. Viv took slow steps but somehow flowed forward like a film being sped up. She coasted to a stop at the edge and stared. They were still there. The dead fish were rotted through, the glitter of the scales obscured by decomposition and maggots. The stench was overwhelming, and Viv held a sleeve up to her face, taking shallow breaths. She stared at the little corpses, littered across the riverbed up to the forest's edge.*

*A motion next to her foot made her jump back in fright.*

*The carcass, a trout when still alive, had flipped over, suddenly and without aid.*

*Viv watched the body flip over, then again. And again. And again. Soon, the other bodies were in motion. They flipped or slithered or heaved themselves, heads over fins, to a spot about ten feet away. The corpses moved in slow, jerky motions — like marionettes, she realized. Viv stepped back to avoid the carcasses. But they ignored her and continued to make their way towards the shared goal. Maggots and larvae dribbled in their wake, rousted from their temporary homes.*

*After a moment, Viv followed the trail of bodies. They were concentrated on a spot, Viv could tell, but kept twisting over one another. Viv stepped closer, careful to keep her feet clear of the bodies. She didn't want to cause more suffering.*

*Finally, the fish stopped moving. A cold wind gusted up from the pile of bodies, and a swirl of flies rose up in circular patterns through the sky. Viv stepped closer and closer until she stopped at the edge. And stared at the symbol that lay upon the pebbled sand, composed of bodies small and large, glittering in the weak sunlight.*

*A key.*

*The bodies formed the shape of a key.*

The cold dawn air had nothing on the chill that hovered over breakfast the next morning.

Viv continued her habit of making a simple breakfast of oatmeal and coffee for everyone. The only concession she made this morning was to offer fresh fruit as well as dried. The rain had thickened overnight so they were forced to huddle in the kitchen tent to choke down their repast and sip at the coffee.

Helen cleared her throat. "Before we get started for the day, I want to check in with folks: does anyone need a ride into Hard Luck?"

Silence greeted her question. Viv and the others eyed one another, to suss out who might leave.

After a moment, Helen continued. "Okay, I'm taking that as a no. If you change your mind later, you will have to finish out the day — no exceptions." Helen zipped up her coat and put on her hard hat. "Let's go."

The rest of the week passed in a blur of pain, misery, and damp for Viv.

The rain continued, a persistent drizzle that seemed never-ending, and a perennial low fog wreathed the homestead and the Fortress. Each day her body was somehow more sore, achier than the day prior. She improved on her trail-building skills in tiny increments with marginal results. At least the others had stopped giving her a wide berth and judgy side-eyes when passing by her on the trail. Viv supposed they were finally becoming accustomed to each other. At night, she nodded off during dinner and after a quick smoke in the parking lot that she half-resented because it forced her to remain awake, she toddled off to bed. The sleeping pad and bag hardly constituted comfort, and during the first few nights, she awoke in the night, shivering. When Helen had passed out additional blankets for everyone, Viv took two.

Despite her fatigue, Viv had terrible dreams every night. She dreamt about crouching on the floor, trapped in that small room, immersed in darkness and alone until the screech of the metal door sliding shut. She dreamt of her mother, during the last stages of the breast cancer that had eventually taken her, which had transformed her hilarious and adventurous mother into a sad, bitter woman. She dreamt about the funeral, how her father had sobbed in the bathroom when he thought no one could hear him. Or how the mortician had used her mother's least favorite shade of lipstick for the viewing.

Viv woke each day feeling like she had survived an obstacle course in her mind.

Today was no different.

Her eyes flew open, and she gasped for breath. *Where am I?*

"Viv, get up. You're gonna be late. You have to make breakfast, remember?"

*Cat,* her mind supplied. She was in the woods, with irritable Cat, timid Morgan, and the others. She was at Grafton Stake. Viv groaned to herself, putting her hands on her head. *The fish and the key. Again.*

Morgan's hesitant query came from across the tent. "Viv, are you okay?"

Viv sat up, grabbed for the clean clothes from her pack. "Yeah."

She almost felt bad for lying to Morgan.

Viv should have known that the rest of the day would be rotten.

After washing up the dishes from breakfast and securing the food and the trash in the bus, Viv gathered up her hard hat and her daypack. She started towards the original homestead when a commotion startled her.

"What the fuck?" she heard Joel say.

Viv turned her head to see what had caused Joel's low expletive. She saw the others gather around him, next to the tools tent by the original homestead, each of them staring at the ground in front of them. She jogged up to the group and stilled in shock.

The tools had been vandalized.

The wooden handles lay in shards, scattered on the ground in dangerous pieces beneath the tent that sheltered them. The metal remnants of the spades and rakes had been twisted, bent out of shape and into something useless. The axes and saws were untouched but thrown afar, a good twenty feet away from the tent's shelter. The extra tool belts not used by the crew had been ripped apart and tossed onto the ground, half-buried in the mud and dappled by rain.

Shock slicked through Viv. *What the hell?*

Joel spoke first. "Did anyone hear anything last night?"

Viv eyed him and realized he was right. She hadn't heard anything throughout the night. She stared at the wreckage. Something like this would have caused noise, a cacophony. Viv shook her head, and a chill rippled across her scalp.

"No, I didn't hear anything," Viv said.

An agreement swept the circle.

"Then what happened?" Cat demanded. "Someone had to have done this. Things don't just break by themselves." Her tone was sharp, but Viv noted the fear in the other girl's gaze, with a pinched look around her eyes and ashen skin.

"Did someone come from town to do this?" Zane offered, with clear doubt on his face.

Devlin shook his head. "Who would do that? Who knows we're up here?"

"I don't know, dude, but someone isn't happy about something." Zane shook his head and took a step back. "This is fucked up."

"Hey, what's going on? What's the hold up?"

Helen's query froze them in place. Viv peered over her shoulder to the older woman approaching the group. She took a silent step aside to make room for the crew leader to join them — and to see the damage. Viv watched as Helen's gaze swept across the tool tent and the area surrounding the shelter. She saw several emotions chase each other Helen's face: shock, dismay, and finally anger, banked by a neutral mask.

"What happened here?" Helen asked in a calm voice.

"We don't know," Cat said. "We found them like this." She gestured to the ground.

"You found them like this?" Helen echoed. Doubt and anger seeped into her calm voice, and Viv was reminded of a clear sky overcome by sudden clouds.

"Well, yeah," Cat responded.

Helen studied the ground again, then scrutinized each of them. "Does anyone have something they want to share?"

The sudden realization immobilized Viv. *She thinks one of us did this, caused this damage.*

"What are you asking?" Joel demanded. His tone was even, but something ugly rested beneath his neutral words.

Helen shook her head. "I'm not an idiot," she said, her sharp words softening as she continued. "*If* one of you did this, please come forward and accept responsibility. You will not be sent home until you've committed a second offense."

Viv felt her brow furrow. "You think one of us managed to do this?" She pointed at the misshapen metal and shattered wooden handles. "*How*? How in the hell could we have bent metal with our bare hands?"

"And in silence," Devlin added.

"I didn't hear a thing last night," Morgan confirmed, worry and fear evident in her voice. She linked arms with Cat, who glared at Helen. Viv was envious of the comfort they had in each other and buried her cold hands deeper into her pockets.

Helen sighed. "Listen, I'm not a fool. We're in a remote area, and hardly anyone knows we're here. The simplest, and most likely, explanation is that one of us did this."

A mutinous silence fell over the group.

Helen pulled off her hard hat and held it by her side. Frustration and fatigue aged her by a decade, and Viv felt a sudden spurt of sympathy for the woman. "Today's plans have obviously changed. Gather up this mess and bag it up. We're headed into town to get more tools and to dump our trash. There will be no excursion this weekend."

Angry scoffs and complaints met her words. Helen held up her hand to forestall further gripes. "Hey, actions have consequences," she retorted in a sharp voice. "This is what happens when you destroy property, at the minimum. No field trip this weekend." Helen frowned at the ground again, then sighed. "Get started. The hardware store opens in an hour or so."

The group scattered amidst grumbles and muttered complaints. Viv moved to follow but paused when she heard Helen call her name.

"Viv, you got a moment?"

She stopped, conscious that everyone could hear Helen's question. She felt how hard they tried to avoid looking in her direction. "I guess."

"Let's take a walk."

Dread unfurled in Viv. *This won't be good.* "Okay."

Helen led them away from the shambles of the tool tent, away from base-camp, and down to the parking lot. She paused next to the bus and turned to face Viv. Helen took a deep breath, then spoke.

"Listen, you may not know this, but I know your uncle, Rick Collens," Helen said.

Viv hadn't know that. "Okay." *Why is this important?*

Helen continued. "He called in a favor, asked to get you on this team to fulfill some court-appointed obligations. He assured me that you were a good kid, a great one, with some recent difficulties." Helen paused as if searching for words. "He also shared that you've had some issues with vandalism in the past."

Anger swamped Viv. Her limbs trembled with the force of her feelings, and she pinched her lips together to control herself. She felt betrayed by Rick, who had shared her past with a stranger and without her permission. *How could he?* Her shoulders sank, and she fisted her hands at her side. Was there any adult she could trust?

When she trusted herself not to cry in front of Helen, she spoke. "So you think I broke those tools? Because I have a history of vandalism and drug use?" Viv noted the lack of surprise in Helen's face at the mention of drugs and inwardly cursed Rick. He had shared that, too. She tamped down further grief, trying to focus on the conversation.

"I'd be a fool not to consider it," Helen replied. "So I'm asking you, directly and with no bullshit: did you vandalize the tools?"

"No," Viv snarled. "I did not." She shook her head, then gave Helen a scathing glance. "You must be a fool after all. How could any of us have done *that*? At night, in silence? None of us are capable of that."

Despite Viv's harsh words, Helen retained her sympathetic expression. "I find that hard to believe. If you decide to own up to it, you can talk with me at any point. If you need anything – a counseling appointment, a phone call to your uncle – I can make that happen. I should warn you, though, another offense, and I'm shipping you home. I can't have a disruptive element here, especially when I have other kids who are trying to get their lives back on track."

The unfairness of the situation — the accusation from Helen, the betrayal of trust by her uncle — slammed into Viv. She felt tears smart in her eyes. She wrenched her gaze away from Helen and stared into the sky, hoping the angle of her head would dry the tears before they fell. She had learned that trip next to her mother's hospital bed. A light drizzle dappled her face.

"Are we done?" Viv heard herself ask.

Helen gave a disappointed sigh. "I guess we are."

# CHAPTER NINE

I t was clear that everyone blamed Viv for the vandalism, and the corresponding loss in privileges.

"Nice job, bitch," Cat muttered at Viv.

Viv paused from picking up a wooden shard. *Did I just hear that?* "Excuse you?"

"Oh, don't play dumb, Viv," Morgan retorted. She held a bag open for Zane to deposit the debris from the vandalism. Zane gave Viv a side-eye and a shake of his head before dumping the assortment of twisted metal and broken wood into the bag.

"What are you talking about?" Viv thought she knew. She dreaded the answer.

"Helen only talked with you," Devlin said, his tone almost gentle. "She didn't talk with anyone else." He shrugged. "It's kind of obvious: she has reason to think it was you who did this." He jostled the bag he held in his hands.

Viv gritted her teeth. "I didn't do this."

"Sure." Zane rolled his eyes.

"How could I have done this?" Viv picked up a shovelhead, bent beyond any useful function, with shards of broken wood sticking out from the metal. "How could I have done this with my *bare hands*? And none of you heard anything last night, right?"

No one had an answer for that, Viv could tell. They all exchanged uneasy glances with one another, discomfort on their faces. Viv felt a small sense of victory unfurl within. At least she had managed to sow some doubt.

Cat scoffed at last, interrupting the silence that had fallen. "Fuck that noise, Viv. You were exhausted this morning. Morgan and I had to yell at you multiple times to wake you up." She smirked at Viv, her eyes brilliant with malice. "Why were you so tired, Viv?"

Viv stared at Cat in frustration as her heart sank in her chest. She couldn't tell them that she had had nightmares every single night since she had arrived at Grafton Stake. Viv couldn't stand to be that vulnerable with this group of hostile semi-strangers. Judgmental strangers, too, by the way they stared at her with speculation and disgust in their eyes. Better they think she was a vandal and a shit-stirrer than a child who had terrible dreams about her mother and the dark.

"I didn't do this," Viv repeated.

No one responded.

Instead, the others turned away from Viv. They managed to clean the mess up quickly, and when Helen was satisfied, she ushered them into the bus for the trip into town. Crowded as they were in the small bus, no one sat by Viv. They took pains to sit next to each other, stacking the gear inside the bus into innovative organizational schemes so that they could avoid sitting next to her.

Viv stared out the foggy window and tried to ignore them. Hurt hammered at her chest, but she refused to cry.

The general mood on the bus had lifted somewhat by the time Helen drove the bus into Hard Luck. It seemed like the others were excited by the change in pace, if angry at the cause for the trip. Helen pulled into the parking lot of the hardware store and parked on the outskirts, careful to ensure that the bus had a respectable distance from the other vehicles. Once parked, she turned in the driver's seat to face the crew.

"Okay, here's what we're going to do," she started in a stern tone. "We are going to replace the tools here, then dump our trash at the BLM office. I'm giving us an hour at the hardware store." Helen nodded down the road, then glanced at her watch. "There is a convenience store a few blocks away. Get yourself a soda or chips for the return trip. I want everyone back on this bus by 11:30 a.m. Understood?"

Nods swept up and down the bus.

Helen turned the crank that opened the bus door. "Let's go."

The others stood and stumbled their way off the bus. Cat smacked into Viv, shoving her aside in her hurry to get off the bus first. "Oops." She smirked at Viv.

Viv glared at her.

Helen led them into the hardware store, which was enormous and more of an agricultural supply store than anything else. The store held livestock supplies, gardening tools and plant starts, and even chicks who rustled around under the red beams of the warmth light adhered to their cage. To minimize distractions, Helen gave them each an assignment to retrieve specific tools in specific quantities. The others responded well to the directions, hurrying to seek their quarry. But instead of giving her a separate assignment, Helen kept Viv nearby. They searched for hazel hoes and shovels together. Viv chafed at the silent punishment but said nothing. Her protests had gone unheard; she didn't bother resuscitating them.

The clerk at the counter, a young woman barely older than Viv herself, gulped at the line of shopping carts that awaited her. "Is this all?"

Helen scanned the three carts in front and behind her. "I think so."

The young woman did not seem reassured. "Uh, I'll ring you up then."

Helen turned to the crew. "Now is your chance to get a snack or take a walk."

The others scattered like dandelion seeds in the wind, chasing each other out of the store and spilling onto the sidewalk.

"Viv, are you going?"

Viv swung a cool stare at Helen. "Am I allowed?"

Annoyance crossed Helen's face, but the emotion didn't make it into her response. "Yes, you are."

Viv nodded, then stepped away. She heard Helen make small talk with the clerk as she left. She stepped outside the hardware store and took several deep breaths. Viv felt her chest loosen with each breath, and the tightness of her terrible morning faded somewhat. She took her time as she made her way to the convenience store, hoping the others on her crew would be gone by the time she arrived.

Hard Luck was in full midday swing, she saw. The traffic from the highway that sliced through town had steady traffic, if a little too fast. Honey's Diner still had a line of customers out the front door and another one at the take-out window. Viv remembered her dinner with her Uncle Rick, only a few days ago. It felt as though much more time had passed.

The convenience store, attached to a gas station, was *busy*. Viv managed to buy a pack of smokes and a candy bar in the hubbub; the clerk was either too busy or didn't care enough to card her. Cat and Morgan eyed her from across the store but didn't approach.

Viv ignored them.

Outside, she walked around the side of the store and pulled out her phone. Ample bars indicated good connectivity, so she shot a text to Olivia. *Got a minute?*

The bubbles popped up. *Yes. You okay?*

Viv almost laughed. *No. It's been a shit day and a shit week.*

Her phone buzzed in her hand. Viv answered.

"What's up, girl?" Olivia's voice had a gravel edge, like hewn stone. Though the older woman was only in her early twenties, she had experienced a great deal of life in a short amount of time. Ollie had been a rock during Viv's first weeks out of rehab, something for which Viv would always be grateful.

Viv gave a half-chuckle, half-sob. "This place sucks, Ollie. And the people are assholes."

"Talk to me," Olivia ordered.

Viv sketched out the events that had occurred over the last few days, culminating in this morning's debacle. "Now everyone thinks I broke apart the tools, and they're treating me like shit," she finished. "I knew this program wouldn't be fun, but this is just *bullshit*."

Ollie paused on the other end of the line. "Viv."

"Ollie."

"Viv, sobriety only works with absolute honesty." Ollie cleared her throat. "You sure you didn't have anything to do with those tools?"

Viv scowled, then sighed. "Yes, I'm sure. I promise, Ollie. If you'd seen those tools, you would know that I couldn't have done that. They were *destroyed*. Absolutely shattered. I'm not that strong." Viv paused. "It's scary, really. I don't know how it happened, especially since everyone swears they didn't hear anything last night."

Ollie inhaled, then coughed into the phone. Viv knew the other woman must have stepped outside for a smoke. "Okay, I believe you."

Viv sighed. "Well, you're the only one." Hurt edged her words, and she stared up at the sky.

Ollie exhaled noisily. "Listen, Viv. You're a good kid. You've made some mistakes, and some people take a long time to trust after someone makes a mistake. Some take forever. You have to accept that. You have what, only five more weeks until the end of this program? Then you have a fresh start, a clean slate." Ollie's voice hardened. "Ignore those fuckers and get through this. Then you come home and go back to your future. Okay?"

Viv nodded, then realized Ollie couldn't see her. "Okay," she replied.

"You've got this, kid."

"I think so."

Ollie took another inhale. "You feeling the urge?"

Viv knew what her sponsor meant. She snorted. "All the time. It only goes away when I'm too tired to care."

"Have you?"

"No." Viv looked up at the sky again. "We're in the middle of nowhere, Ollie, and I don't think anyone else on the crew has a history with the stuff. We don't even have alcohol out here.

Ollie gave an inelegant snort. "You'd be surprised."

Viv thought of her comfortable upbringing, the large four-bedroom Craftsman in the suburbs. The tutors her parents paid for to supplement a public education. The trips to Chicago and Los Angeles before her mother had become too sick to travel. No one in her family had a history of addiction. At least, not publicly. Viv's experience had been a surprise – and a disappointment – to her father. "Yeah, I know."

A silence fell over the call.

Then Ollie spoke. "You ready to finish what you started?"

"I have to, don't I?"

Ollie snorted again. "That's the spirit."

Viv gave a choked laugh. "Yes," she said, her voice getting stronger. "I'm finishing this."

"Good."

In the distance, Viv could see Helen and several of the crew members gathered around the bus in the parking lot of the hardware store. "Ollie, I've got to go."

"Okay, kid, knock 'em dead."

"Thank you, Ollie. Really."

"Ain't a thing, kid. You're one of the good ones."

Viv's throat closed up at Ollie's kind words. She had needed to hear them, especially after this morning. "Thanks." She coughed to clear her throat. "Catch you later."

Viv hung up — and a clang echoed behind her.

She spun around.

Joel and Devlin stared at her, almost tucked behind the dumpster next to the store. Devlin held a cigarette in his hand, Joel a soda. Both of them stared at Viv.

Viv went on the offense. "Eavesdrop much?"

Devlin inhaled on his cigarette. "Sorry, sweetheart. No one cares about your boyfriend."

Joel spoke before Viv could. "Not a boyfriend, Dev – her sponsor. You didn't catch that bit?"

Viv stared at Joel, her eyes wide. Fear thrummed through her. She felt exposed, *seen*, as though a predator had her in its sights. She hated that vulnerability. Hated *him* for a moment.

Dev ground out the cigarette. "I didn't catch that." He sounded uncomfortable with the topic. "We should get back to the bus."

Viv stalked away before she could hear Joel's response.

This day had gone from bad to worse.

## CHAPTER TEN

Saturday dawned clear and bright, the first day without a drizzle or a torrent.

After a quick breakfast and quicker coffee, Viv left the campsite to go for a walk around the property. It was not her first choice. She had thought she would have relished being still, to be lazy over the weekend, but the simmering discontent from the others, all directed at her, drove Viv out of the camp and up along the trail they had just created earlier that week. The sunlight strengthened as the morning waxed on. Viv had to remove her coat due to the warmth. She found herself at the junction where she first saw the obelisk, the sentinel to the graveyard. She stared up the hill from the fresh trail. After a moment, she walked up, following the faint path laid by the entire group that Thursday afternoon.

The obelisk stood, bright in the sun and slick from recent rain.

Viv stood next to the hewn monument and examined the graves. She thought of Helen's revelation, that the graveyard housed victims of neglect and abuse. Viv shivered. She almost put her jacket back on.

Movement distracted her from her thoughts, and Viv leaned forward, gazing into the pasture. A weeping willow tree rested near the back of the cemetery, and from beneath the draping tendrils, Viv saw a small figure step forward.

A boy in pajamas stood obscured by the willow branches.

Viv stilled.

The boy stepped forward in a stuttering, jerky step. His pajamas, with a pattern of straight lines and too large for his slight frame, fluttered in the air despite the lack of a breeze. He had light hair, Viv could tell, though she couldn't quite see his face. He staggered another inch forward, and another.

Viv didn't move.

The boy stopped, then peered up at her. Viv could see his face. Black eyes glowed from within a pale white face. He stared at Viv, his head tilted. After a moment passed, he lifted his arms and pushed up a sleeve of his pajama smock. He rolled the sleeve several times, tucked it into the crook of his pale and bony arm. The normalcy of the action didn't prepare Viv for what happened next.

The boy dug his fingers into the skin of his forearm. Deeper and deeper until the skin severed and burst, like an overripe tomato.

Viv gasped, then started forward.

She stopped as she watched him dig his fingers even deeper into his scant flesh. His blood seeped, then rushed to the surface of his skin. The boy's fingers wiggled within his own flesh, searching for a grip. Once he had a hold, he pulled the flesh up and away from his small frame. The flesh came up in a deliberate motion, slow and steady. The ragged edges dripped blood onto his legs and feet, staining the grass beneath the willow tree.

The boy smiled.

His teeth were rotted daggers.

Viv stared at him, then took a step back. She heard a gasping, sawing sound coming from her and realized it was her breathing. She tried to steady her breath but couldn't. *Don't show your fear. He will see it.* Viv edged back, past the obelisk and then away from the clearing. *Don't run. Do not run, Viv.*

A black bird burst through the foliage next to Viv.

She screamed, folded into herself. Her heartbeat hammered against her head, and she sobbed out an incoherent plea. When no attack came, Viv turned to the sky to see dark wings beating away. She whipped around to the willow tree.

The boy was gone.

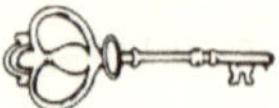

Viv didn't tell anyone at basecamp what she saw. What would be the point? If no one had believed her denials about the vandalized tools, they certainly wouldn't believe her about...whatever she saw. Her mind had tried to whisper the truth several times as she half-jogged, half-walked down the trail back to camp. She shut the whispers out, shaking her head and rolling her shoulders. She didn't check behind to see if anything — or anyone — followed her. Viv just moved forward.

*Whatever I saw, it's not important,* she told herself. *Five more weeks. That's it. Five more weeks.*

Viv had lunch duty for the following week and decided to stick with the tried and true: peanut butter and jelly sandwiches, fresh fruit, and trail mix. She prepped the lunches on Sunday night, listening to the relaxed conversation that swirled around her. None of the conversation was aimed at her, of course. The others were distant and cool towards Viv, still bitter about the camp-bound weekend.

A few feet away from the camp's edge, Helen snapped shut her satellite phone. A frown dug lines between her brows and around her mouth. She marched back into camp, pausing by the firepit.

"Hey, listen up," she called out.

The others gathered around the firepit. Viv continued with the sandwiches but moved around the table so she could see Helen.

"What's up, H-Bomb?" Zane had tried to make several nicknames work for the team leader, each more painful than the last.

Helen grinned at Zane. "That was terrible."

Zane shook his head. "I get no appreciation, no love."

Helen's smile faded before she spoke. "I've had a call from my contact at BLM. They are changing the timeline for us a bit. Due to new availability of the contractors, they want to bring the construction crews in two weeks, rather than at the end of our tour."

Viv watched the others look at each other, then at Helen.

"So...what does that mean?" Joel finally asked.

"That means we need to finish our gut job of the original homestead and the rest home before they arrive," Helen replied. The frown was back. "We have a fairly tight turnaround. Not a lot of wiggle room."

"Does this mean we won't have to build trails again?" Viv had never seen Cat so happy.

Helen gave Cat a sardonic glance. "We will switch our focus for the time being, yes."

Cat rested on her heels. "Thank god."

Helen shook her head. "I wouldn't relax so fast. Both buildings have old furniture and garbage to remove. We'll likely encounter rodents or small wildlife. These structures have had a lot of wear and tear over the years. It's going to be a big job, a tough one," she admitted. "Everyone will be required to wear a mask and a hard hat for your own safety, and it won't be pleasant or comfortable."

Cat's face fell.

Devlin spoke for the first time, his face twisted in distaste. "Wait, are you talking about rats?"

Helen stared at the young man. "Yes. There will be rats."

Devlin winced.

"Maybe," Helen amended. Viv thought the team leader was trying to reassure Devlin. "Probably."

Devlin sighed.

"Starting tomorrow, we'll gut the original homestead," Helen continued. "I'll designate a trash spot in the parking lot that we'll have to use until the dumpster arrives on Tuesday." She scrutinized the group. "Any questions?"

The relaxed mood had waned during Helen's recitation. Shoulders had sunk and faces had fallen. Still, no one spoke.

"Then enjoy the rest of your evening," Helen advised.

The others scattered in the wake of Helen's announcement. Cat, Morgan, and Devlin wandered to the parking lot for a smoke. Viv eyed them as they left, wrapping sandwiches in tinfoil. She wondered idly if Morgan was a third wheel but decided it was no concern of hers. She'd get her evening smoke after they were gone from the parking lot; Viv didn't feel like making small talk.

"Do you need help?"

The query jolted Viv out of her thoughts. She stared up at Joel, who stood next to the table on which she had set up a sandwich assembly station of sorts.

Joel nodded to the stacked lunches. "Do you need help?" he repeated.

Viv watched him with an unblinking gaze for a moment. She had avoided Devlin and Joel after the phone call to Ollie. She hadn't wanted to face them, hadn't enjoyed knowing that they knew so much about the worst parts of her life. Then Viv dropped her eyes and wrapped another sandwich.

"I'm almost done," she replied.

Joel surveyed the table: sandwiches had been made but not yet wrapped. Fresh fruit lay in an unorganized pile at the edge of the table. The bags of chips and trail mix rested in haphazard piles at the opposite end. Nothing had been assembled into the day packs. Joel peered back up and into Viv's face.

"Seems like it," he drawled with a light smirk. Clearly, he was not convinced.

"Thanks, though." Viv wrapped the last sandwich, staring at the work in front of her. She hoped Joel would get the hint.

A pair of raw-boned hands, large and covered in the swelling blisters they all sported from a week of unaccustomed activity, entered the periphery of Viv's vision. Joel reached for the fruit. "I'll do this, then."

Viv threw the sandwich onto the table. "I don't need your help."

Joel stared at her, unreadable. "I know."

"Then you can leave."

"I can do this for you first."

"Why won't you take a hint?" Viv scoffed.

Joel flushed, his frustration palpable. "Because I'd like to apologize."

Viv fell silent, taken aback. She studied Joel with new eyes. He shifted from one foot to the other, uncomfortable. His black hair, shaggy and overdue for a cut, flopped into his eyes. Despite the faint flush still staining his cheekbones, he met her gaze. "I'm sorry. I didn't mean to listen to your conversation," he said. "I won't tell anyone."

Viv snorted. "No, Devlin will do that for you."

Joel shook his head. "He won't. He gets it. Besides, he's wrapped up in Cat." He paused. "Again, I'm sorry. Won't happen again."

Viv looked away from Joel. *He's so earnest.* She wanted a cigarette. Or something stronger. "Okay. Thanks."

Joel inched closer. "Can I help with the lunches?"

Viv cut him a sideways glance. "Only if you're bored."

He gave her a full grin.

A flush warmed her face, and she stared back down at the sandwiches. Her fingers gave a slight tremble as she packaged the sandwiches, one after another. She couldn't remember the last time someone had smiled at her like that. *Maybe this will turn out well.*

*Maybe things do get better.*

## CHAPTER ELEVEN

Helen did not fool around with the safety gear.

"No, you have to wear the hat *and* the mask, Devlin," Helen said. "This isn't a negotiation."

"It's muggy and gross," he said. His eyes held a mute plea to the team leader. "And it's so *ugly*."

"Are you whining?" Zane inquired. "It sounds like you're whining. It's pathetic. Just so you know."

Cat glared at Zane, her eyes baleful over the mask that enveloped her face.

"Zane, not helpful." Helen turned back to Devlin. "You must wear the mask for your own safety. You will likely encounter mold and other contaminants in the house."

Devlin sighed, then pulled the mask from under his chin and settled it over his face. Viv could only see his eyes, simmering with discontent, beneath the hard hat, and the edges of his cheeks around the mask. "This sucks," came his muffled voice.

"Thank you." Helen ignored his complaints. "Everyone, hats on, masks up. We're going in." She led the group up the steps to the homestead. Viv saw that stone steps walked up to a wide front porch, covered by the extended roof and thus somewhat sheltered from the elements. Two large windows graced the front of the house, one of them boarded up with recent slabs of plywood. Pulling a rusty key set out of her pocket, Helen unlocked the front door and pushed it open. The hinges groaned in protest, the door shuddering and wincing its way ajar.

Helen stepped into the house, then waved the others into the homestead. Viv was the last to enter.

"We're going to survey each room, decide what needs to be done, and start our work. Got it?" Helen's instructions were clear, despite the mask.

Viv watched the line of hard hats nod their agreement.

"Good."

Helen made short work of diagnosing what needed to be done in each room. The homestead was bigger than Viv expected. The home seemed smaller, humbler from the worn exterior. But within, the homestead boasted large, expansive rooms with good light from many windows. Warped wooden floorboards were laid throughout both stories of the house, covered with a thick film of dust. The wainscoting along the hallways was waist-high and rotted along the top. The main rooms on either side of the entrance foyer were empty save for cobwebs and dust. Peering through a door that marched from the front room to a back one, Viv saw a large kitchen in the rear of the home. Stairs that seemed in good repair to Viv's unpracticed eye led up to the second floor.

Upstairs were four smaller rooms, a bathroom, and a large linen closet. The linen closet held a ceiling trap door that led to the attic. Helen led everyone up the stairs, and Viv was careful about where she placed her feet. Since dust coated every surface, the journey through the house had sent it in a flurry, and Viv heard Morgan sneeze despite the mask. Zane coughed.

They crowded onto the landing next to the top of the stairs, and Viv gazed around. Large windows graced both ends of the hallways, looking over the front and back of the homestead. Viv could see the worn molding and thin glass. Each of the doors had antique handles, the ornate, clear glass kind. A few were broken. The doors to each room were made of the same warped wood found on the first story of the home and differed only in the patterns of accumulated stains.

When she peered down the hallway, Viv saw a thin chain of rusted metal hanging from the ceiling. She followed the chain up and saw that it was the makeshift handle to an attic trap door. Viv eyed the trap door, then shook her head to herself. Given the state of the house, she did not want to go into the attic. Helen turned left and opened one of the doors to a room. Everyone else filed through the narrow doorway, while Viv leaned against the doorjamb.

"This is the worst room," Helen said. "Which isn't saying much."

Viv gave a soft snort of agreement.

The house was filled with trash, and in complete shambles. The walls had been covered in graffiti, likely by local trespassers seeking a lark. Some of the messages were harmless, even normal. One inscription instructed viewers to call Matt for a good time with near illegible numbers given below. Others had painted occult, helter skelter, and gang signs cribbed from television shows that Viv had seen. But most of the messages held simple warnings about Grafton Stake.

*Haunted AF.*

*This place is evil.*

*Murder Valley.*

Viv stared at those inscriptions the longest before turning away. In this room, the floor was littered with beer bottles, whole and broken. A discarded sleeping bag with torn lining lay in the corner. Faded wallpaper, a calico print where Viv could see through the graffiti, lined the top half of the room. The bottom half was edged with rotted wood wainscoting with clear termite damage.

"So, you've seen the condition of the house," Helen started. "It's bad but salvageable. My contact at Bureau wants the trash and the worst of the rotted wood removed. Since they want to turn this into a museum of sorts about the mining history of the region, they want to keep the 'original character' of the house, rather than bulldoze it and start fresh."

"Was there a lot of gold mining on this property?" Joel asked, casting a doubtful glance through the room.

Viv shared his skepticism.

"Not a great deal of successful mining on Grafton Stake, no," Helen admitted.

Viv saw the skepticism deepen on Joel's face. Helen must have, too, because she shrugged, then continued. "I know. Usually, we'd want a site associated with a successful history of gold mining activity to house a museum about the history of gold mining. But there aren't any available buildings in town. The city council of Hard Luck thought if we cleaned the original homestead and the asylum — I mean, the residence home — up, add a few trails and campsites, it would bring in some tourism."

Morgan stumbled in the corner of the room, her sudden motion interrupting Helen. Viv watched Morgan reached out to the wall to steady herself, staring at the opposite corner of the room with a peculiar expression on her face, one of faint disgust and worry.

"Morgan, everything okay?" Helen inquired.

Morgan didn't respond. She continued to stare at the corner, her brows pulled into a deep V of concentration. Fear skittered across her face, and she shuddered. Viv followed the other girl's gaze into the same corner, which held a small chair and table set that had clearly been built for a child. Nothing remained on the tabletop. Viv figured that years of trespassers had destroyed anything that had once been there.

"Morgan."

Helen's sharp voice cut through the fog. Morgan started, then turned to Helen, still bracing herself against the wall with one hand.

"Are you okay?" Helen asked, concern evident in her voice.

Morgan nodded. "Yeah."

Helen wasn't convinced. She studied Morgan for a moment. She must have decided against pursuing the issue. "Okay, here's the plan."

Viv had been assigned to clearing out trash from the second-story rooms. Helen had given her heavy-duty trash bags and instructions for where to put the trash until the industrial dumpster arrived. Viv pulled on her thick gloves, grateful that her uncle had insisted on several pairs of good work gloves prior to arriving in Hard Luck.

The others had been assigned to clearing trash in the other areas of the homestead: Morgan and Cat in the main rooms downstairs, Zane and Devlin to the kitchen. Helen and Joel had ascended to the attic on the rickety and frail stepladder that came down from the trap door. Their footsteps were muffled thumps above Viv's head, with thick dust drifting down like sooty snow from between the ceiling boards. The first time they tossed trash onto the second-floor landing, Viv had almost come out of her skin in fright at the loud bang. She grew accustomed to the noise after a while.

Viv found a wide assortment of trash in the rooms: broken beer bottles, food wrappers, bent spoons and used needles, signs of sleepovers or temporary habitation. After a quick consultation with Helen, she found a medical hazardous waste bag for the drug-related debris. Helen wouldn't let Viv handle it, insisting that an adult had to take responsibility for the spoons and the needles. Viv didn't protest. However, she suspected that she had had a great deal more experience with those items than Helen.

After the trash had been cleaned from the rooms, Viv started on the furniture and the rotted boards. She moved any furniture in good condition to a cleared space in one of the barns. "Original furniture will help sell the character of the place," Helen had advised. Rotted wooden floorboards and wainscoting were to be removed with a pry bar and tossed into the waste pile. Viv lost count of the many, many trips she made between the garbage pile in the parking lot and the original homestead.

Viv found that she liked yanking the rotted boards from the walls. Often, they came apart in her hands, shattering into slivers and shards of wood that embedded themselves into her gloves and clothes. Some boards were in better repair and more stubborn to remove, coming off the walls nearly whole. A persistent smell, a mix of mold and damp and something rotten, wafted up with every board she removed. But despite the smell and the debris, Viv was surprised by how much she enjoyed the work. Soon, each room was empty of the distractions and seemed almost clean. *Ready for something new*, Viv thought, then rolled her eyes to herself. The expression was a bit too obvious.

She worked for several hours, pausing to eat lunch at noon. Joining the others at the basecamp, Viv removed the facemask and hard hat with gratitude, taking what felt like her first deep breath in hours. The others were dusty and haggard, with a line of soot and filth that encircled their faces around the edges where the facemasks had rested. Sweat had dotted everyone's brow and had glued their hair to their scalps. Sitting down in a camp chair, Viv wiped her face with a cleansing wipe. Without a mirror, she couldn't tell how successful she had been in getting the dirt off. She was simply grateful to feel somewhat fresher.

Viv inhaled two sandwiches during the quiet lunch, during which only Joel and Helen had talked much. Everyone else appeared to be too tired. Morgan seemed to have withdrawn entirely into herself.

After lunch, Viv returned to the upstairs rooms to continue removing the rotted boards from the walls. As she gripped a board and braced herself to pop it off, she heard an odd noise, like paper being crinkled.

Viv paused to listen.

Nothing.

She gave the board in her hands, still attached to the wall, an experimental wiggle.

Paper, or something like it, rustled again.

Viv stopped, leaned forward to peer into the space between the wall and the frame of the house. The space was too tight and too dark. Without a flashlight, she couldn't see anything. Viv stepped back. *I'll have to remove the board to see what's there*, she thought. She pulled off one board, then another and yet another. It seemed as though the rustle of paper grew louder to Viv as she removed board after board. A new smell, beyond that of rot and damp, floated up *Something metallic*, Viv thought.

The final board came off the wall.

Viv peered in. She saw a small package, about the size of a large journal or sketchbook, wrapped in paper and knotted with old twine, resting on the floor between the former wall and the frame of the homestead. She crouched, then leaned in to lift the package with gentle hands. *Light*, she thought, *and not a book or a journal*. The paper wrapped around the package crumbled in Viv's hands, causing her to jump in fright. The contents spilled out into Viv's hands in a sudden tumble, and she stared at her cupped hands.

She didn't quite know what she held.

It was a medley of odd items. They didn't seem like they belonged together, not really, and Viv frowned. A round leather medallion with an evil eye symbol, similar to the one found on the obelisk, was branded into the surface on one side. One chicken leg lay beneath the leather medallion, with faded red and yellow feathers attached above the twisted foot. Viv traced the edges of a dirt stained, ivory and dark wood rosary, entangled with the chicken claw. Bone fishhooks and a baby's sterling silver rattle rested beside the medallion. Faded flower petals and dead stems of lavender. Two foreign coins, one small and one medium, with different languages on each, lay at the bottom of the pile.

Viv disentangled the items from each other and laid them on the floor with care. She studied the array of items, each one disparate from the next. What was the connection between these items? Why had they been wrapped in paper and hidden in the very walls of the house? Who had placed them there?

"Viv."

She jumped, her heart leaping into her throat.

Helen and Joel stood at the doorway of the room. Helen gave Viv a quizzical glance, her brows raised, followed by a smile that was obvious even through her safety mask. "Sorry to startle you." She studied the floor. "What do you have there?"

Viv unfolded from her crouch and stood up. "I found these in the walls."

Helen cast her a sharp glance. "In the walls?" she echoed.

"Yes, behind the boards," Viv confirmed. "They were wrapped in paper and twine. I didn't tear it," Viv added on, a little defensive in case she had stumbled onto a valuable artifact of some kind. "The paper was so old, it just crumbled in my hands."

Helen walked into the room and bent down to examine the collection. Over her bent head, Viv found Joel watching her with unreadable eyes above the sooty facemask.

After a moment, Helen stood back up. "An odd assortment," she said. "Wrap them up and put them on the bus. We'll drop them off at the museum this weekend."

Viv looked away from Joel. "The museum?"

Helen nodded. "If all goes well this week, we should be able to catch the Mining Days Festival in Elk Canyon this weekend. The regional history museum there may want these items for their collection." Helen continued to study the objects at her feet.

*If all goes well this week.*

Viv hunched her shoulders against the reminder of last week's vandalized tools and the unfounded — *untrue* — accusations by Helen. Rather than try to defend herself again, Viv reached down to gather up the items with angry jerks of her hands. She rose, and turned to leave the room. "I'll put these away."

She left, ignoring the others.

## CHAPTER TWELVE

*T*he boy in the pajamas stood across the clearing.

Viv waited at the edge of the graveyard. The sun was absent from the sky, but there was enough light to see the boy. She wore a patterned smock so large that it draped over and off of one shoulder. The smock's edge came to her knees, her bare legs and feet buried in the tall, dewy grass that swayed without a breeze.

Despite her lack of clothing, Viv wasn't cold.

In fact, she didn't feel much of anything.

*Viv watched the boy in the pajamas hopscotch across the graveyard, jumping from one unmarked headstone to another. He jumped and jumped, clearing improbable distances in leaps and bounds. He crisscrossed, double-backed, then leapt forward. Soon, too soon, he stood before Viv.*

*Viv could hear her heartbeat in her ears. Her breath sawed in and out, in and out, like a human metronome. Sweat rolled down her spine, dripped onto her thighs.*

*The boy grinned at her, the rotted daggers of his teeth gleaming wetly through thin blue-white lips. His black eyes glowed with anticipation, too large for such a thin face. Viv watched as he pulled his pajama smock off of his frail frame and tossed it onto the grass between them.*

*Viv gasped.*

*Bruises stained his thin torso like a gruesome watercolor portrait. Scars, old and new, were etched into the pale skin. An open wound across his shoulder drained pus and seeped pitch-black blood. His ribs pressed his skin like they were trying to escape his body. Each of his knuckles were raw, with more black blood wrapped around the joints.*

*The boy stared at Viv. His grin grew wider and wider, until it cut across his face. He drew a single hand up and brought it to his chest, his sharp nails pressed against the taut skin. In slow and precise motions, he carved into his chest with his nails. Up and down, then back up again. Across one way, then a circle. The speed of the carving was a constant and slow pace, but the blood dripped faster and faster, until streams of the dark ichor rolled like a river down the boy's chest.*

*He never looked away from Viv, grinning the entire time.*

*Viv trembled in the grass.*

*After what seemed like an interminable amount of time, he stopped. He let the bloody hand drop to his side.*

*Viv's gaze drifted down to his chest. A blaze of pain lanced across her own chest, and she could feel wetness stain her breasts, the smock clinging to the sticky fluid. She didn't look down. She couldn't wrest her eyes from the boy.*

*A key.*

*The boy had carved a key into his chest.*

Viv jolted awake with a cry.

She felt tears on her face and a pain across her chest, her breaths erratic and shallow.

Morgan and Cat stirred, unhappy to be woken up.

"What?" Cat snarled.

Morgan just moaned, then turned over.

Viv pressed a hand on her chest. Her fingers searched beneath her top and found no wetness or blood but... she paused at what felt like a scabbed over wound. She traced the edges of the abrasion across her shoulders and down her torso.

*What on earth is happening?*

"Nothing," she lied. "It's nothing. Sorry about that."

Later that morning, Viv examined her chest in the camp bathroom mirror. A single bare bulb lit the small space with faint illumination. The injury seemed faded, with white tracery across her skin, as though it had occurred years earlier. She stared at the symbol of an ornate key was etched across her chest in jagged motions, uneasy. Then she buttoned up her work shirt.

She avoided her gaze in the mirror.

She felt very alone.

The industrial dumpster arrived that morning. After a miserable meal of semi-frozen waffles from Morgan, Helen directed the crew down to the parking lot to transfer the accumulated trash and wooden debris into the dumpster.

The arrival and the transfer of trash took longer than Helen had expected so she called for an early lunch before turning Viv and the others back onto the original homestead.

The sun had drifted out from behind the ever-present cloud bank, turning the day warm and bright. With that many bodies in close quarters, the homestead grew warm and almost muggy. Sweat rolled down Viv's back as she stood and shifted the armload of rotted boards to her shoulder. Placing the boards in the discard pile next to the path that led to the impromptu parking lot, she glanced up in time to see Joel and Devlin struggle as they removed a large piece of furniture out of the homestead.

"Need help?" Helen called out from nearby, wiping her gloved hands on her work pants.

"We're good, thanks," Devlin grunted. "I think that Cat needs help on the first floor, though."

Viv tried to sneak into the homestead without being seen.

"Vivienne."

*Not fast enough.* Her shoulders sank and she turned to Helen. "Yeah?"

"Help Cat out?" It wasn't really a question nor a request.

*Damn it.* Viv nodded. "Sure." She kept her voice neutral.

Viv walked through the entrance and then the foyer of the homestead. The main room to the right had been gutted and now resembled a skeleton of its former self, with barren support beams and empty space. Viv peered through the main room on the left. This room still needed work, with many of the rotted boards still on the walls. Viv stepped further into the room and scanned every corner.

There was no sign of Cat.

Viv wandered through the room and into the large kitchen. Like the first room, the kitchen had been cleared of furniture and rotted wood. Only the enormous stone hearth and the maple mantle remained in the room. The many windows, designed to let in light by which to work, were mostly broken. Thus, Helen had tacked up weather-proof sheeting to protect the interior. The resulting sunlight that emerged through the sheeting was eerie, casting a muted sepia color throughout the room.

"Cat?" Viv called.

No answer.

Viv headed upstairs. She paused at the door of each room and peered within.

Again, no sign of Cat.

At the end of the hallway, Viv saw the ladder to the attic fully extended to the floor. The trap door was wide open, the entrance to the attic a black blot on the ceiling. Viv stepped closer, coming to a stop at the bottom rung of the rickety ladder.

"Cat?" Viv's voice floated up like it had wings. "Are you up there?"

No answer.

Viv sighed. She *had* to look in the attic to confirm Cat wasn't there. Then Viv could tell Helen that she couldn't find Cat. Viv started up the ladder, only pausing when it swayed beneath her. The ladder steadied and she continued up. Her head cleared the entrance into the attic, and as she climbed further into the room, she pulled herself off the ladder and onto the floorboards in relief. Her feet dangling through the entrance, Viv surveyed the room.

Cat sat in the corner, still. Her facemask and hard hat lay next to her, discarded. She leaned over an antique trunk, blackened by age, her hands resting on the upright lid.

Anger flared through Viv. Why hadn't she responded to Viv's calls? "Cat, what the hell?"

Still, no response.

Viv's brow furrowed and she studied the other girl for a moment. Something about Cat's absolute stillness triggered an alarm in the back of her mind. Cat was *too* still, and it reminded Viv of animals that froze out of fear, to fool nearby predators into thinking they were part of the scenery.

"Cat?" Viv called, this time in a gentle voice.

A smothered moan forced its way out of Cat, the sound full of aching grief.

As Viv edged closer, Cat gave a violent start. She spun around to stare at Viv. A medley of emotions crossed the other girl's face: Terror, grief, shock.

A bone deep coldness settled over Viv.

Something was wrong.

"Cat, are you okay?"

Cat's face crumpled. Instead of tears, she began to laugh, short bursts of hysterical laughter. "Oh," she gasped, "it's you." Cat shook as she emitted short bursts of the false laughter. Viv shivered. The sound raised the hairs on the back of her neck.

Viv watched Cat, uneasy. She knew the other girl to be snarky, confident, unshakeable. The Cat before her was a *mess*, with mucus and tears dripping down her face, her eyes reddened from crying. After a moment of indecision, Viv sat next to Cat, careful not to get too close in case the other girl objected.

"Cat, are you hurt?" she asked.

"No," Cat gasped out. "I'm fine."

Viv cast her a doubtful look. "Sure."

Cat snorted through her tears. "I'm *fine*."

"Okay." Viv steeled herself for her next words. "Do you... need a hug or something?"

Cat gave Viv a withering glance.

"Oh, thank god," Viv sighed in relief.

Cat choked out a rusty chuckle.

They sat in silence for a few minutes as Cat wiped her face with the sleeve of her work shirt. Unfortunately, Cat was only successful in grinding dirt further into her face. But Viv didn't say anything.

Cat sighed. "I guess we need to tell Helen."

Viv shook her head. "I wasn't planning to tell anyone."

Cat grimaced, and fresh tears welled in her eyes. "Not about this," she pointed to herself. "About *that*." She gestured at the antique trunk.

Viv switched her gaze from the trunk to Cat. "I don't understand."

"Look. It's in there," Cat muttered. "Just...be careful. Don't get too close."

*That's not exactly comforting.*

Viv leaned towards the trunk, and peered into the darkened depths.

Human bones, patinaed with age and of every size, lay within.

## CHAPTER THIRTEEN

V iv tried to gasp in shock, but instead choked on an exhalation of air.

Most of the bones in the pile were intact, dried and worn by time. A few were held together by a thin, almost transparent, flap of skin and dried ligaments. A sour taste burned down her throat, and Viv swallowed down her bile, forcing herself to examine the remains To make sense of what lay before her eyes. A small calico dress were twisted around a set of small remains. Viv saw old leather shoes, riddled with moth holes and pest damage, on the feet. That last detail broke her heart. Viv tried to hold in the sudden sob that rose in her chest.

*Her shoes were eaten by bugs*, she thought, dazed. *God, I need to get out of here.*

Viv threw herself away from the trunk, tripping over her hands and knees.

She met Cat's gaze. The other girl stared back, understanding and shared horror on her face.

"You're right. We need to tell Helen."

"We need to call the police," Cat said, almost as though to herself.

"Let's leave. Now." Viv's tone became firm with sudden purpose. Cat hurried down the trap door ladder and Viv followed, stumbling as the ladder swayed with speed. Viv fled down the stairs and stumbled out of the house, heavy breaths sawing in and out of her.

She let Cat break the news.

Helen thought it was a joke at first.

She was not amused.

But after she confirmed the truth of Cat and Viv's story, she emerged from the attic with an ashen, grim countenance. She secured the trap door to the attic and told everyone to go back to basecamp for the remainder of the afternoon. She called the police on her satellite phone, her bleak expression and somber tone obvious from a distance.

Cat huddled in a camp chair before the fire Devlin had started, her arms wrapped around herself. Viv stood apart from the others. She felt her skin itch with nerves as her mind roiled. Whose remains were those? How many people had been dumped in that trunk? How had that small child passed away? Viv hunched into herself, trying to contain the feelings and the thoughts that threatened to erupt. She wondered how long those people had laid forgotten in the trunk, enclosed in a dark and cramped space.

Forgotten. Alone.

In the distance, gravel crunched beneath tires.

Viv glanced up at the noise. The police had arrived, and they pulled into the impromptu parking lot to park next to the industrial dumpster that had only arrived that morning. *Only this morning? It feels like years ago.* A second car, a white SUV with a discreet logo from the county coroner's office on the driver and front passenger doors, followed shortly after. Viv watched Helen greet the men, then lead them into the homestead and up the stairs.

*I need a smoke.*

Viv strode down the path to the parking lot. She hid behind the dumpster, then lit a cigarette. The first inhale felt like a benediction, a blessing to chase away the fear and the sorrow from earlier.

"Can I have one?"

Viv almost jumped out of her skin.

Cat stood a few feet away. She eyed the cigarette in Viv's hand.

Viv pulled out the packet from her back pocket, offered it to Cat. The other girl then borrowed the lighter and took her first inhale with a practiced ease that told Viv that Cat had smoked before, often. They smoked in silence, twin plumes rising in the damp air. After she finished her first, Viv pulled out another and offered a second to Cat. The girl accepted. A few minutes later, Cat spoke.

"I had a miscarriage a few months ago."

Viv stilled. She stared at the ground at her feet, uncertain what to say.

"I didn't want the pregnancy, but it was still hard when it happened, you know?" Cat took a deep inhale. "My parents were furious. They sent me to a Catholic school to avoid that kind of thing."

Viv didn't know what to say. *I'm sorry* seemed insufficient. Viv opened her mouth to speak but Cat continued.

"When I saw those bones, looked at the little one... I thought it was my punishment." Cat stared into the sky. A tear slipped from the corner of her eye and down her face. "For not wanting mine."

A breath stuttered out of Viv. Her heart turned over in her chest, aching at the obvious sign of Cat's pain and sorrow.

"That's not true," she said.

Cat cast a withering glance at Viv, the effect marred by the tears that slid down her face. "Oh? Because the world is fair and nothing bad like that would happen?"

Viv snorted. "No. Because not everything is about you."

Cat stared at Viv in shock. Viv felt a twist of remorse at her harsh words and was about to apologize when a chuckle trickled out of Cat. The other girl continued to chuckle, shaking her head.

Viv sighed. "Sorry. I don't try to be an asshole."

"It just comes naturally?" Cat inquired with a smirk.

Viv grinned back. "I'm sorry." She nodded in the direction of the homestead, and her smile faded. "That was rough."

Cat's earlier mirth subsided. "Yeah, it wasn't great." She ground out the cigarette. "But... thank you. For being there."

Viv stared at the cigarette in her hand, the ember tip glowing. "Yeah. Of course." She watched Cat for a moment. "Are you going to be okay?"

"Probably not," Cat replied. She shrugged. "Nothing new there. You?"

"Oh, sure," Viv said. "Fantastic."

Cat's weak chuckle followed her back up the trail.

"Hey. Can everyone gather here for a minute?"

Helen's subdued greeting roused Viv from her staring contest with the campfire. The older woman appeared exhausted. Her shoulders sloped down and the bags under her eyes seemed deeper, darker. Beyond Helen, three men stood. Viv eyed them: Two were dressed in tan and brown police uniforms while the third wore a blue, ill-fitted variation of a lab coat. *The county coroner.* The man didn't appear old enough to be a coroner. He was young, with a fresh face that reminded Viv of high school football and homecoming dances.

Helen continued once she had everyone's attention. "These gentlemen want to take your statements. They'll start with Cat but they want to talk with each of us. Privately."

The older cop was clearly in charge, his silvered temples like the wings of a bird and his skin resembled aged leather. He stepped forward. "Which one of you is Catherine?"

Cat stood up from her chair. She seemed nervous, tucking her hair behind her ear. "I am."

"This way, please."

The other cop, dark hair and mid-thirties, scanned the remaining crew members. "I'd like to talk with Vivienne."

"That's me."Viv followed the younger cop towards one of the barns but not too far away. Viv noticed his last name embroidered on the uniform: Burton. He pulled out a pad and a pen, and scribbled a few words before scrutinizing h er.

"Vivienne, I have a few questions but first I'd like you to walk me through what happened."

Viv sketched out the encounter in the attic in terse words and a monotone voice, hoping to keep the interaction as short as possible. Cops always made her nervous. Burton watched during her grim recital, taking a steady stream of notes on his pad. Her voice broke a few times when Viv tried to describe the bones.

"The bodies were dried, not fresh?" Burton queried.

Viv shivered. "Yes."

After a few more questions, Burton closed the police pad and thanked Viv for her time. The remaining statements took the better part of an hour. Viv watched Helen join Burton, the older cop, and the county coroner near the homestead to confer in quiet tones. She could hear the steady hum of their voices but couldn't make out what they were saying. Finally, Helen gathered everyone to the campfire.

"Colts and Burton have an update to share with you."

"Well, the bones are quite old." The older cop began with a slightly nasal twang. He continued, rubbing the back of his neck as he spoke. His shirt shifted with the motion and Viv saw the name Colts embroidered on the uniform. "Greggs, our coroner, confirmed that the bones have been that way a while, perhaps even for over a hundred years. We won't know until we test some more, but those people are likely patients from the asylum." Colts glanced at Helen, trepidation on his face. "You tell them about the history of this place?"

Helen's brow was furrowed. The corners of her lips turned down. "Yes."

The older cop gave a single nod, then turned to the crew members. "Then you all understand why this discovery isn't that unusual, given the background of the Grafton Stake." He shook his head. "We conferred with Ms. Whiteaker, and we're going to let the project continue. We know you all have a tight timeline to keep. Just stay out of the attic until we've had a chance to remove the trunk."

"We'll switch our focus to the residence home starting tomorrow, keep out of your way," Helen added.

Colts frowned. "Residence home?" he echoed.

Helen pointed to the Fortress. "Where the patients stayed?" she offered.

The cops exchanged a quick look, something like disbelief passing between them. The older cop spoke again. "That's a generous name for that hellhole. Lot of people died in that place."

Helen's brows dipped deep into a grimace. "I know. We found the grave-yard."

Colts nodded. "Well, we appreciate you staying out of the homestead until we retrieve the remains. We'll be by tomorrow morning to wrap everything up." He glanced over to the coroner. "Greggs, you got anything to add?"

The young man shook his head. "Awfully creepy up there," he announced in a cheerful voice. He seemed impervious to the tense atmosphere that pervaded the group. "I can see why it's the stuff of teenage dares."

Colts sighed. Viv watched him fight to keep from rolling his eyes. "All right. Thank you all for your time." He nodded at Helen and turned to leave, with Burton and Greggs close behind him.

Freed from the cops and the coroner, Viv's gaze wandered through base camp. The late afternoon had seeped into night. Stars studded the dark sky, a thin strip of faint light that shone against the black outline of the forest canopy.

Sudden fatigue washed over her, and Viv just wanted to drive back to the Har'
Luck Otel, sketchy as it was, to shower and sleep for twelve hours.

She wanted to get away from this disturbing place.

Helen sighed. "Well, that was a shit day, huh?" It was the first time Viv had
heard the team leader curse.

"So, boss, we're going to work on the Fortress tomorrow?" Zane asked.

"Sounds like it," Helen replied. "Everyone should turn in early tonight.
Try to sleep, at least." Helen didn't sound optimistic about their chances. Viv
shared her misgivings. Grafton Stake had revealed more and more secrets since
their arrival: The beached, desiccated fish at the river's edge. The graveyard of
abandoned, nameless souls. The vandalized tools, and now forgotten human
remains in an antique trunk. Viv stared at the Fortress in the twilit darkness, the
copper panels of the roof shimmering with the light from the campfire.

She shivered.

She thought of the boy with the key engraved on his chest. What did he want?
Had anyone else seen him? And if not, why did he appear only to Viv?

What other secrets did this cursed place hide?

Breakfast was charred half-frozen waffles. Black on one side, pale beige and raw
on the other. When Morgan was distracted by clean up, Viv tossed hers into the
trash, then ate trail mix instead. *Good thing I had a second cigarette this morning.*

The others seemed short-tempered or fidgety. Viv watched Devlin and Cat sit
next to each other, with nary a word between them, eating their waffles in grim
counterpoint. Zane stood up, then sat down, and up again, his face puckered
into a worried frown. Finally, he started gathering trash to help Morgan out
of what seemed like boredom. Morgan appeared frazzled. Viv eyed Joel, who
choked down a single waffle before drinking a quart of water. *Probably to wash
away the taste,* she thought.

Helen was subdued, and Viv had caught her watching the homestead several times, a thoughtful expression on her face. Viv wondered how the woman felt about finding those remains in the antique trunk.

Viv's gaze surveyed the homestead and then turned to the Fortress. The large, three story building lay northeast of the homestead. *Close to the graveyard.* She shook herself, trying to escape the shiver that tapped along her spine. The ever-present rain and mist dappled the Fortress, and the empty windows were black with darkness. Looking at the black windows, Viv thought of her dream, her nightmare, of the tight and dark room with no light and no space to stretch her legs. And cold. So cold.

She wondered if the Fortress held such rooms.

## CHAPTER FOURTEEN

U p close, the Fortress was larger and more weathered than Viv had expected. The stone had been worn down by the damp Oregon weather for decades. Overgrown shrubbery at the base of the Fortress, a discordant concoction of wild roses, briars, ferns, and nettles, threatened to take over the first floor. The wild mess of sharp greens seemed to reach up to the sky as if to pull the Fortress into the ground. A short flight of stairs led up to the large oak double doors, hemmed in by stone and wrought iron brackets.

Viv watched Helen first remove the padlock from the chains that secured the double doors, then unweave the length in a careful motion. The older woman laid the padlock and the chains aside.

The soft clank made Viv jump.

Helen pushed open the first door, then the second. The doors squealed apart, and the hinges emitted a vigorous protest as Helen forced the oak doors wide and braced them against the walls of the entrance foyer with two large stones from outside. The others followed up the steps after Helen, trailing up in a single line.

Viv was last.

She took her time, dragging her feet with each step. She really didn't want to go into the Fortress.

Once inside, Viv glanced around. The light inside was dim and eked through the broken windows. The deep shadows in the corners and along the ceilings pressed into the scarce daylight like a hungry, desperate creature. The narrow entrance led to an open floor beyond, and as the group trudged forward, Viv saw that the open space spread almost to the back of the first floor of the Fortress. The wide room had high ceilings; the lavish tile floor had more broken squares than complete ones, all of them a stained white background with Delft blue floral motifs. Broken chairs and tables littered the room, the wood either shattered by local vandals, or worn down by damp and too much time.

Helen faced the group, her face decorated with false cheer. Despite the wide grin, Viv could see the tension that tightened her face.

"Let's get started."

Instead of splitting the group up like the day prior, Helen kept them all together on the first floor. Each of them worked to clear out the old furniture, shattered tiles, and trash from trespassers. Most of the garbage consisted of empty chip bags and broken beer bottles. Cat found a desiccated sleeping bag and made a face.

Working from the foyer to the opposite side of the first floor, the crew made slow progress. Plumes of dust and slivers of wood swirled throughout the air. No one spoke much.

Then the injuries started.

Zane was the first.

"Goddamn," Viv heard him shout. Lifting her head from the debris pile she had gathered at her feet, Viv gazed across the room to Zane.

He rose from a crouch, holding one hand with care.

"Zane, what is it?" Helen barked. She made her way to his side. The others paused to gather around. As Viv approached, she saw a fingertip of Zane's glove stained with blood, seeping into the fabric like ink into paper.

"Cut myself." Zane winced.

"Let's wrap it up outside," Helen urged. "Everyone else, keep working. Take extra care when working with items that could cause damage." She ushered the tall boy out the double doors. As Viv returned to work, she could hear snatches of the murmurs out front.

The next injury occurred less than an hour later.

"Ouch!"

Viv stilled. "Morgan, are you okay?"

Morgan held her arm, which bore a long deep scratch beneath the torn sleeve of her work shirt, with her other hand. "I got scratched." She shook her head. "It hurts."

Helen appeared from around the corner. "Did someone get hurt?"

Viv nodded to Morgan. "She has a deep scratch. It probably needs a bandage or something."

Helen sighed. "Okay, Morgan, outside. Let's get you cleaned up."

Lunch was quiet and tense. Hardly anyone spoke, and Viv doubted that the cause of the silence was fatigue. She picked at her own sandwich and fruit. Despite the morning's hard work, her appetite had waned.

By early afternoon, the team had cleared most of the debris from the first floor. Behind the front room with the porcelain tiles, they discovered the remains of a large kitchen. Only the stone hearth, a collapsed table, and a few cooking pots remained.

Cat dropped a large pot on her foot, having lost her grip on the worn handles.

"Fuck." She gritted out.

Helen appeared from behind Viv, almost like magic. "What happened?"

"What do you think happened?" Cat snapped. Her brows slammed over her eyes and the girl let out a short whimper of pain.

"Cat dropped that on her foot," Viv answered before Helen could respond. She pointed at the pot on the ground.

"Cat, go outside and take a break." Helen shook her head. "Let me know if you think something is broken or sprained."

Viv watched Cat limp out of the kitchen. She heard Helen sigh. The older woman started to massage her temples with both hands. "No more injuries," she muttered to herself. It sounded like a prayer, or maybe a demand. Helen studied Viv, her lips twisted to the side. "Are you alright? No injuries or scrapes from today?"

Viv thought of the key symbol scratched across her chest only yesterday, but she only shrugged. "I'm okay." She had kept her distance from Helen after the debacle with the vandalized tools. The older woman's disbelief in her innocence had made Viv wary. Slow to forgive and even slower to trust.

Helen studied Viv for a moment, then gave a slow nod.

*BOOM.*

A crash echoed from the front room.

Viv winced.

Helen swore, then rushed out of the kitchen. Viv followed at a slower pace.

Joel and Devlin stood at either ends of a shattered table that now rested on the floor of the front room. Both shook their hands, pain on their faces.

"Do I want to know?" Helen sighed.

"We misjudged the width of the door, slammed our hands against the frame," Joel said.

Helen massaged her temples again. "Are you okay?"

The boys answered at the same time.

Devlin winced. "Yes?"

"I think so," Joel said.

Helen sighed, then glanced at her watch. "Okay, we're done. Let's clean this up and call it a day. A long day."

"Thank god," Cat muttered somewhere from behind Viv.

The cleanup didn't take long. The others seemed keen to stop for the day and redoubled their efforts to clear up the front room and the kitchen.

Finally, they were done.

Viv watched Helen do a silent headcount over the group, her lips moving as she named each of the crew. Suddenly, she paused.

"Where's Morgan?"

Viv looked around, seeing the others do the same.

Morgan wasn't in sight.

"Is she still in the Fortress?" Zane asked.

"Vivienne, Cat, check inside the Fortress," Helen said. The rest of us will walk around the building and check the barns."

Viv and Cat started up the short flight of stairs. Viv pushed open the heavy wooden door, which slammed shut once she let go. *Dark. It's really dark in here.* The late afternoon light, already made weak by the grey overcast skies outside, poorly illuminated the front room. Viv wished she had brought a flashlight. She cast a quick glance at Cat. The other girl was apprehensive, her eyes wide and her body tilted towards the door, as if ready to run at a moment's notice.

"Let's check the kitchen," Viv said. She led the way across the large front room, her work boots staccato-ing across the tile floor. The noise somehow seemed bigger in the empty room. Cat followed behind her, almost on her heels.

The kitchen was empty and silent. The large hearth, cleared of pots and cooking utensils, looked like an open maw of a beast — ready to swallow anyone who drifted too close. Viv shivered, then shook herself. *Silly. Stop it.*

"Do you hear that?" Cat asked suddenly. She tilted her head, listening for something.

"What is it?" Even as she spoke, Viv could hear what Cat spoke of. A faint murmur reached her ears and Viv strained to listen. "Is it – is it coming from upstairs?"

Cat's eyes were wide. "I think so."

Viv walked over to the narrow staircase that led from the kitchen to the second floor. "Morgan?" she called out. "Are you up there?"

The murmurs stopped.

A chill chased down Viv's spine.

Then the scratches on her chest, etched in the key shape, blazed with renewed pain and she almost gasped aloud, catching herself at the last moment. She rubbed her hand against her chest. Viv turned to Cat and saw the other girl shake her head in a vigorous denial.

"I'm not going up there," she hissed. "Hell. No."

Viv agreed with her but... "What if she's hurt?"

"Then she would call for help," Cat retorted in a harsh whisper.

Viv peered up the stairs. They were darker than the rest of the kitchen and narrow enough to only permit one person at a time. She could see faint daylight at the top, likely from the windows.

The murmurs started again.

The hair on the back of Viv's neck stood up.

"Morgan?" She called again. "We need to go."

Heavy footsteps creaked across the floorboards above her head.

Viv stepped back from the staircase. *What was that?*

The footsteps continued, then paused.

When the heavy tread started again, Cat fled. Viv watched the other girl run from the kitchen and out into the front room. A heavy door slammed shut a few moments later.

Viv envied the other girl her presence of mind. Viv felt trapped to the floor, her feet glued in place. *Run*, her mind shrieked. *Move*. Still, she couldn't.

The footsteps altered in rhythm and after a moment, Viv realized they were drawing closer. She peered up the staircase — and saw work boots coming down the steps, slow and steady.

Viv heaved a sigh of relief.

It was Morgan.

But her relief came too soon, Viv realized. There was something different, something *wrong*, about the other girl. Her eyes were wide, the whites evident even in the semi-darkness. Her pupils were dark pinpoints among a blue sea, and her lips trembled as they held a grotesque grin. Her lashes fluttered rapidly, her hands held still at her sides.

Viv took another step back. "Morgan?"

Morgan's smile stretched further across her face, stretching her lips into thin lines of forced mirth.

Viv shivered. *Something is not right.* "Is everything okay?"

Morgan gave a slow nod. "Of course." Her voice seemed higher, lighter than Viv had heard before.

Viv cleared her throat. "Everyone is looking for you. We should go." Viv paused. "Who were you talking to? Upstairs, I mean."

The too-large grin on the other girl's dimmed for a moment, then burst forth again.

"No one."

## CHAPTER FIFTEEN

Helen gave Morgan a sharp admonishment for wandering away.

Viv watched Morgan nod and grin during the lecture, then nod and grin some more. Helen's obvious frustration didn't seem to register with Morgan, and as Viv watched the odd behavior, she grew more uneasy. Morgan had clearly spoken to either herself or someone else.

Maybe *something* else.

Cat took some teasing from Zane and Devlin for having fled the Fortress after hearing the footsteps.

"Ooh, did you hear a ghost?" Zane decided to poke at the already irate girl.

"Yep, she found a ghost and got the hell out of there," Devlin cackled.

"Oh, shut up," Cat retorted, then stomped ahead of the group.

Viv hadn't joined in on the teasing. She understood why Cat had fled. Viv only wished she had done the same thing.

"So did you find a ghost?" A quiet voice inquired.

Viv turned, then studied Joel. His dark eyes were serious, not jocular, and studied her face.

"No ghost."

"But you heard something," Joel prodded.

Viv cut a sharp glance at Joel.

"You're clearly upset," he continued. "What happened?"

Viv thought for a moment. What could she share that wouldn't convince Joel she was crazy? "Cat and I heard... something," she offered. "Morgan was talking to herself."

"What?" Joel was taken by surprise, Viv could tell.

Viv shrugged. "Yeah, I'm not sure. It was... creepy," she admitted. "Cat was right to be nervous."

Joel didn't say anything for the rest of the walk back to basecamp.

At basecamp, Viv was surprised to see three men standing around the firepit. She recognized the coroner's representative from the day prior but didn't know the other two men. They wore tan uniforms with patches that identified them as members of the Department of Fish & Wildlife. Helen greeted them with obvious affection and warmth, and they stood just outside the camp to murmur in low voices to one another, the conversation punctuated by frequent laughter.

The rest of the crew had settled in for dinner around the campfire when Helen had waved farewell to the men. She dished up her own dinner, a hodgepodge of kielbasa and turkey stuffing, and sat down. After a moment of silence from the group, Helen glanced up from her dinner to see the crew watching her with expectant expressions.

Devlin spoke first. "Who were those guys?"

Helen swallowed her food first. "Friends, colleagues. You met the coroner last night. He came by to retrieve the trunk and gather up any additional evidence." Helen paused. "Based on the bones, the littlest one was a girl, less than a year old when she passed. They also think there might be remains from twelve other people in the trunk."

Viv recoiled. She saw the news ripple through the others like sudden waves on an ocean shore. Shock and disbelief stained their faces. Viv set her bowl on the ground, her dinner forgotten.

"It's awful," Helen agreed with the unspoken sentiment that hovered over the crew like a fog. "But the coroner believes that the deceased passed decades ago, which means the project should be able to continue without any bureaucratic interruptions."

"Yay." Cat spoke in a flat voice, her sarcasm a sharp knife through the night.

"And the others?" Joel asked. "Who were they?"

"Department of Fish and Wildlife," Helen answered between bites of her dinner. "I asked that they come out and take a look at the fish we found by the river."

Viv glanced away from the fire. "Did they find anything?" She thought of her dreams with the fish, arranged in a glittering key composed with dead flesh.

Helen shook her head. "We don't know anything yet," she replied. "Most of the fish have completely decomposed but they retrieved a few samples and will run some tests, make sure the water is safe." Helen shook her head again. "They were surprised and a bit disturbed by the fish. Walters and Novik haven't seen anything like that before. It's doesn't seem natural."

*Because it* isn't *natural.* But she didn't say anything aloud. *Only four and a half weeks left. I can do this.* She eyed Morgan, who had finally lost the manic grin and the pinpoint pupils sometime during dinner. Viv watched the other girl stare into the fire, her food mostly untouched.

*I will do this.*

*I can't go back to the detention center.*

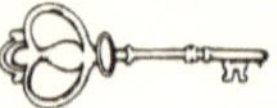

*Viv could hear the murmurs down the hall. She folded into herself, a tight ball of shivering limbs. She bowed her head against her knees.*

*They were coming.*

*The footsteps started on the opposite end of the hall, drifting closer with intermittent pauses and stops. Viv could hear the others across the floor, each of them secluded in tiny rooms with a single window, recoil and blanch away from the doors. She could hear the rustling of worn, dirty thin gowns like the one she wore.*

*The footsteps started again. They were coming.*

*Viv stared at her bare feet against the raw wood floor. Her toes were dirty, thick grime wedged under the untrimmed toenails. Slivers of wood buried themselves into the soles of her feet. Bruises covered one foot. She didn't remember how they got there.*

*The footsteps paused outside the door.*

*Her door.*

*She could feel his gaze upon her, like an unwanted caress. Viv stared at the floor and imagined herself invisible, melting into the floorboards and walls like rain against the earth.*

*She didn't dare meet his gaze.*

*A key was inserted in the lock.*

*Viv screamed.*

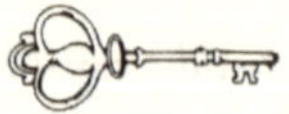

Viv jolted awake. The symbol burned into her chest, an anchor weighing down on the breaths that sawed in and out of her. *Just a dream. It's just a dream. Please let it be just a dream.*

Viv sat up in her sleeping bag. She shivered as the cold dawn air kissed the nape of her neck and shivered down her back. Viv checked her phone. 5:43 a.m. *Too early*, she moaned inwardly. But she knew she wouldn't get back to sleep anytime soon. Viv started to crawl out of her sleeping bag but paused when she heard a rustle from across the tent.

Morgan was awake.

The other girl had sat up and turned towards Viv, a familiar grotesque grin marring her sleepy eyes and face. Her disheveled hair wove a bizarre halo around her face.

"Vivienne, are you well?" Morgan asked.

Viv couldn't remember when Morgan had ever called her by her full name. "Yes. Go back to sleep, Morgan."

Morgan grinned wider. "Only if you're certain."

Viv eyed the other girl, then swallowed back her discomfort. "I'm certain. Go back to sleep."

Morgan laid down in an abrupt motion, like a deflated balloon, not bothering to pull the sleeping bag over her body. Viv watched as the grin disappeared from the girl's face and her eyes slammed shut.

Viv dressed in the darkness in hurried motions, wincing whenever she made a loud noise. She jammed her boots on and stepped away from the girls' tent, finally taking a deep breath.

She wanted to be as far away from Morgan as possible.

## CHAPTER SIXTEEN

The cigarettes in the parking lot hadn't soothed Viv like usual.

When they returned to the Fortress to begin the day's work, her nerves jangled against each other. She eyed the facade of the building with trepidation, her dread mounting as she climbed the stairs. It was almost a letdown when they entered the front room to find it empty, looking just as they had left it the prior afternoon. Helen made quick work with the assignments, dividing the boys into a team to clear out the third floor and the girls into a team to tackle the second floor. When Helen assigned them to the second floor, Viv and Cat exchanged a worried glance over Morgan's head.

Viv studied Morgan, who smiled her usual smile — not the grotesque expression from earlier in the morning — and shuddered. She agreed with Cat. *This won't end well.*

The large room on the first floor of the Fortress had a grand staircase that led to the second and third floors. Unlike the narrow staircase found in the kitchen, these steps were wide and deep. Rails lined either side of the stairs, and Viv ran a light hand over one as she ascended the stairs to the second floor. At the small landing atop the staircase, a small desk and chair was tucked into an alcove. A wide hallway marched across the entire second floor, echoed by a series of doors leading to separate rooms. Viv counted. There were twelve rooms in total.

Viv wandered down the hall and stopped in front of a room with a door that stood slightly ajar. She peered within – and recoiled.

The room was tiny, narrow, and long. A slender bed frame, empty of its mattress, leaned against the back wall beneath a sliver of a window. The floors boards were raw, unpolished wood. The walls were defaced with graffiti, modern and old. A pile of wood laid in the opposite corner of the bedframe, and it took Viv a moment to realize that the wood had once been a chest of drawers.

Viv stared at the room, her eyes unseeing. A deep shock, like touching an electric fence, rippled through her. She *knew* this room.

She recognized it from her dream.

But that wasn't possible.

Was it?

The morning passed in a daze for Viv.

In mechanical movements, she emptied the cruelly narrow rooms of trash alongside Morgan and Cat. The slender doors to the small rooms made it difficult to wrestle out the intact bed frames. Viv had to instead take a hammer to the frames to bend and twist the metal until they could fit through the doorways. Cat proved to be more than useful, and the two of them made a decent team. They avoided Morgan in an unspoken pact: The other girl alternately grinned and frowned throughout the morning; she also chattered to thin air every now and then.

After a few false starts, Viv realized that Morgan wasn't talking to her. Or Cat.

Or anyone that Viv could see.

"Morgan, who are you speaking to?" Helen had asked during a mid-morning break.

Morgan had quieted and stared at Helen from beneath her lashes. After too long a silence, she grinned the wide, toothy smile and spoke. "Catherine and Vivienne."

Helen had cast a dubious glance at the other girls, who had stared at Morgan with dismay and distrust. "Sure," Helen had replied.

Helen didn't ask again.

"Damn it!"

The shout, followed by a crash, came from above. Viv paused and peered up to the ceiling.

"Should we even go?" Cat asked. She wiped her face with a damp handkerchief.

Viv didn't want to. She had had enough unpleasant surprises. "I guess we should, right?"

"Right." Cat looked grim.

Upstairs, Viv saw that in the place of the residential rooms there were two large rooms, opposite of one another and on the east side of the building. Helen and the boys were gathered in one of the large rooms. Inside, several narrow, long tables stood waist-high. Leather straps with brass buckles dangled from each corner of the table. A leather pillow rested on one end of each of the tables. Cabinets with broken glass doors lined the back walls, filled with blue, brown, clear, and green bottles. *Medications*, Viv thought.

She fingered the six month sobriety coin she wore around her neck.

The on-going argument between Helen and Devlin tore her attention away from the medication cabinets.

"Devlin, I need you to calm down," Helen was saying.

"I'm calm," he said through gritted teeth.

Devlin was not calm.

"I know Grafton has an upsetting background," Helen began. "I get it. If I had needed medical attention in the nineteenth century, I would not have wanted to come here. But let's focus on the here and now, on this job."

"What's going on?" Cat asked. She stepped closer to Devlin.

"Devlin isn't happy about the history of this place," Helen replied.

"No shit," Devlin huffed. He swept an arm around the room. "*Look* at this room. It's a torture chamber. You can't tell me otherwise. Look at this!" He grabbed a leather strap from the corner of a table. "These are *restraints*. To hold people down. Without their consent. How the hell are you not upset by this?"

Helen shook her head. "I understand why you're angry. I do." She sighed, then continued. "This place gives me the creeps, too. So let's take an early lunch. We'll return after we've had some time to cool down." When no one moved, Helen raised her arms and started to make sweeping motions. "Everybody out. Let's go. No dallying."

Morgan gave a sudden chuckle, staring at one of the long narrow surgery tables near the medical cabinets against the back of the room.

Everyone froze.

"Something funny, Morgan?" Helen barked in a testy voice.

Morgan's head flung up, surprised. Viv stilled just outside the room and studied the other girl, ignoring Joel when he bumped into her. *It's like she forgot we were here*, Viv thought.

Morgan cleared her throat. "N-no, nothing funny."

Helen stared at the girl but didn't say anything.

Viv exchanged a glance with Cat.

Something was *wrong* with Morgan.

After lunch, Helen swapped the teams: The girls would work on the third floor while the guys would finish the second floor. As Viv cleared out the tables and the debris from the large rooms on the third floor, Viv better understood Devlin's upset earlier in the day. The dual rooms, complete with medications cabinets, tables equipped with restraints, and big windows for good lighting, were clearly medical theatres or offices of some kind. Given how bad medical care must have been back then, Viv was sure that the rooms held the echoes of many painful episodes.

Viv avoided the medication cabinets in both operating rooms as much as possible. Pain meds had been her drug of choice before rehab. She was somewhat relieved that most of the bottles were empty or broken. The few bottles that contained anything had precious little liquid that moved like sludge in a swamp.

Viv was simply relieved to toss it all away.

Late in the afternoon, on one of the many trips to the dumpster parked in the impromptu parking lot, Viv saw a flicker in the corner of her eye. Turning her head, she saw the boy in pajamas with black glowing eyes. He stood a little ways up the hill, staring at the Fortress. Feeling Viv's gaze on him, he turned to stare at her.

He grinned.

The key symbol ached across her chest.

Then he disappeared.

Viv shuddered. Taking a few deep breaths, she continued down the trail. *He's not real. He can't hurt me. He's not real.*

She ignored the burn from the scratches on her chest.

Saturday dawned bright and clear.

Viv appreciated the change in the weather as she smoked her requisite morning cigarette. She took a deep inhale, grateful that she didn't have to go back into the Fortress for two more days. Tracing the key symbol scratched onto her chest, which had refused to heal, Viv's fingers bumped into her sobriety coin. She wrapped her hand around it, where it lay against her chest, and she thought about the past week.

The remainder of the past week had passed with grim determination to get through the Fortress as quickly as possible. Viv had assumed she had been the only one affected by the Grafton Stake. But as the week had worn on, she saw the same signs on everyone present: Dark circles carved beneath tired eyes. Grim lines carved into haggard faces. Short tempers. And Morgan continued to whisper into the air. She only paused when someone addressed her directly, and even then, she only offered simple answers with a grotesque grin. It was unnerving.

Viv could hardly stand sharing a tent with the other girl. She wanted to say something to Helen but didn't quite trust the older woman to believe her.

She ground out her cigarette and headed to the basecamp. Time to go to town.

## CHAPTER SEVENTEEN

T he Mining Days Festival was larger than Viv expected.

Helen had driven them into Hard Luck and then kept going past the town limits, up to a large stretch of flat grass. Even early in the day, the parking lot was almost full and Helen paid the twenty dollar fee without protest. In the distance, Viv could see carnival rides: A colorful Ferris Wheel rose above a carousel and a small roller coaster. As they spilled out of the car, Devlin let out a whoop of joy and Zane laughed. They appeared young and carefree to Viv, a marked contrast to their demeanor at Grafton Stake. Even Cat seemed excited.

Helen corralled them in the front of the van. "Let's go over rules: Before you ask, yes, you may have an advance on your stipend. Make it last for the day. The buddy system is required: Find a buddy, or two, and stick with them for the rest of the day. You will need to check in with me at noon. Plan to meet me at the base of the Ferris Wheel. Lastly, be back at the van by 5:00 p.m. Do not make me search for you." Helen studied each member of their group. "Any questions?"

No one spoke. Viv could see Devlin and Zane practically vibrating with excitement.

Helen pulled out her wallet. "Your money and your admission passes. Have fun."

Viv found herself buddies with both Joel and Morgan. She was grateful for Joel's presence; she hadn't wanted to be alone with Morgan. Judging by the side-eye he cast Morgan, Joel agreed with her. As they drew closer to the festival entrance, the muted sounds of enjoyment grew louder. Viv could hear children squeal with glee, the loud rush of the mechanics on the carnival rides. A small red balloon floated up into the sky, beyond the reach of the child who had lost it

.

Viv received her blue ink stamp of a miner's pick upon entry, along with a festival map and a handful of tear-away tickets. These, the cheerful grandma at the booth informed them, were to be used at the ring toss and other game booths. Inside, color rioted and competed for attention: Red pennants outlined designated walkways, blue balloons and streamers decorated the booth tops, yellow tablecloths rested atop booth fronts. The food court lined the edge of the large pasture, shaded by a row of thick trees. Viv could smell butter and sugar, hot dogs and BBQ.

Viv wandered the festival with Joel and Morgan, walking up and down each aisle. She refused any of the carnival rides except the Ferris Wheel. Viv pretended disdain for such things but really, she refused to admit that she often got motion sickness. Instead, she focused on the booths. The vendors ran a wide gamut: Many of them were local artisans with handmade scarves, soaps, candles, and the like. Some of them hawked cheap stuff that Viv had seen on television infomercials, the ones that came with a lifetime guarantee and cheap gold stickers promising 100% customer satisfaction. Opposite from the food court, on the far side of the festival, several booths were dedicated to educating attendees about the region's mining history. Viv was not surprised to find most of them deserted.

The only popular booth amongst that row bore a sign: "Become a Gold Miner — Pan for Gold — Success Guaranteed." Viv watched as children stood on stepladders and stools around a low tub filled with a few inches of water. Black sand lined the bottom of the tubs, and even from where she stood, Viv could see shining flakes peek through. The kids held plastic miner's pans, cautiously circling the shallow dish in a clockwise, then a counter-clockwise motion, as instructed by the grizzled old man with a single gold tooth who ran the set up. Viv grinned when one of the little girls found a few flakes at the bottom of her pan and screamed her glee.

Viv walked on. She saw the usual ring toss and balloon dart booths, and a photography stand where you could get a Western-themed portrait done. A low tent draped in rich purple fabric stood at the end of one row, a small plaque with a single word rested atop the entrance: "Psychic. Fortunes Told, Past Lives Remembered." Viv studied the tent before turning away. She didn't want to hear about her future. Her present was uncomfortable at best. And she knew too much about her past.

Viv just wanted to get through the next four weeks.

At noon, they checked in with Helen and the others by the Ferris Wheel.

Viv almost didn't recognize the others at first: They were so *happy*. Cat had gotten her face painted, a swirl of bright flowers that dappled her brow and cheekbones. Morgan seemed like her old self again, with glitter strands woven into her hair and a smudge of cinnamon sugar dusted across her face. Joel wore a balloon crown, for which Devlin would not stop heckling him. And Zane had astonished the group by buying two dozen mini doughnuts from a vendor that specialized in bizarre flavors — and promptly eating them, one by one, despite the groans and protests of the group.

"Man, we share a tent," Devlin had groused. "I'm going to have to *smell* this later."

Zane had only smiled, his teeth stained by the maple sriracha sugar donuts.

Her phone buzzed in her pocket. Viv stepped away and checked the screen. It was her uncle.

*Helen mentioned you'd be at the Mining Days Festival this weekend. You there now?*

Viv tapped at her phone. *Yes.*

*I'll be there in an hour. See you soon, kiddo.*

Relief coursed through Viv, and she felt her shoulders unknot. She would see her uncle soon, and she could tell him about the weird things occurring at Grafton Stake. Maybe he could do something? Viv wasn't sure. Talk with Helen, explain all the creepy things Viv had experienced over the last two weeks? Viv shook her head. She would figure it out later. She cast a glance at the group and seeing that they were occupied — Zane was begging Cat to try the pickle nacho doughnut — Viv dialed a number.

The phone rang. Then, "Viv, how are you doing, kid?" Ollie's voice was the same. No nonsense yet affectionate.

"Hey, Ollie." Viv cleared her throat. "How's it going?"

"Good enough. Where *are* you? I hear children screaming in the background."

Viv filled her in on the day trip to the Mining Days Festival. "It's a treat of sorts, for good behavior," Viv finished. She eyed the table with the crew. Cat had refused the pickle nacho doughnut but conceded to trying the salted chocolate. Morgan stood behind her, braiding her hair in a wispy fishtail style.

"Good behavior, huh?" Ollie paused and Viv could hear her sponsor soothed her irate toddler. Ollie returned after a moment. "I wish I had good behavior here," she muttered.

A corner of Viv's mouth kicked up.

"But that's good news, right?" Ollie continued. "No more incidents?"

Viv shrugged before she realized that Ollie couldn't see her. "It's okay, I guess."

Ollie paused. "What does that mean?"

"The place is creepy as hell, Ollie." Viv shuddered despite the midday sunlight. "There is something wrong with the house, the 'rest home' — even the land."

Ollie's voice sharpened. "Do you mean someone's threatening you?"

Viv paused, then spoke. "Or something."

At last, Ollie spoke. "What's really going on?"

"What do you mean?"

"I don't believe in ghosts or things that go bump in the night, Viv. Not the Halloween, supernatural ones. So, again: What's going on, kid?"

Viv sighed. "I wish I knew how to explain." She tried again. "One of the other girls, she seems... different than when we started. She was the most cheerful of us, normal, you know? But over this last week, she *changed*. She talks into thin air sometimes and she doesn't smile anymore. She just... grins at you. It's awful, honestly."

"Is it possible that she's messing with you?" Ollie was skeptical. "People do weird shit for weirder reasons."

Viv rolled her shoulders, trying to loosen them. "I don't think that's it. I think there is something wrong with her."

"Like she needs a mental health intervention or something?"

"Maybe. Probably."

"Tell the team leader," Ollie advised. "And then refocus on your shit. Your sobriety is what matters, not someone else's troubles." Ollie paused. "How are things on that front?"

Viv sighed. "Good. I'm still clean. I haven't used for one hundred and eighty-four days."

"Keep adding to those numbers, kid."

Viv almost smiled. "Thanks, Ollie." The usual combination of pleasure and anxiety sent a frisson through her. Most days, Viv didn't feel proud of her sobriety. It felt tenuous, like cotton candy facing a rainstorm, and Viv couldn't make herself trust the circumstance. Or maybe she didn't trust herself to continue the fragile state. But she knew that Ollie understood.

"Okay, I gotta go. My kid is a monster," Ollie announced, her cheerful manner contradicting her words. "You gonna be okay?"

"Sure," Viv lied. "I'll be fine."

Viv met her uncle outside one of the educational booths at the festival. Uncle Rick talked with an older man who vended the booth for the Hard Luck Historical Museum, their conversation punctuated by frequent laughter. Viv stood on the outskirts of the conversation, not wishing to interrupt. Finally, her uncle caught sight of her.

"Hey, kid." He stepped forward and swept her into a large hug. "It's good to see you."

Viv gripped her uncle with tight arms. He felt like a refuge after these last two weeks. Even if he had spilled too much about her history with Helen.

"Hey, hey." Her uncle stepped back and held Viv by her shoulders. "Are you okay? What's wrong?"

Viv shook her head. "Nothing," she lied. "I'm glad you're here."

Uncle Rick studied her for a moment. "You look... tired."

No need to lie there. "I am," Viv admitted.

Her uncle shook himself. "Let me introduce you to Leonard, then we'll walk around." He turned to the older man, who had sparse white hair up top and a full white beard, and dark eyes that twinkled with mirth. "Leonard, this is my niece, Vivienne. She's part of the team that works under Helen Whiteaker, on the Grafton Stake project. Viv, this is Leonard Fuller. He runs the Hard Luck Historical Museum."

Viv nodded at the man. "Hi."

"Grafton Stake, huh?" Leonard shifted on his feet, then leaned forward. "That's a big job. Helen has her work cut out for her. You all do."

She nodded again. "Yeah." Viv didn't know what else to say.

Leonard opened his mouth, then closed it. He glanced at Rick, then back to Viv. "Is... is this job the best fit for a group of teenagers? I mean, is it safe for everyone to be so remote and doing this kind of physical labor?"

"Leonard, what are you really saying? You know Helen does superb work with these teams," Uncle Rick replied.

Leonard nodded at Viv. "This one should be in school, not traipsing about those woods with dangerous tools."

Viv tensed. She wondered how her uncle would respond. *Please don't tell him anything, Uncle Rick.*

"Viv... is exploring her options." Her uncle's tone discouraged further questions. He turned to Viv. "How's the job going?"

"It's okay," Viv replied. "We've made trails, and now we're working on the homestead and the Fortress."

Both men exchanged a puzzled glance. "The Fortress?" Leonard echoed.

"Yeah, the three-story building? With the copper roof and all those rooms?"

Leonard's expression cleared. "Ah, the residential home." He chuckled. "I understand why you call it the Fortress. It's an imposing building, especially being in the middle of nowhere like it is."

"Doesn't that building have a history, Leonard?" Uncle Rick elbowed Viv, a grin on his face. "Haunted, isn't it? Full of ghosts and goblins?"

Leonard gave a weak smile and shook his head. "The whole place has a shameful history," he admitted.

"I found the graveyard," Viv offered.

Leonard winced. "Horrifying, isn't it? An absolute nightmare."

"Does anyone know who those people are?"

Leonard studied the sky for a moment before answering. "No, not real well. I have some records in the museum of who entered the home on Grafton Stake. But we have no idea who is buried in which plot and I don't have a complete list of everyone who stayed at the rest home." Leonard paused. "Some people left before they died of neglect or abuse. Not many, of course, but a lucky few got away. Those were the ones whose families started the inquiries with the local sheriff, got the town riled up. You probably know that the Graftons had to flee town, and quickly."

Viv had remembered that from Helen's account. She opened her mouth to ask another question but Rick interjected.

"Hate to interrupt, Leonard, but I know my niece has to be back on the bus in an hour or so." Rick glanced at his wristwatch. "I want to buy her a treat before she heads back into the woods."

"Definitely." He nodded at Viv. "If you're in town, come by the Hard Luck Historical Museum for a bit. I'll give you a tour, show you some of the Grafton Stake artifacts."

"Okay. Thanks," she added.

Her uncle steered her towards the food court. "Leonard is a good guy. Runs the museum on a shoe-string budget and volunteers most of his time. He used to be a fire-fighter for the district."

Viv didn't know what to do with this information. "Cool."

Uncle Rick insisted on treating her to an enormous elephant ear, a fried dough concoction dusted with sugar, cinnamon, and butter. Viv wasn't especially hungry but her uncle seemed determined to do something nice for her. She didn't want to refuse the kind gesture, as simple as it was. And she certainly wasn't going to get elephant ears on the job, so she acquiesced. They found a spot under the shady trees behind the food court. Rick had half-finished his own elephant ear before Viv had even taken a few bites.

"How is the job?" Her uncle queried. "Tell me everything."

Viv thought of the boy in his pajamas, who peeled back his flesh and scratched her chest with a key-like symbol. The Fortress with the ominous surgery tables and medical supply cabinets. The dead fish, the vandalized tools, and Morgan, with her episodes of an unusual demeanor.

*Would he believe her?* "It's okay," Viv lied.

Her uncle frowned, then waved his doughy treat at Viv. "Okay? C'mon, give me more to work with, kiddo."

"It's a lot of work," Viv offered.

"And?"

"Now I know how to build a trail?"

"Christ, it's like pulling teeth," her uncle muttered. "What about your crew mates? What do you hate or like about the job? C'mon, Viv, share a little."

Viv let out a huff of annoyance. "Fine. It's creepy as hell, okay?"

Her uncle swallowed the last bit of his elephant ear before answering. "What, Grafton Stake?"

"Yes." Viv shook her head. "Why didn't you tell me? Before I started the job?"

Her uncle frowned. "Because you didn't have any other option, Viv," he retorted in a sharp voice. "It's either this or going back to juvie. I wanted you to take this chance, not use a few ghost stories as an excuse to refuse the only opportunity you'd get to fix the mess you'd gotten yourself into."

His harsh words stung Viv. She opened her mouth, but he continued.

"Yeah, that place has a dark history. But not many places around Hard Luck have a happy one." He started counting on his fingers. "The KKK used to set up shop a few towns over. Probably still there, even though they deny it. And believe it or not, this town had a witchcraft scare decades ago." Her uncle shook his head. "No place is perfect, Viv. You must realize that."

"I know." Viv's tone could cut ice.

"This is your last opportunity," Rick said. "If you don't want to do it for yourself, do it for your mother."

Pain slammed into Viv's chest. Her breath stuttered while her heartbeat hammered in her ears. Her eyes welled with tears.

Rick seemed to realize that he had gone too far. "Kiddo, I'm sorry—"

"What time is it?"

Rick glanced at his wristwatch, then cursed. "You have to head back to the bus now. Look, I'm sorry I was harsh. But I worry about you. I want good things for you — and the last year hasn't been good."

Viv didn't reply. She stared past her uncle, focusing on a gnarled knot that stretched across a tree trunk. A slight breeze blew by, barely cooling her flushed and hot face.

Rick cursed again. "Let me walk you back to the bus."

"I'm fine."

"Viv."

"I said I'm fine." Viv shifted her gaze from the knot just beyond her uncle's shoulders to focus on his face. Her uncle's own face sank when he read her expression. Shame and sadness drooped the corners of his mouth. "I can find my own way."

## Chapter Eighteen

Viv dreaded the return to the Grafton Stake. The others seemed to share her sentiments: The bus was quiet, and hardly anyone spoke. The high spirits of the Mining Days Festival were now subdued, or absent.

Her uncle's words haunted her on the return trip to the Grafton Stake. *He was right*, she admitted to herself. The last two years hadn't been good ones. Her mother's death and her father's retreat into his own grief had created a vacuum of affection, love, and normalcy. So Viv filled it with friends, her mother's prescription pain medication, and petty vandalism. It landed her in juvenile detention, a hell unlike anything she'd experienced. She wondered if the patients from the Fortress had felt the same way she had about juvie.

Viv trudged up the parking lot and into basecamp, her feet dragging with every step. She eyed the homestead and the Fortress. Rick may have been right about her past but he failed to understand the present.

There was something *wrong* with this place.

*Four more weeks*, Viv reminded herself. *Four more weeks.*

The work on the Fortress continued the following Monday. Viv was grateful to be assigned the second floor again. She hadn't wanted to be around the medical supplies, however old and dubious they were. The day passed in a haze of fatigue and more injuries: This time, Joel received a nasty scrape from a falling beam. Devlin smashed his thumb between cabinet doors. And at the end of the day, Cat found a long scratch up her leg. She couldn't remember what had caused it.

Viv watched the others compare injuries over dinner that night. The symbol etched onto her chest burned and itched.

The boy with the dagger teeth smiled in her mind's eye.

The confrontation came the next day, after dinner. Viv heard the noise before she saw it.

Zane stumbled out of the boys tent, tripping on the tarp edge that peeked from beneath the tent. His hair disheveled and his brow furrowed, he glared back into the tent. "It wasn't me," he gritted out, anger clear in his voice.

Joel followed him out of the tent, Devlin close on his heels. "No?" Viv could almost taste the skepticism in his voice. "Then who? Who would steal from others and hide the thefts in your belongings?"

"D'you think I'm really that stupid?" Zane retorted. "Why would I hide items I 'stole' with my own stuff? I'm not an idiot."

Joel scoffed, his doubt and disdain obvious.

Helen stepped out of the kitchen tent. "Hey." Her voice cracked like a sudden gunshot. "What is going on?" She wiped her hands on a towel, standing between the boys.

Joel stared at Zane. "Well?"

Zane stepped closer. "Well, what?"

Joel shook his head. "This one" — he pointed at Zane — "has been stealing our stuff. Hiding it in with his bags."

"That's bullshit!" Zane exploded.

"Then explain how our stuff ended up in your stuff," Joel invited. Sarcasm coated each word like honey.

A tense silence fell over the group.

Helen sighed, then rubbed her forehead. "Let's start at the beginning. Zane and Joel, with me. Everyone else, finish your dinner."

No one touched their dinner.

Instead, Viv and the others strained to listen into the angry conversation that Helen mediated between Joel and Zane. Viv couldn't catch everything said but she watched Zane as he defended himself from Joel's accusations. His arms swung in wild motions and he retorted in short bursts of anger. But Viv watched his eyes grow resigned, sad. Then his shoulders sank. *He knows he won't win this one*, Viv thought. She thought of her own experience with the vandalized tools. She knew she hadn't touched those tools; she didn't have the strength nor the inclination to do that kind of damage. But no one had believed her, either.

*What would happen to Zane?*

Helen had folded back the large flap of the boy's tent and entered before lowering herself to examine a pile of items next to a sleeping bag and disorganized hiker's pack. Zane stood on the outskirts of the camp, his back turned to them as he stared at the Fortress. Anger and frustration rose from his shoulders like steam. Viv noticed that the others, clustered around the campfire, tried not to watch and failed. She was doing the same thing.

Inside the tent, Viv saw Helen shake her head before rubbing a hand over her face. Standing, she told Joel something before stepping outside. She went up to Zane and had a quiet conversation, her face set in disappointed lines.

Joel brought out a handful of items from the tent and laid them on the kitchen table. He beckoned the others to join him.

"This stuff belongs to you all," he said. "You should claim what's yours."

Viv studied the table. A medley of items, some valuable and some not, rested before her: A leather wallet, with a couple of green bills clearly visible from the edges. A billfold that doubled as a checkbook, overstuffed with credit cards and receipts. A delicate bracelet, set with a few gems. A simple smartphone, the battery dead. A book with worn covers featuring a spaceship. A switchblade. Lastly, a hairbrush.

With a start, Viv realized the brush was her own. *I thought I had lost it.*

She looked up to see the others glance at one another, troubled. Finally, Cat spoke.

"Zane stole these?" she asked. Her usual hauteur was gone, and she seemed... vulnerable. Young.

Joel gave a grim nod. "He denies it but I saw them mixed in with his stuff."

Viv shook her head, then spoke. "Why? He had to know he would get caught. That doesn't make sense."

Joel shrugged. "I don't know why. He just did it."

Devlin spoke for the first time. "But... Zane *loves* this work. Out of all of us, he's the one who really likes being here. He even asked Helen about getting a job with BLM." Devlin shook his head, and Viv watched him rotate the wristwatch in anxious motions. "Why would he jeopardize that?"

Joel hunched his shoulders. "I don't know, okay? I just found this."

"Listen up." Helen's voice cut through the tense conversation like a knife.

Viv watched Zane storm away from the campsite, towards the homestead and beyond.

"Zane has chosen to leave the project." Viv's head snapped around to focus on the team leader. Helen's careful words matched her neutral voice.

"What?" Devlin was shocked.

Joel looked ill.

"Since I can't leave you alone on a build site, we will drive him into town tomorrow morning, then return to finish clearing the Fortress." Helen paused. "I know you have questions but please respect Zane's privacy."

"This is bullshit," Cat muttered.

"Cat, do you have something to share?" Helen inquired, her voice a warning.

"Yes. This is bullshit," Cat enunciated as she stared down the other woman.

"I understand you're upset. I had hoped for a different outcome." Helen shook her head. "Wrap up for the night. We have an early day tomorrow."

Viv shook her head. She remembered the vandalized tools, the shock of the accusation and how unfair it felt. How lonely she had felt when no one believed her. *Was it only a week ago?* Viv shivered despite the warmth of the campfire.

Three and a half weeks, she reminded herself.

The weather for the drive into Hard Luck was bleak and matched the mood of everyone on the short white bus. Zane had stomped onto the vehicle without speaking to anyone, then slammed his pack beside himself onto the bench seat so no one could join him. He almost vibrated with palpable hurt and anger, his face set in harsh lines as he stared out his window. Viv doubted anyone would have chosen to sit next to him.

The acute discomfort of the entire bus made the trip seem longer than usual to Viv. Eventually, finally, Helen pulled into the parking lot for Honey's Diner. After a brief consultation with a sleepy woman who ran the bus kiosk inside, Helen returned and waved everyone off the bus. The cold, damp air slapped against Viv's face as she stepped out.

"The bus is running late. We'll be here for a while," Helen said.

Viv's shoulders sank. She shot a quick glance at Zane, who clearly wasn't thrilled with the news.

"How late is late?" Cat asked.

Helen shrugged. "Couple hours, maybe?"

A small wave of discontent swept through the group. Zane's jaw clenched. Viv thought he might be grinding his teeth.

"We got time to kill. Any suggestions? Zane and I need to wait here but you could walk around town," Helen offered.

Viv watched Morgan and Devlin cast a dubious glance up, then down the main thoroughfare of Hard Luck. Joel hunched his shoulders, his hands deep inside his pockets.

"A walk through town?" Cat drawled. "Thrilling."

"What about the museum?" Viv interrupted.

Everyone turned to stare at her.

"What?"

"The museum. The Hard Luck Historical Museum, I think." Viv glanced at Helen. "I think I saw a booth at the Festival. Met Leonard there."

Helen seemed relieved. "Good idea, Viv."

No one spoke.

"Then the museum it is." Helen pulled out her phone and pulled up the hours. "It opens in a few minutes. Go ahead and start walking over."

Joel didn't respond. Cat and Devlin shrugged. Morgan stared at the mountain range behind Honey's Diner.

Helen sighed. "Then I'll see you all back here in two hours."

# CHAPTER NINETEEN

The Hard Luck Historical Museum was... humble.

The museum was a worn, square wooden single-story structure next to the town jail and sheriff's department. Painted in an eye-smarting shade of bright blue, the small building appeared as though someone's aunt with too many cats lived within rather than a historical museum. Nevertheless, a small neon sign read 'Open' in the window.

Joel led them up the steps and inside. A cheerful, loud bell announced their presence.

"Be there in a second," a voice hollered from another room.

"No rush," Joel called back.

Viv studied the cramped space. The room was lined with cabinets fronted with clear glass. Within the cabinets rested newspaper articles, postcards, letters, and small artifacts. Viv saw a watch fob, a small revolver, and medical instruments on the cabinet shelves. Saws of every size and shape were mounted to the walls, indicating the region's history with the lumber industry. There didn't seem to be any organization to the array.

Leonard bustled into the room, then paused when he caught sight of the crowd before him. "Oh." He cleared his throat. "Good morning. How can I help you all today?"

Viv glanced around the group, then shrugged. "We're here to look around, if you don't mind."

Leonard beamed at them, his thin hair a wispy halo around his head. His tobacco-stained teeth peeked at them through his wide grin. "Don't mind at all. Let me give you a tour. It'll be a short one," he added with a chuckle.

Leonard launched into a clearly familiar, often-repeated spiel about the museum and the long history of Hard Luck, Oregon. He led them around two small rooms and Viv listened to the lecture with half an ear. She didn't quite care about the mining boom, quickly followed by a bust of dramatic proportions. Viv hardly noted the long succession of failed sawmills in the area, a novelty since lumber was so abundant in the area. "Lots of people speculate this is what solidified the town name as 'Hard Luck,'" Leonard added. "It seemed hard to catch a break around here." He chuckled at his own joke.

Cat rolled her eyes.

Then Leonard mentioned the name Grafton.

"What was that?" Viv interrupted.

Leonard paused in mid-flow. "Sorry?"

"You mentioned the name Grafton," Viv said. "What about them?"

Leonard studied Viv for a moment. "You're Rick's niece, aren't you? We met at the Mining Days Festival."

Viv shifted from one foot to the other, aware of the eyes upon her. "Yes." She didn't elaborate.

Leonard nodded. "Good to see you again. As I said, the history around the Graftons isn't especially pleasant. They were one of the earliest white families to move to the area, which we know because we have census records dating back to 1845. They tried their hand at everything. Mining, farming, even beekeeping and making mead." Leonard winced. "All of the ventures were failures, spectacular ones. That led them to the decision to open up the rest home."

Viv leaned forward.

"At first, the home seemed like a refuge for those who couldn't stay with families or those whose families didn't want them," Leonard continued. "The home was the first of its kind in the region and made Hard Luck a destination of sorts among desperate families, unfortunately. The Graftons took in people with challenges or difficulties, folks we'd call people with disabilities today. Didn't matter the nature of the illness or malady, the family took 'em. Built that great asylum — excuse me, rest home — and spared little expense in doing so."

Leonard shook his head. "They built the place but had no idea how to care for people with different needs. They weren't medical people, so they had no idea what they were doing. Just out to make a profit. They kept collecting patients like baseball cards and before long, townspeople started asking questions. Why did people enter the rest home but never leave? What was the exact nature of the treatment?"

Leonard held up a finger. "Hold on. Let me grab something." He ducked into an adjacent room for a minute. Viv heard him rustle through what sounded like paper, followed by a thump and a low curse. She cast a glance at the rest of the group: Cat and Devlin huddled near one another. Joel's brow was furrowed and his eyes dark with an emotion Viv couldn't read. But her gaze stopped on Morgan. Unease rippled through her body as Viv stared at Morgan, and she wrapped her arms around herself.

Morgan had a familiar grotesque grin on her face again.

The other girl's eyes gleamed with mania, and her nose quivered, as though cold despite the warmth of the small room that contained several people. Her grin stretched across her face, wide and too open, her teeth and expression reminding Viv of a rabid dog.

Leonard returned to the room and paused when he saw Morgan. "Excited about history, huh?" He chuckled.

Morgan didn't blink. "Yes, I am." Her voice went up a register, higher and thinner. *Like a child,* Viv thought. Gooseflesh pebbled Viv's arms. She took a discreet step away from the other girl.

Leonard laid down the items he retrieved from the room behind him: A scrapbook with pieces of paper that trailed off the pages and flapped around the edges, and a tray of small items. Viv stepped closer, then swallowed. On the tray, against the worn black velveteen speckled with flecks of rust, lay an old-fashioned syringe. The needle was enormous, the glass chamber even more so. It seemed like a child's toy to Viv. Next to the syringe were a few empty bottles, the labels promising a restorative cure for different maladies such as sleeplessness or hysteria. A narrow roll of loose woven fabric, the original white made beige by age, rested next to the bottles. After a moment, Viv realized they were bandages.

Then her eyes settled on the next item: A tarnished silver ring with a filigree of flowers, berries, and leaves wreathed around the edges. Delicate chains of varying lengths, and studded with silver beads for further decoration, stretched from the ornate ring and were attached to several keys. In contrast to the ring and the elegant chains, the keys were utilitarian. A silver metal coating had long worn through along the sharp edges to show brass beneath.

Leonard flipped open the scrapbook, drawing Viv's eyes away from the keys. "After about a decade in the business, the rumors had gotten pretty bad. One family raised a ruckus, filing a lawsuit when the Graftons wouldn't, or maybe couldn't, produce their daughter, who had come for the restorative properties of the home and the climate. The lawsuit even made it to some national newspapers and it brought a lot of unwanted scrutiny down on the Graftons." Leonard stopped on a specific page within the scrapbook, then swapped the scrapbook around in a 180 degree motion. "Here are some of the clippings."

They crowded close to the counter, peering at the scraps of yellowed paper with elegant newspaper typeset. Each of the headlines seemed more extreme than the next.

"Rest Home is Charged with Neglect, Murder, and More!"

"Sanitarium Lost Daughter, Family Charges."

"Lawsuit Alleges Murder in Oregon State."

Leonard flipped a page in the scrapbook. "The Graftons eventually had to let law enforcement onto the property. The sheriff and his posse were astonished at the conditions, but according to lore didn't try to arrest the Graftons until they found the mass grave site with only numerals on the headstone. To this day, we don't know who is buried in which plot. Or even if there are multiple bodies in a single plot. The family fled that night." Leonard's lips curled into a sneer. "Those cowardly bastards left their patients behind and uncared for — which may have been a mercy, to be honest."

Devlin's voice startled Viv, and she flinched in surprise. "They didn't catch any of the Graftons?" he asked, skepticism clear in his voice. "Not a single one?"

Leonard shook his head. "The family left everything except cash and portable valuables behind. If I have to guess, they likely went south. There were rumors of another asylum in northern California but..." Leonard shook his head. "I doubt we'll really ever know. It was easy to get lost and start a new life in those days."

"What happened to the patients they left behind?" Joel asked.

Leonard flipped a page in the scrapbook. "According to the state newspapers, most of the remaining patients were returned to their families or shipped up to Salem." His finger rested on the edge of a clipping. "However, given what the medical field was at that time, I'm not sure their lot improved a great deal."

Cat leaned forward to examine the tray on the cabinet top. "What is this?" She pointed.

"Ah, that is a chatelaine." Leonard beamed at Cat. "A chatelaine is a household tool that many women used back in the day. They would attach it to their belts, with the chains and keys and other useful items — scissors and the like. That way, they would always have ready access to whatever daily items they needed. The purpose is highly practical but you can see that this one is a piece of art, being made in sterling silver and molded with flowers." Leonard leaned on the cabinet top, then ignored the ominous creak that accompanied his action. "This chatelaine was found at Grafton Stake. We think it holds the keys to the locks within the rest home, and was likely worn by the family matriarch."

Viv stared at the tarnished silver and the worn keys arrayed on the tray. *They were locked in. The patients, the victims, were locked in their rooms.* She remembered how small the rooms were within the Fortress, the narrow strip of space made even more confining by the area occupied by the beds and wash stands. They were dark, too, because the thin sliver of a window afforded so little light. Viv shook her head, to chase away the chill that settled on her shoulders. She tried to take a deep breath, but the breath stuttered in her chest, and she coughed. Panic flickered at the edges of her mind. *They were trapped.*

Morgan interrupted her thoughts.

The other girl leaned forward to stare at the chatelaine on the tray. Her grotesque grin had etched a too large crater across her face and her lips gaped open like a canyon, her teeth sharp stalagmites against the darkness of her mouth. Her eyes were too wide, Viv noticed, the whites too evident. Only a thin rim of blue separated the whites from her pinpoint pupils. *She looks high.*

"Pretty," Morgan crooned. Her voice rang like a clear bell through the museum, still in the unusually high register of someone much younger.

Leonard eyed Morgan, then took a step back. "Yes, the chatelaine is very pretty."

Morgan peered up at Leonard. Somehow her grin got wider. "I like it."

"I see that." Leonard seemed nervous now.

A silence fell over the group. Viv could tell that the others had noticed Morgan's strange manner and they were unnerved by it. Cat took a step closer to Devlin, almost burrowing into his side. Joel gave Morgan the side-eye and shifted on his feet. Viv met Cat's gaze and saw the same discomfort she felt in the other girl's expression.

Morgan didn't seem to notice. She continued to grin down at the chatelaine.

"Uh, was there anything else you want to know about the Graftons? Or Hard Luck?" Leonard continued to watch Morgan with a wary glance.

"I don't think so." Joel scanned the room. "We should probably head back."

"Back to Grafton Stake?" Leonard turned from Morgan. A flicker of curiosity crossed his face. "Are you enjoying the work?"

No one answered.

Finally Joel spoke, his eyes on Morgan. "It's fine."

Viv admired his ability to lie so well.

## CHAPTER TWENTY

L eonard seemed eager for them to leave.

Viv couldn't blame him.

Morgan had flinched when Joel reminded her to leave with the group, to head back to the bus station. Viv had exchanged an uncertain glance with Cat, both of them agreeing to an unspoken sentiment: Something was *wrong*. The group was quiet, and Viv noticed that everyone tried to stay as far away from Morgan as possible. Once outside, the grin had faded somewhat as Morgan wrapped her arms around herself, but the sheen of mania persisted in her eyes.

Helen and Zane were still at Honey's Diner, next to the bus kiosk. Helen nursed a cup of coffee while Zane stared into the distance with red rimmed eyes.

"Hey, how was the museum?" Helen greeted them.

No one spoke a moment. "Okay," Cat answered, casting a glance at Morgan.

Helen studied the group. "Did something happen?"

"No." Joel and Devlin spoke at once.

Helen's face turned skeptical. "That's not suspicious." She gave a heavy sigh. "One thing at a time," she muttered to herself.

A large bus rolled into the diner's parking lot, coasting to a stop several feet away from the entrance.

Helen stood. "Let me get your bag, Zane," she offered.

Zane glared at her. "No, thank you." His words were icicles, cold and sharp and painful.

Helen nodded, her expression sorrowful. "You have your ticket?"

Zane rolled his eyes and didn't answer. He started towards the bus, his backpack slung across his shoulder and a ticket in his back pocket. He paused, then turned back to the group. He ignored Helen and focused on the others.

"I'm not a thief and I didn't take your shit," he started in a low voice. He seemed to struggle with his next words. "Watch yourself when you go back, okay? There's something wrong with that place. It's... cursed or something."

Viv stared at Zane. Dread pebbled her flesh and she shivered. She thought she was the only one who had noticed how bizarre, how *wrong*, the Grafton property was.

"Zane, wait," Viv called out. She jogged across the damp pavement up to the boy and gave him awkward hug around the backpack. She stared into his eyes as she stepped back. "I know you didn't do anything." Viv kept her voice low.

Zane's eyes widened. "Why didn't you say anything?!"

"I'm sorry," Viv hissed. "What was I going to say, 'It's not him, it's ghosts'?"

Zane shook his head. "Well, whatever is going on at that shithole, I'm done."

"I'm sorry," Viv said. "I... I should have said something. Take care, okay?"

Zane snorted and turned away. Viv watched as he tossed his bag in the storage area in the undercarriage of the bus before settling himself in a seat.

He did not look at any of them.

They finished clearing the Fortress on Friday, two days after Zane left. Viv had never been so happy to leave a building behind.

Injuries and minor accidents had continued to plague them. Cat had incurred a nasty bruise on her shoulder from a falling beam; only her hard hat had saved her from a more serious injury. Everyone, including Viv, wore bandages and wraps for cut fingers, scratches, and lacerations. Morgan was the only one who had somehow managed to avoid any injuries.

The field trip for the weekend was subdued. Helen had taken them to a nearby cave system two towns over, through which Viv and the others could climb through a large lava tube that had adjacent caverns, stone shelves, and crannies. Midway through one of the smaller caverns, Devlin had turned off the flashlight as a joke. Viv's heart rate had accelerated abruptly and she had started breathing too fast. Panic had beat like the wings of a bird through her mind. The close confines of the cave combined with the utter and complete darkness reminded Viv of her dreams, of the small rooms in the Fortress. Viv hadn't realized she had made low whimpers of pain until Joel had yelled at Devlin to turn the flashlight back on. Helen had had to guide her out of the cavern. Viv had been silent with shame and embarrassment on the precarious trip to the surface, her vision filmed with tears. "Caving isn't for everyone and that's okay," Helen had said, patting Viv on her shoulder.

Viv hadn't bothered to correct Helen. They had emerged into the daylight, and the bright sun and the heat had felt like a balm against an angry wound.

"I'm fine now," she had lied, her face turned up to the sunlight. "I feel better."

Viv woke up early on Monday, anxiety curled through her body like smoke. Her morning cigarette did little to quell her nerves, so she had a second.

It still didn't help.

Viv was back on breakfast duty for the crew. She laid out the oatmeal and the various toppings with robotic motions: dried fruit, nuts, drizzles. Her fatigue made every action seem more difficult to complete, every object a hundred times heavier than it would have otherwise been. Her pants had slid down her hips a few times and she had to return to the girls' tent to fashion a makeshift belt with a piece of rope. She had lost more weight than she had realized. The work was hard on their bodies.

The chronic lack of sleep hadn't helped, either.

After breakfast, Helen outlined the plan for the week.

"We've finished the Fortress so we will return to the homestead this week," Helen announced. "The renovation crews are coming sometime next week, so we'll need to finish the homestead by then. I suspect we'll be back to making trails and campsites by Thursday or so." Helen glanced through the group. "If you have questions, ask them now."

Everyone shook their heads or shrugged.

Helen sighed, and Viv could see the weariness etched across the older woman's face. "Okay. Up and at 'em, team."

Clearing the homestead was better than the Fortress. The building itself was smaller, with fewer items and less garbage from trespassers. The work moved along at a steady clip, and in contrast to the Fortress, no one had incurred an injury in the homestead. *At least, not yet,* Viv corrected herself.

However, by midweek Viv couldn't shake a suspicion that weighed on her shoulders like an anchor: It had been too quiet.

"Ladies, where's Morgan?" Helen's voice interrupted Viv's focus and she glanced up. The older woman stood at the doorway of the room in which Viv and Cat worked, gathering garbage and debris. Worry ran harsh tracks across Helen's face though she tried to offer them a smile along with her question.

Viv glanced at Cat, her eyebrows raised. "I haven't seen her for most of the day," she admitted. Viv didn't share that she had actively tried to avoid the other girl whenever possible. Morgan's strange behavior had seemed to cease somewhat as they stopped working in the Fortress. But Viv had caught Morgan a few times as the other girl stared into the distance and silently mouthed an entire conversation with an unknown recipient.

It never failed to send ice through her veins.

Cat shrugged. "I haven't either. I thought she was outside."

Helen gave a single nod. "Okay, good to know." Her brows furrowed deeper into her eyes, contradicting her acknowledgement.

"Is...is Morgan missing?" Cat asked, surprise in her voice.

"No." Helen's denial was quick, definitive. "I'm sure she's wandered off. I'll find her."

Helen stepped away from the doorjamb, and Viv heard the older woman make her way through the hall and down the steps. Viv turned to Cat.

"Do you think she's missing?" Viv asked.

Cat shook her head, her eyes sweeping the room with disgust and fear in her gaze. "Knowing this hellmouth, probably," she said. Viv watched Cat wrap her arms around herself. "Zane was right. This place is cursed — an actual nightmare come to life."

Viv nodded to herself. Cat and Zane were right.

Grafton Stake was cursed. Or haunted.

Or *something*.

Viv swallowed hard against the alarm that flooded her body. She rubbed her hands together in brisk motions, hoping to dispel the nervous energy. *Only a few more weeks. I can do this. I have to.*

By mid-afternoon, Helen could no longer pretend all was well. Viv watched as the crew leader struggled to stay calm as she pulled the crew members into a huddle.

"I don't want anyone to panic," Helen started.

Devlin paled at Helen's opening gamble. "What now?"

Joel frowned. "Jesus," he cursed in a low, tight voice.

"Too late," Cat muttered.

Helen frowned at them. "Not helping," she snapped. Viv watched her take a deep breath before continuing. "I can't find Morgan in the Fortress, or the basecamp, or the homestead. No one has seen Morgan since approximately 10:00 this morning." A tremor shook through Helen's voice before she steadied it

.

"Before I call it in to the authorities, here's what I'd like us to do: I want Joel and Devlin to walk along the riverfront and search for Morgan. Cat and Viv, go up to the trail system we created and look around. I'm going to check the campsites, the parking lot, and the buildings again." Helen bent to pick up some equipment at her feet. As she straightened, she continued. "Everyone gets a walkie-talkie, set to this shared channel. Do *not* change the channel. Everyone will wear an orange vest and a hard hat." Helen handed out the equipment before putting on her own vest. She took another deep breath.

"Normally, I'd never ask any of you to engage in this kind of work," she admitted. "But we're so remote and we only have three to four hours of true daylight left. If we can find Morgan before the night falls, we increase her chances of avoiding hypothermia or... anything else." Helen's voice trailed off, her face grim.

The reality of what Helen was asking them to do crashed down on Viv. *She thinks Morgan is injured. Or even dead.* Viv thought of how she had tried to avoid the other girl for the last two weeks, disturbed by the odd behavior and mannerisms. Viv tried to remember if she had even greeted Morgan earlier that morning, or thanked the girl for her efforts at making dinner, despite the inedible results. Guilt and shame traced through her insides, harried by worry.

What if Morgan were hurt? What if something terrible *had* happened?

Helen had continued talking. "Check in on the walkie-talkie every twenty minutes. If you find her, let us know immediately." Helen studied the sky with a calculating glance, then back at the crew.

"Be back before dark. No exceptions."

Viv led the way to the trail the crew had made their week onsite, Cat close to her heels. They didn't speak during the fast hike, either to save their breath or because they didn't know what to say. Soon they reached the newly made trailhead. Viv scanned the ground before them, surveying the freshly turned dirt for something. A footprint or a torn piece of clothing. Some evidence that Morgan had been there.

She found nothing.

Viv glanced back at Cat. "Do you see anything?"

Cat shook her head. "I guess we should walk down the trail?" she offered.

Viv stared down the trail. The thick canopy of the evergreen trees shaded the dirt path, making the walk seem dimmer than the surrounding woods. "I guess."

"Well, do you have a better idea?" Cat snapped.

Viv simply stared at the other girl. "No," she replied in a flat tone.

Cat flushed but glared back at Viv.

They walked up and down the trail in silence. Viv peered into the underbrush and past the thick trees, hoping to see Morgan or some sign of her. But she didn't see anything unusual on the trail, just berry bushes, saplings, boulders, and grasses. Walking along the trail, Viv strained to listen for a sound that would lead them to the other girl. To her surprise, she heard...nothing.

No bird song or insects or small creatures rustling through the bushes. The wind was still. The forest was silent.

The walkie-talkie crackled to life. "First check-in."

Viv jumped and almost dropped the device. Cat placed a hand on her chest, gasping for air.

"Joel and Devlin, have you found anything?" The static echoed in the woods.

A pause. Then, "No, nothing yet." The response was garbled.

"Cat and Viv, any updates?"

Pressing the button, Viv spoke. "We haven't seen her."

A longer pause. "Okay, keep looking. The next check in is in twenty minutes." The walkie-talkie crackled as Helen signed off.

Viv and Cat continued down the trail, further and further away from the homestead and the Fortress. They peered and examined and leaned into every bush. They stepped on every boulder to gain a greater line of sight, hoping to see something.

Anything.

A second check-in occurred, then a third, each with the same news.

Still no sign of Morgan.

The daylight faded as they walked and walked. Twilight seeped across the sky like ink from a tipped bottle. Finally, Cat stopped and crossed her arms.

"She's not here," she announced. "We're not going to find her here."

Viv glanced around the woods, then nodded. "You're right," she admitted.

Cat gazed at Viv, her eyes worried and the corners of her lips downturned. "You know, there is a place we haven't checked." Her voice trembled on the last word.

Viv stilled. "The graveyard."

Cat didn't answer. She stared into Viv's eyes, trepidation scrawled across her face.

"We have to check," Viv said. "Right?"

Cat sighed. "I know we should. But..." her voice trailed off.

"Yes," Viv answered the other girl's unspoken statement with a wince. "I know."

Viv led them back up the trail. She paused at the junction that led to the graveyard and stared up the hill. She studied the grass in the near twilight and her gaze sharpened. She bent down to examine the earth. "Cat, do you see that?"

Cat stopped next to her. "I think so?"

A faint path bent the grass underfoot and led up the hill, in the direction of the graveyard. The line in the grass barely there, so thin that Viv almost didn't notice it. Viv glanced at Cat. "She may be up there."

Cat was pale; she looked nauseous. "Let's find her, then."

Viv scrambled up the hill and almost slipped several times in her urgency. At the top, the obelisk in hewn black stone rose up to greet her. It seemed like a warning in the growing darkness. The pasture spread out before her and Viv continued forward, then slammed to a stop. She rocked on her heels, trying to make sense of what she was seeing.

She heard Cat exclaim behind her. "Morgan! She's here, oh my god, she's here." Cat tried to push past Viv.

Viv flung up an arm to bar Cat's movement. "Stop," Viv hissed through gritted teeth. "*Look.*"

Cat stopped. She saw. And fell back, almost behind Viv.

"Oh my god," Viv heard the other girl whimper from behind her.

But she couldn't take her eyes off the scene before her.

Morgan stood several feet away, near the center of the graveyard. Dressed in a white gown that gleamed like bone in the twilight, Viv saw that the garment was old-fashioned, with flounces at the hem and on the chest. The hem trailed in the wet grass at Morgan's feet. Long sleeves covered her arms, and Morgan's long hair draped down her gown and around her body like ropes, the ends of her hair coated in a sticky fluid. Viv's eyes trailed over the gown. Red stains, etched in symbols that resembled keys, were traced across the fabric. Morgan's hands were coated in red, and Viv realized, in a distant corner of her mind, that the red was blood.

More blood dripped from her scalp, a gory crown that haloed her white face and wide eyes. Her lips were stained red, and more fluid dribbled from her mouth as Morgan's face stretched into the familiar too wide, grotesque grin. Feathers, blue and black and red, rested on the ground at Morgan's feet, also stained with blood.

Morgan turned from the sky and focused on Viv. The grin grew wider.

"Hello." The high, thin, childish voice was back.

"Have you come to join us?"

## CHAPTER TWENTY ONE

Viv called in the discovery on the walkie-talkie. Helen appeared within ten minutes, with the boys in tow. They came to a stop next to the large black obelisk, where Cat and Viv stood, huddled together.

And stared.

Viv watched the emotions flicker across the others' faces like channels on a television but faster: Shock. Disbelief. Horror. Worry. Pity. Discomfort.

Finally, Helen called out. "Morgan? Are you injured?"

Morgan turned away from the gravestone she examined at her feet, turned to stare at Helen. "Hello." The same high voice whispered across the wind to where they stood. "Have you come to join us?"

Joel took a step back. "Holy hell," he muttered. Devlin wrapped an arm around Cat. Viv just shivered in place.

To her credit, Helen didn't flinch. "We've come to see if you're okay, Morgan," Helen answered. "Do you need medical attention? Are you hurt?"

Morgan's face stilled. Then her eyes crinkled above a playful smile. "You're silly," Morgan accused. She giggled, and fresh blood dribbled from her mouth and down her chin. It splattered onto the gown below.

"Oh Jesus." Joel shook his head. "This is not good. Not good."

"Shut up, Joel," Cat hissed.

"Guys." Helen's low voice whipped across the clearing. "Quiet. We need to get Morgan to safety."

Viv stared at Morgan. Feathers were affixed to her bare feet with dried blood and as the other girl wandered from gravestone to gravestone, a feather or two would slip from her feet to rest on the black hewn stones. Morgan chattered about nothing and everything to no one in the same high, childish voice. She skipped and lunged and twirled, her bare feet leaving a long and twisted trail of feathers throughout the graveyard. Twilight had deepened, making the bone white gown seem spectral, almost intangible. The blood-soaked locks of hair appeared as black ropes that ensnared Morgan in a vise.

Viv looked back to Helen. "How are we going to do that?"

Helen didn't answer. Instead, she stared at the young woman, dressed in blood and feathers and twilight.

Viv shivered.

In the end, Helen had to call for an ambulance from a hospital in the neighboring town for Morgan.

As the darkness continued to deepen, Morgan refused to leave the cemetery. Viv and the others each took a turn, trying to cajole the young woman past the obelisk and down the hill to the camp. But Morgan continued to ignore them, her head tilted as though listening to sounds or noises the others weren't privy to. She wandered from gravestone to gravestone, and chuckled and babbled and danced. When Helen started forward to offer a jacket to Morgan, the young woman stilled.

Her mouth widened until it was a gaping crater on her face, and screamed. She continued to scream until Helen backed away.

Falling silent, Morgan continued to wander the cemetery.

They didn't try to help Morgan after that.

All of them remained by the obelisk, cold and growing colder, and watched the damaged young woman pace and sing and whisper nonsense. Viv shivered as she watched the other girl. She couldn't seem to get warm. Did Morgan felt the cold at all? Did the temperature even register in her altered state?

*She is possessed. Haunted.* Rationally, Viv knew Morgan's condition could be the result of a mental health issue but... The shivers that had cascaded across her body now turned into full on shakes. Viv felt icy from the inside out. *There's something truly wrong with her, with this entire place.*

Finally, the ambulance and the police arrived an hour after Helen's terse call on the satellite phone. From the edge of the graveyard, Viv could see the flashing lights turn up the gravel road and into the impromptu parking lot. Joel ran down to greet them and to guide the newcomers up to the graveyard.

The ambulance EMTs and the police picked their way up the dark hill. The police held high-powered spotlights to light the path, and the EMTs carried a stretcher between them, padded thick restraints nestled on the white padded board. A third EMT walked behind them. When they arrived at the obelisk, she recognized the police officers from a week ago — had it really only been a week? — from the inquiry with the human remains in the antique trunk. The officers stared at Morgan in shock, disturbed by the state of the blood drenched girl. The EMTs simply examined Morgan and then glanced at each other with a shared resignation.

The EMTs started forward. As the EMTs approached, Morgan began to scream and scream. She screamed until her voice went hoarse, then continued to moan in a garbled whisper when her voice gave out. The police had had to help the EMTs restrain Morgan to the gurney. The girl whipped her body back and forth, tried to lunge away and kick and flail. Blood flew from her stained mouth, the hoarse horror in her voice echoed her eyes. The wide eyes had slitted to narrow, feral gleams of white and black on the girl's face.

Viv had to turn away at that point. It was too much.

The police led the EMTs down the hill, spotlights held high. Morgan's piteous moans, made hoarse from her screams, rippled through the night and trailed after the somber party. Helen led Viv and the others after the emergency personnel. On the outskirts of the basecamp, Helen paused.

"Wait here," she instructed. "They may have questions for you." She waved to the kitchen tent. "Get something to eat if you can manage it." The group watched Helen follow the police down the path to the parking lot.

Viv heaved a deep sigh. She settled a camp chair in front of the firepit, though no fire burned within. She just needed to sit, to process, for a moment.

Cat paced around the empty fire pit. "What the hell was that?"

Devlin shook his head. "I have no idea," he muttered. "It was creepy as hell, though."

Cat kept pacing. Viv wished she would stop. The anxious movement disturbed her, poked at her already raw senses. "She had blood all over her," Cat said. The other girl finally stilled, apprehension scrawled across her face. "Was it hers? Or s-something else?"

"She also had feathers all over her feet," Devlin added. "Did she kill some birds or something?" He shook his head. "What a fucking nightmare," he muttered.

Joel appeared with an armful of kindling and logs; Viv hadn't realized he had left the campsite. "Does anyone know if she had health issues before she came here?" He bent to start a fire.

Viv met Cat's gaze, then Devlin's. They each shook their heads.

"I don't know her that well," Cat admitted. "She said that she was here to fulfill a court order but seemed normal otherwise. A little... quiet sometimes. Kind of a follower, you know?"

"That doesn't tell us much," Devlin pointed out. "None of us are here because we wanted this."

"I know," Cat snapped. Viv watched the other girl wrap her arms around herself. "Sorry," Cat offered in a low mutter.

Faint flames blew to life in the pit. Joel crouched over them and fed the fire with larger sticks and small logs. "There is something wrong with this place," he muttered. He glanced up. "I mean, every week seems to get worse."

"No shit," Devlin muttered.

Viv turned from the empty firepit. "Why Morgan?"

Joel frowned at her. "What?"

"Why did they target Morgan?"

"'They'?" Devlin echoed.

Viv met his gaze, then waved a hand at the forest around them. "Yes. *Them.*" She dared him to deny what they all knew to be true yet unspoken. Something — *someone* — lurked in the woods. Someone wanted them gone. Viv and the others were not welcome.

She watched Devlin swallow hard, his Adam's apple bobbing in his throat. He twisted his watch around his wrist a few times. "I don't know, man," he finally answered.

They fell silent when Helen appeared with the police officers.

"I think you all remember Colts and Burton," she began. "They want to ask you some questions. Please share everything you know with them."

Colts stepped forward. "We'd like to talk with you one-on-one. This may take some time." He nodded at Viv. "May we talk with you first?"

Viv pulled herself out of the chair with reluctance. She wasn't keen on revisiting what she saw. "I guess."

She followed the officers to a spot several feet away from the camp. Almost immediately, Viv missed the warmth and light of the now large campfire. She could hear the others bustle in the kitchen tent, putting together a belated dinner. Her stomach rumbled in response. Viv couldn't believe she was hungry after the day's events.

"Miss?" Colts tried to get her attention.

Viv looked away from the campsite to focus on the two men before. "Yes?"

"Can you describe what you witnessed today?"

Viv stared at Colts. She hardly knew where to start.

"Perhaps you tell us when Morgan first went missing?" he prompted. Viv thought she saw a faint echo of compassion pass over his face.

Viv sketched out the day's events as quickly as she could. She wanted to be done with it, to bury the memory of Morgan wandering the graveyard in bare feet and blood. Of Morgan's screams, growing more and more hoarse, as the EMTs had to restrain her to the gurney. Despite the cold of the evening, she didn't shiver. Viv was numb, impervious at this point.

Throughout the recital, the police officers peppered her with interruptions.

"When did she go missing? At what exact time?"

"Does Morgan have any enemies among the crew members?"

"Why did you look for her in the graveyard?"

"Why didn't you attempt to provide aid to her?"

At the last query, Viv stopped. She gave Colts and Burton a scathing frown. "You saw her, up in the graveyard. It took all of you to subdue her and get her onto that gurney." Viv grimaced as guilt washed through her despite her rationalization. "How could any of us have helped her?"

After a quick glance between themselves, the police continued.

They asked how well Viv had known Morgan, and how long. Did the girl have enemies within the crew? Did she have a history of mental health issues? Where was Morgan from? The questions went on and on. Viv could only answer, "I don't know," or shrug. She knew so little about any of the crew members, let alone Morgan. Viv only wanted to finish her sentence, then go ho me.

Finally, the officers let her go.

Viv choked down a hasty dinner. The others were quiet, waiting their turn with the officers as they sat around the campfire. The ambulance had long since left, and Viv listened into the difficult conversation Helen had with Morgan's parents on the satellite phone. Viv could hear faint echoes of anger and fear come through the phone's receiver, followed by Helen's calm apologies and repeated reassurances that Morgan had received medical attention. When Helen returned to the campfire, she looked as though she had aged a full decade: Deep circles beneath her haunted eyes cut heavy shadows into her face. Tense lines wrapped around her lips and etched between her brows. Helen settled into a camp chair, her head in her hands.

No one spoke.

The flames in the fire crackled and snapped.

## CHAPTER TWENTY TWO

Devlin was the last of them to be questioned.

Finally, the police were done. Helen followed them down to the parking lot, their conversation a quiet murmur in the dark. Everyone stared into the flames, waiting for Helen to come back. When Helen reappeared at the edge of the circle of firelight, her eyes were red-rimmed and even more haggard than before.

"How is everyone doing?" Helen hazarded at the group.

No one responded.

"Yeah, that's about what I figured." Helen sighed, then scrubbed a hand over her face.

"Did you hear anything about Morgan's condition?" Viv asked. "Will she be okay?"

"The EMTs managed to sedate her for the ride to the hospital but I haven't heard anything else," she admitted. Helen paused. "The police may be back tomorrow for further questioning."

A ripple ran through the group. Viv sat up but Cat beat her to the question.

"Why?" The other girl frowned. "We don't know anything."

Helen stared into the fire. "Morgan had bruises and scratches all over her body." She paused. "Many of the bruises resembled handprints. Thankfully, though that word hardly applies here, that's the extent of her injuries. There wasn't any sign of a concussion, no contusions. The blood wasn't even hers. It was from an animal, likely a bird. Or several of them," Helen amended.

Viv remembered the officer's query: *Did Morgan have any enemies among the crew members?* The question made sense now.

Joel's question interrupted Viv's thoughts. "Do they think one of us did this to Morgan?" His voice rose with each word, like an alarm bell gaining volume.

Helen sighed, her gaze rueful and sad. "They have to explore — and eliminate — every possibility."

Cat shook her head. "But...no one was alone with Morgan," she said slowly, as if putting together the pieces of a difficult jigsaw puzzle. "The guys were with you, Helen, and Vivienne and I were alone in the homestead. None of us would have been able to sneak away without the others noticing."

"I explained that to the officers," Helen replied. "I told them it was my belief that Morgan had some kind of mental health break, and that the injuries were self-inflicted." Helen shrugged. "We will know more tomorrow. The police promised an update on their investigation and the BLM made it clear to me that the continuation of this project hinged on the outcome of that inquiry."

"Wait, they're going to cancel the project?" Devlin asked.

Helen shrugged. "If the police believe one of us injured Morgan, then yes. In a heartbeat. They can't afford that kind of liability. It doesn't matter that your parents all sign waivers in cases of injuries — the BLM won't leave itself open to that kind of legal action."

Viv studied the others, their faces alternately dimmed and brightened by the light of the campfire. She couldn't read their faces in the darkness, couldn't get a sense of who would be glad to leave and who would be disappointed.

"I'm not sure when or if we'll get more updates. The hospital has to be careful in cases with minors." Helen swept a glance around the campfire. "You all should turn in, try to get some rest." Helen turned away from the fire. "We'll know more about the project tomorrow."

The police called early the next day.

Viv could hear Helen's hushed conversation outside the kitchen tent. The others fell silent over bowls of oatmeal. The call was short, Helen's tone relieved and grateful. Afterwards, Helen made a second call. This conversation was longer, more detailed. Viv listened to Helen recite the same reassurances again and again.

"No, the police do not suspect anyone on the crew."

"They believe the injuries were self-inflicted."

"Yes, a random incident."

"No, no relation to the remains in the trunk. The police believe those remains are possibly over a century old."

"Yes, we are on track to finish the project on time."

Viv glanced at the others. Joel studied his oatmeal but didn't eat, stirring the contents in the bowl. Cat nibbled on a slice of toast, her wide eyes focused on the tent flap entrance, as though waiting for Helen to appear. Devlin had given up all pretense of eating and tilted his head to better listen to the conversation outside.

Finally, Helen hung up. When she didn't appear in the kitchen tent, Viv stood. She tossed her bowl into the wash basin, then stepped outside. A light drizzle greeted Viv and she pulled the hood of her jacket over her head. Behind her, she could hear the others scramble up and follow, a series of clunks as the abandoned bowls and silverware clattered within the basin.

Helen studied Viv and the others with a knowing gaze as they approached. "How much did you hear?" the older woman asked.

"Most of it," Viv answered. Why lie? The truth would save them time.

Helen nodded. "I suspected that." She sighed, then shifted to face the four of them. "So, good news first: Morgan is at the hospital and seems well on her way to a full recovery." Helen paused, then continued. "Morgan shared with the police that she has no memory of last night's events. Nor does she remember much of this past week. But she's lucid and seems herself again. Her parents are furious but haven't threatened legal action against the BLM. Yet," Helen added.

"She doesn't remember last night?" Devlin echoed, his face perplexed and his eyes worried.

"Probably a mercy," Helen muttered. Then louder, "No, nothing. Apparently, she was upset to wake up in the hospital."

The image flashed through Viv's mind: Morgan, adorned in feathers and blood and twilight. *Have you come to join us?* The high childish voice echoed in her mind. Viv shook her head, trying to clear the memory. She glanced up in time to catch Cat's question.

"What about the project?" Cat watched Helen, her hands buried in the sleeves of her hoodie. "Are we still working here or what?"

Helen sighed. "Since the police believe that Morgan's injuries were self-inflicted, the project lead at BLM has given us the tentative go ahead to keep working, to finish out the next three weeks."

No one spoke at Helen's words. She continued. "We will return to the project tomorrow. But before we do, I want each of you to consider whether you want to stay on." Helen shook her head. "I've never had a project go sideways on me, not like this. We've had vandalism—"

Viv flinched at this, the unfair accusation still raw for her.

"—literal corpses in trunks, theft, injuries, and now *this*." Helen gestured up the hill, in the direction of the graveyard. "It's been... wild."

Joel snorted.

"So I want you all to take the rest of the day and think. Figure out if you want to remain on the project." Helen held up her hands to forestall any comments. "For those who are here to fulfill a requirement, I can write a letter on your behalf and try to get you some good faith credit for time served on this project." Helen checked her watch, and then glanced back up at the others. "Let me know of your decision by noon, and I can have you on the last bus out of Hard Luck by the end of the day."

Viv retreated to the parking lot for a smoke.

She lit up and took the first inhale. The smoke streamed from her nostrils and she studied the tall evergreen trees through the mist that had followed the morning's drizzle of rain. She thought of what she had learned from Leonard about the history of Latimer Stake. The corrupt family, out to profit off the suffering and misery of vulnerable people. The lack of justice for the patients, long since dead, as the family fled the region and into the ether. Viv thought of the desiccated remains in the trunk. Viv wondered if they would ever know who those people were.

"Can I have one?"

Joel stood before her. He nodded at the cigarette in Viv's hand. "Spare a smoke?" he repeated after a moment of her continued silence.

Surprise flickered through her. "I thought you didn't smoke."

"I don't."

Viv studied Joel for a moment. Dark circles swathed his eyes, and his hair was disheveled. *He looks like how I feel. Tired. Scared.* Without a word, Viv pulled one out of the packet and lit the cigarette for Joel. She watched him inhale.

Joel stared into the trees, then spoke. "Are you going to stay?"

Viv stared at the gravel around her feet. "I'm not sure." She took another inhale.

"Why are you even here?" Viv startled at Joel's query. She found him studying her with a puzzled expression. "What did you do?"

"My mother died. Breast cancer." Viv hadn't meant to share that. She took a quick drag on the dwindling cigarette. Her eyes watered, and she stared up at the sky.

From the corner of eye, she saw Joel still. He watched Viv through the mist and the cigarette smoke, waiting for more.

Viv ground out her first cigarette, then lit another. "Things went... bad afterwards. The usual. A few drugs, some vandalism. My father didn't know what to do with me. Still doesn't," Viv added under her breath. She shook her head to herself. Viv barely remembered the months following her mother's death. They blurred together, a horrid quilt of patched, painful scenes, stitched together by despair and fury and destruction.

"Shit," Viv heard Joel mutter. Then, "I'm sorry."

"Thanks." Viv cleared her throat, coughing past the emotion that had wedged in there. "I spent a short stint in juvie. I won't go back there again." These last words were a promise, low and fervent. Viv nodded towards the campsite. "After I got out of rehab, this was the only alternative. I was lucky my uncle knew of this program and offered the judge on my case a different option."

Joel snorted. "Lucky. Yeah, we're so lucky."

Viv met his eyes. A giggle bubbled up, more hysteria than real mirth. Joel grinned back and the open, almost carefree expression made him seem younger, happier.

Then the smile slid off his face. Joel sighed around the cigarette perched between his lips. "I'm really sorry. About your mom."

Viv swallowed hard. "Thanks."

"I'm not sure my parents will let me come home early," he admitted. "They were so pissed and disappointed." Joel inhaled. "The disappointment was worse, honestly."

Viv thought of her uncle's words at the Mining Days Festival, his frustration and sadness bleeding into anger. But she preferred his reactions and sharp words, which were honest and straightforward, despite the hurt they caused. It meant that he *cared*, cared enough to get salty and pushy with Viv, to demand better from her. Her father would simply retreat into his shell and treat her with an icy disdain that pained her almost as much as her mother's death.

"Yes. It is." She cleared her throat. "How did you end up here? You don't seem... like us."

"Like you?" Joel echoed. His brow furrowed.

Viv waved at the woods around them. "Broken. Bad."

"You believe you're broken and bad?"

"I'm not talking about me," Viv retorted. *Idiot.* She hadn't meant to reveal so much. "Why are you here, Joel?"

Joel finished the cigarette, then pinched the smoldering end between two fingers to smother the coals. "I fucked up."

"How original."

Joel scowled. "Look, this isn't... easy." He shook his head, then rubbed a hand over his face. "My cousin got into some bad shit. He's a few years younger. Kind of lost, you know? Seeking attention, any kind. My uncle... he's not the greatest d ad."

Joel took a step closer, his voice hushed. "One night, he texted me. Said he needed help. And my dumb ass didn't ask why. I just met up with him — only to find out that he had stolen a car." Joel chuckled without mirth. "A fucking Kia. Who steals a Kia?"

When he didn't continue, Viv prompted him. "What happened?"

"What always happens: someone called the cops. They found us two hours later, miles away, arguing over what to do." Joel ran both hands through his hair, then shifted from one foot to the other. "I wanted to return the car, then go home. He... he didn't. He just didn't *care*. He stole someone's car and didn't care about how it would hurt them." Joel met Viv's eyes, and she almost flinched at the sorrow within. "I gave up on him that night. Not to the cops — I'm not a snitch. But I knew I couldn't help him. Not anymore."

A crow cawed from a nearby tree. They watched the bird fly up into the gray sky and disappear into the persistent fog.

"I'm sorry." Viv didn't know what else to say. "Really."

Joel nodded. "Thanks." After a moment, he continued. "So that's why I'm here. I got a deal because it was my first offense, and I wasn't the main offender."

Viv studied Joel, with his sad and frustrated eyes. Envy welled up in her, and she wondered if Joel's cousin would ever realize how lucky he had been to have had a champion. Someone who cared enough to come out into the night to help, to fight alongside him. She wondered how the last year of her own life might have been different had she had someone like Joel pushing for her.

"Hey, what are you guys doing?"

The question caused Viv to flinch. She saw Cat make her way down the trail from the basecamp, her eyes jumping between Viv and Joel.

"Talking," Joel said.

"Smoking," Viv replied.

Cat looked between them, then smirked. "Uh huh. Viv, I need a smoke."

Viv sighed, then tossed the pack to the other girl.

"Thank god." After a few moments, Cat ground out the cigarette beneath her tennis shoe. "So we're all staying." A question lay beneath her words.

Viv turned to study the path that led up to the basecamp. She could see the homestead and the Fortress from where she stood, the edges of the buildings blurred by distance and smoke. She thought of the boy in the old-fashioned pajamas. The symbol scratched onto her chest, an elaborate motif atop on a narrow spine of a key, had never fully healed. It still pained her. *They are angry and they want* something.

Viv just didn't know what.

But if she left, where would she go? Her court order unfinished, she would go back to the juvenile center. The judge had made that very clear. Her uncle wouldn't be able to shelter her nor would her father intervene on her behalf. Viv almost snorted at that thought. No, Viv would have to stay and see this through.

"Yes," she finally answered Cat. "I'm staying."

## Chapter Twenty Three

At noon, no one chose to leave.

Helen had asked them three times, determined to give them multiple opportunities to change their minds. Still, everyone stayed. Viv wondered if Devlin stayed out of stubbornness or if he simply didn't have anywhere else to go. She didn't ask. Helen seemed both relieved and chagrined by their decisions.

Viv was glad to return to trail building the following morning. While she hadn't gotten any better at the work, and still dropped tools, tripped over nothing, and was a general menace due to her ineptitude, she was grateful to be away from the homestead and the Fortress. Being outside, away from the narrow rooms in the Fortress or the dusty interior of the homestead, was a relief. The trail was wet and cold and muddy during most days. Viv became acquainted with every fern and boulder that lined the new trail that led to the river's edge and the start of the campsites.

But at least she wasn't trapped inside those buildings.

Viv should have known the peace wouldn't last. It was the following week when Viv first spotted him.

It was mid-afternoon and they had just finished the trail that led to the river's edge. Viv sat on a boulder during her break and wolfed down the trail mix by the handfuls. This work never failed to make her hungry. Glancing up, Viv almost choked on a raisin.

The boy in the pajamas stood next to a tree, only six feet away. A single hand rested on the trunk as he watched her.

Chills slithered across Viv's skin, pebbling her flesh in goosebumps. She met his gaze, staring into the black, empty eye sockets.

He scowled.

Viv felt her brows furrow. She hadn't seen that expression on his face before.

The boy in the pajamas scowled harder. Then he opened his mouth and spoke, his daggered teeth jagged against the thin blue-white lips.

No sound came out.

Viv shook her head, trying to understand. What was he trying to say?

The boy spoke once more. Again, no sound.

"I don't understand."

The boy screamed but no sound emerged. His clear anger made his eyes thin, severe dark brushstrokes against his face, his mouth a canyon of black on the blue-white face.

The key symbol on her chest blazed in pain. Viv gasped, bent double at the shock and hurt.

"Vivienne."

Viv jerked. Helen stared down at her, concern and wariness on the older woman's face. "Who are you talking to?"

Viv cast a searching glance at the tree.

The boy was gone.

Viv turned to Helen.

"No one," she lied.

Over the next few days, Viv realized that the others were also seeing the ghosts. She had caught Cat staring at the river one morning, the other girl's gaze intent and frightened. Cat's rigid posture felt familiar to Viv, a natural reaction to seeing something profoundly unnatural. Viv watched Cat take slow steps away from the river, her skin pale and limbs tense. When Devlin had reached out to touch Cat on her shoulder, the other girl had jumped, letting loose a scream that had Helen running across the campsite.

"It's nothing," Cat had assured them. "Devlin surprised me."

But Viv had seen Cat cast a glance over her shoulder at the river a few moments later, her brows twisted together with worry. *She saw something. Was it the little boy?*

Viv couldn't bring herself to ask. She was afraid of the answer.

What if there were more ghosts?

*Two more weeks*, Viv promised herself. *Only two more weeks.*

Joel was the next one to see something.

He had dropped an armful of logs and kindling at the edge of the campsite one evening, startling everyone in their camp chairs. Viv watched Helen sink back down into her chair with a heavy sigh. Joel had apologized, gathering up the wood with a distant expression on his face. Throughout the night, he shot repeated scowls at the Fortress. Viv followed his gaze once, then stilled when she saw what he saw. She squinted past the firelight, trying to get a better look.

A woman in a bone white gown stood at a window in the Fortress, her long dark hair twisted into ropes around her body. Dark stains crowned the woman's head and black fluid dribbled down her front.

The resemblance to Morgan was uncanny.

Viv swallowed hard. She turned to Joel to see if he saw the woman, and found him watching her, a question in his eyes. *Do you see it, too?* Viv gave a single nod. Relief, then worry, cascaded over Joel's face. He turned again to spy the spectral woman in the window and Viv followed his gaze.

The woman had vanished.

Neither Joel nor Viv said anything to the others.

Viv dreamed of her that night. The symbol scratched on her chest ached and bled the next morning.

Devlin seemed to be the last one on the team to see something.

He was also the first to say something.

He shared a smoke with Viv most mornings, silent and bleary-eyed as they struggled to wake up fully. One morning, huddled under a tree to shelter from the rain, he spoke.

"You see them, too, right?"

Viv cut a sharp glance at Devlin. The boy stared at her through the smoke, his gaze steady. "Yes."

Devlin exhaled. "The woman in the window of the Fortress... she looks like Morgan. Or maybe Morgan looks like her. A little boy in pajamas with the creepiest damn grin you've ever seen. An older woman with missing legs. She drags herself up and down the trails, close by the riverside." Devlin shuddered, then took a hasty drag off his cigarette. The ember tip glowed in the semi-darkness of the morning.

"I've seen the boy," Viv said. "He was the first. I saw the woman in the window a few nights ago."

Devlin nodded. "They're ghosts, right? What else could they be?"

Viv shook her head, then hunched into herself. "I don't know. I guess?"

"If they're ghosts, they are memories or... energy, maybe, of the bad shit that happened here." Devlin continued as if he hadn't heard Viv, almost to himself. "Terrible memories. But they can't hurt us." Devlin glanced at Viv. His eyes pleaded for an affirmative. "Right?"

Viv thought of the symbol on her chest. She hadn't done that to herself, she knew. The boy in the pajamas had somehow done it to her. And Morgan... the girl had changed during her time at Grafton Stake. Viv bet that the woman in the window had been at fault, somehow.

Viv stared at Devlin.

The answer in her eyes didn't comfort Devlin.

He shivered. "Well, shit."

The sightings grew worse over the following week.

Viv first saw the woman without her legs near a new campsite they had built earlier in the day. It was mid-afternoon but the faint daylight under the canopy of the trees was made further dim by the mist that came off the nearby river. Viv saw a flicker of bone white at the corner of her eye, and though she *knew* better — her mind shrieked at her to turn away, to keep working, to ignore the summons — Viv turned to look.

A middle-aged white woman with shorn blonde hair, cut at jagged lengths, laid on the trail. She propped herself up by her arms, her hands stained in black fluid and dirt. Her gown, an old-fashioned garment, was ripped and torn. The edges of garment ribboned behind her, resting on the trail. Her legs were missing, Viv saw. Clean bandages wrapped around her thighs, the cleanest cloth the woman wore. Viv then met the woman's eyes.

That was a mistake.

Agony and fury swirled across her face, a grimace interrupted by black sockets. The woman bared her teeth at Viv.

Viv's heart stuttered, then kicked up an irregular rhythm. She stepped back, afraid.

The woman moved. She stretched one arm forward, the motion jerky and disjointed. The woman grasped the ground before her, then pulled. She inched forward, dragging her body across the dirt. The woman repeated the motion with the other arm. Another inch. Over and over and over, the woman came forward.

Towards Viv.

Viv stepped back. *What the hell?* Fear flooded her limbs. A voice in the back of her mind begged her to run, to flee. The woman dragged forward, inch by inch, her fingers scrabbling in the dirt for purchase. Viv met her gaze again.

The black sockets burned with a dark flame. *Give them to me.*

Viv jerked back. The woman had spoken without moving her lips. Viv shook her head, trying to clear the intrusive words from her mind.

*Give them to me.*

"I don't know what you want," Viv cried.

Still, the woman came forward, empty sockets burning.

*GIVE THEM TO ME.*

"What do you want?" Viv yelled. Deep breaths sawed in and out. Her chest burned in pain and she doubled over, grasping at the raw edges of the symbol etched across her chest.

"Vivienne!"

Viv's head snapped around.

Helen stood a few feet away, with Joel, Cat, and Devlin arrayed at her back. The team leader seemed irritated yet worried. Looking at the others, each of them with a grim, tight squint around the eyes and their lips set in firm line, Viv knew that they *knew*. Had they seen her? The woman without her legs? Viv looked back at Helen, puzzled. Why couldn't Helen see them?

"Vivienne, are you okay?"

Viv straightened, then glanced over to the dragging woman.

She was gone.

But Viv saw something, a movement that glistened in the faint daylight. Ignoring Helen's repeated queries, Viv stepped forward and closer to stare at the ground where the woman without legs had dragged herself. She stilled when she realized what she saw.

Desiccated slugs and snails stretched out before Viv, a mosaic of life and death in muted shades of brown, grey, and black.

She stepped forward and realized that the ones closest to her were somewhat fresh, alive, with delicate antennas that wafted around in the damp air. The snail shells were fragile, many of them cracked. As Viv trailed her gaze down the stretch, they shriveled unto themselves, the slime and the damp drying the further down the trail she looked, until she saw only dead things where the trail went crooked and bent towards the river, out of sight.

Viv shivered. *That was her trail. Wherever they are, that's where she was.*

"Goddamn it, Vivienne!"

Helen's angry curse pulled Viv away from the trail. "What?"

Helen calmed at Viv's attention. "I've been trying to get your attention for the last several minutes," she grumbled, heaving a sigh. "Are you okay?"

Viv stared at Helen, then the others.

"No."

Helen's head jerked back in surprise. "No, you're not okay? Do you need anything?"

A sound bubbled out of Viv before she could stop it. *A laugh,* she realized with a distant horror. *I'm laughing.* "I'm not okay. None of us are okay." Viv couldn't stop herself.

Helen eyed her with a wary expression and Viv knew the other woman was thinking of Morgan, worried that Viv would follow a similar fate. "Helen, don't worry," Viv offered, finally sober. "I'm not okay but then who would be? There is something broken about this place. We all know it." Viv pointed at the others behind Helen. "They know it — they just don't want to risk sounding crazy." Viv shook her head. "I'm not okay. But I'm going to finish this. A little over a week, right?"

Helen stared at Viv, her brow furrowed. Viv could see the older woman wrestling with a decision and wondered which decision it was: Acknowledge something off about the Grafton Stake? Take Viv to the hospital? Penalize Viv for her outburst? Viv felt a calm settle over her as she waited for Helen's response.

Finally, the older woman spoke. "Viv, take a break and get some water. Everyone else, let's get back to work."

The others avoided Viv during her break. But at lunch, Joel sat down beside her. "You okay?"

Viv met his eyes, then looked away at the kindness in his gaze. She shrugged. "Sure."

Joel snorted. "Liar."

"You saw her, too. Don't tell me you didn't."

After a moment, Joel gave a nod. Relief washed over her. She was right: The others had seen the woman.

"Did you see the slugs and the snails?"

Joel shuddered. "Yes." He paused. "She was the first one I saw."

"You've seen others?" Viv's voice was sharp. "Besides the woman in the window? The one who resembles Morgan?"

Joel nodded. "The little boy, too."

They didn't speak for a moment. Viv tried to eat her lunch but couldn't muster any enthusiasm for the peanut butter jelly and trail mix combination.

"Why do we see them?"

Viv put down the sandwich. "I don't know."

"Do they want something?"

"I don't know." Viv remembered the strident command from the crawling woman. *Give them to me.* She shivered. "Maybe?"

Joel sighed, frustration clear in his voice.

Viv agreed with him. She was tired, exhausted, by Grafton Stake: The ghosts, the dreams, the incidents. For a brief moment, she wanted to go home. But then she remembered all over again that her mother wasn't there, and grief seeped into her like steady rain. Only her father remained at the house that was no longer her home. Still. *Better than this place. A little over a week left.*

She hoped that they would make it.

## CHAPTER TWENTY FOUR

At first Viv didn't believe Joel.

It was near the end of the day.

"That is a sick joke," she hissed, glaring at him. Viv swept a glance around the new campsite they had just finished to see if Helen was nearby, if she had overheard. Helen was gone but Cat raked sand into the new tent bed nearby. She cast a quizzical glance at Viv's hiss. Viv scowled again at Joel.

Joel shook his head, his face serious. "I'm not joking, I swear: I can't find Devlin."

Viv studied the tall boy. He stared down at her, his dark eyes worried and upset. His hair looked as though he had run his fingers through it many times. "You're serious."

"Yeah." A sigh gusted out of him. "I'm worried as hell."

Her heart sank. She thought of Morgan. Would they find Devlin in the cemetery, dressed in feathers and blood and a smile, out of his mind? "Have you checked the graveyard?"

Joel stared up the hillside, a grimace on his face. "Not yet."

"Where have you checked?"

"Riverside, homestead, and the Fortress," Joel replied. "Nothing."

"Have you told Cat or Helen?"

Joel shook his head. "I didn't want to worry them without a reason."

"We need to check the graveyard."

But the graveyard was empty.

Viv and Joel stood at the obelisk. She scanned the edges of the cemetery and swept her gaze through the flat pasture. Viv searched for anything that signaled Devlin walked through the headstones.

She found nothing.

Viv sighed. "He's not here." She winced as she stated the obvious.

"Damn," Joel muttered. "What now?"

"We should tell Helen," Viv said.

"Wait." Panic limned Joel's voice. "Do you see that?"

Without waiting for Viv, Joel started forward in low crouch. Viv followed him to the edge to the pasture, past several of the headstones embedded into the turf: 87569. 34209. 25943. Joel paused, then pointed. Viv followed the direction of his finger — and stilled. The underbrush next to the graveyard had been wrenched aside, leaving a large hole that led into the darkness of the woods. A red black fluid edged the leaves and branches, and slicked the path forward, the color difficult to make out in the fading light of the day.

A wristwatch lay on the ground.

Viv recognized it. Cat had teased the boy for wearing an old fashioned analog device.

It belonged to Devlin.

Helen called in search and rescue.

Then she had rounded Viv and the others up. "Pack your clothes and identi-fication, and get on the bus," Helen told them. Despite the unnatural calm that she wore like a mask, Viv could tell Helen was exhausted. "Leave everything else behind for now."

The drive into town was brutal. Viv heard Cat sniffle to herself two rows behind her, and after a moment's hesitation, she unbuckled herself and made her way back to Cat.

Cat glared up at her. "What?" Tears clouded her eyes and stains were tracked down her face.

Viv felt a wave of warmth and affection. Cat never changed. "Move over." She thought Cat would refuse but after a moment the other girl slid over and stared out the window. Viv sat down next to Cat and buckled her seatbelt.

"You should wear your seatbelt."

Cat gave her a snide glare. "Yeah, sure. That's what we need to focus on right now."

"I'm sorry."

More tears welled up in the other girl's eyes. Cat quickly turned to stare out the window again. She didn't respond but after a moment, she reached over and grabbed Viv's hand in a grip that was almost painful.

Viv held on and didn't say anything.

Helen checked them into the Har' Luck 'otel again, and Viv realized that the manager, an odd duck with odder manners, hardly registered with her this time. *I can deal with this kind of weird.* Viv and Cat shared a cabin; they had even got the same cabin Viv had shared with Morgan. Pushing open the door, Viv wondered about Morgan. Was she well? Then she thought of Devlin and ice congealed in her chest.

She hoped they would find him. Soon.

Tossing her bags on the bed closest to the door, Viv left the cabin to meet the others. They were going to Honey's Diner for a late dinner. But she stilled when she saw her uncle at the front office, talking with Helen in hushed tones.

"Uncle Rick?"

Her uncle looked up and a wave of relief crossed his features. He strode over and Viv found herself wrapped in a tight hug. She sighed in relief and leaned into the hug for a long moment.

Uncle Rick pulled back and gave Viv a quick scan. "How are you doing, kiddo?"

Viv stared up into his eyes. "Not great," she admitted.

Rick's face softened. "Helen filled me in. I'm glad you're safe, and in town. We will do everything we can to find Devlin."

"'We'?" Viv echoed. A suspicion bloomed in her chest. *No, no, no.*

Her uncle was puzzled. "Yeah, I'm part of the local Search and Rescue unit."

*No!* "Uncle Rick, please don't go out there," Viv begged, grabbing at his arms. "Please. You don't know what's there. That place is cursed."

Her uncle wrapped her in another hug. "Don't worry, kiddo. I've done this many times before. I'll be fine," he said.

"No, you're not listening." Viv pushed her way out of the hug. She grabbed his arms with a tight grip. She had to make him understand. "Please don't go out there."

"Vivienne."

Viv fell silent. Rick rarely used her full name.

"I have to go. Devlin is missing and we can't lose him. I promise you, I'll be okay," he said. "Stay close to Helen. I hope we have an update for you soon."

*He won't listen.* Her shoulders fell. After a moment, Viv gave a nod.

Her uncle squeezed her shoulder in reassurance, then nodded to Helen. Viv watched as he crossed the parking lot to get into his beat-up Datsun, an old but reliable little monster of a truck he called the Beast. The truck rumbled and sputtered to life, and then Viv watched him drive away. Tears slipped down her face, and she wiped them away in impatient motions.

*Please come back. I can't lose you, too.*

*Viv flipped through the scenes like pages in a book, catching crumbs of sensation within each one.*

*The fish at the riverside, the carcasses a hopscotch of glittery scales and rot. The smell was unbearable, rotted meat and something worse, and Viv gagged, shivering in the cold. Then she saw the boy in the pajamas as he peeled back the tender flesh of his forearm, blood first seeping and then rushing from the tear. Viv could smell something metallic, almost taste the tarnished copper blood at the back of her throat. The woman in the window of the Fortress, superimposed on Morgan like a pair of negatives in the same photo, dressed in a bone white gown of feathers and blood and twilight in the graveyard. Viv felt a feather brush her cheek and settle into her hair. By the time she had reached up to touch the feather, the older woman without legs had dragged herself along a path from nowhere, salting the earth with the trail of the desiccated flesh of slugs and snails in her wake.*

*Viv stretched her hands out in front of her. She tried to push the images away but they crept closer, bled through the cracks between her fingers like smoke. She shook her head again and again.* I don't want this. I don't want any of this.

*The symbol on her chest shimmered, then lanced with a sudden pain.*

*"Give them to me." Viv heard the old woman's voice.*

*Viv shook her head. "I don't know what you mean."*

*"Give them to me." A lighter voice, high and childish, joined in.* Morgan, Viv *thought.*

*"Please," Viv begged. "Please stop."*

*"Give them to me." A growl echoed in her ears, deep and menacing.*

*Others joined in, a cacophony of voices: Young and old, every gender. Each distinct and there were so very many. Viv knew who they were: Patients, prisoners, of Grafton Stake. All of those who resided, suffered, and died at the Fortress. Viv shook her head and placed her hands over her ears, trying to block the noise. She couldn't think, only feel, and she felt too much. The noise, the smells, the pain.*

*Something made her open her eyes. She glanced up — and flinched. They were there. The boy in the pajamas, the woman with the slugs, and a new spirit — a young woman with an erstwhile crown of black hair and thorns in a stained gown. They arrayed themselves before her, an ominous triad. Viv felt the weight of their stare like stones upon her chest. The thorn crowned woman lifted her arm in a sudden flash and plunged forward.*

*Viv screamed.*

*The woman had stabbed her.*

*Viv gasped and choked, blood bubbling to her lips. The wind whistled through her ears and Viv felt fluid pulse out of her body to the tune of her heartbeat and weep down her body, between her breasts and onto her stomach. She grabbed the woman's arm and pulled in a feeble motion, trying to dislodge her arm and the knife. Viv glanced down at her chest and flinched in surprise. It wasn't a knife.*

*It was a key.*

*Silver, with an ornate motif on the head, the slender spine of the key stretched forward and was embedded in her chest, the edges of the open wound raw with fresh blood. The young woman in the thorned crown reached towards her. Grasping the delicate key with both hands, Viv watched in horror as she reached forward with bloodstained hands and broken nails and gave a sudden twist.*

*Viv cracked at the first turn of the key, then shattered at the second. Pieces of her, jagged flesh and shattered bone, tumbled to the ground. She saw the three, each adorned in their own crown of flesh or bone or feathers, jeweled with matted blood that winked when caught by the light.*

*The triad grinned and grinned and grinned.*

*Viv screamed.*

Viv drank four cups of coffee at Honey's Diner that morning.

Helen watched her from the bench seat across the table, her brows pleated in concern.

Viv stared back. "What?"

Helen shook her head. "Nothing."

It was clearly something. But Viv didn't have the energy to pursue it. She had been up since dawn, unable to sleep because of the dreams. In the bathroom, she had found that the wounds on her chest had begun to ooze a yellow pus that smelled of rot. Faint smears of blood dotted her chest and ribcage. Viv had scrubbed at her body in furious motions during her shower, ignoring the pain. She wasn't foolish; she knew she needed medical attention. But Viv worried that if she told anyone, they would force her to see a doctor. To leave Hard Luck.

And she couldn't — wouldn't — leave until she knew Uncle Rick was safe.

Viv watched the traffic outside the window. Hard Luck remained unchanged: Two buses had rolled into the small town off the main road, pausing only long enough to off and on-load passengers and baggage. Honey's Diner had been packed during the morning rush but had since slowed down. Now mostly older folks lined the breakfast bar and chatted with the waitresses. Retirees, Viv guessed. She turned back at Helen.

"Have you heard anything yet?"

Helen shook her head. "When I hear something, you'll know."

Cat shifted next to Viv, her gaze down and focused on the largely untouched pancakes on the table before her. The other girl had cried the night prior, in the shower. Viv could hear the whimpers and gasps. She had pretended not to notice when Cat had come out of the bathroom, her eyes rimmed in red and still wet. But she had given the Cat the extra blanket she had found in the closet.

Joel seemed to be the only one with an appetite. With horror and something like admiration, Viv had watched him eat a plate called the Farmer's Bounty, laden with every kind of meat, potato, and egg concoction. After a moment, she had to stop watching. It was too much.

After breakfast, they wandered the town in the light, ever present drizzle. They peered into boutique shops filled to the brim with the modern farmhouse aesthetic. Viv bought a pack of smokes from the convenience store. They skipped the grocery store and the town municipal buildings. Coming across the Bureau of Land Management building, where she had first met Helen and the others weeks ago, Viv was surprised by how small a structure it was. It had seemed larger, more imposing, when she had first seen it. She thought of all that had happened since: Zane leaving after the accusation, then Morgan being taken away on a gurney. Devlin was missing. Half the team: gone, in a matter of mere weeks. The ghosts weren't calming down; in fact, they had increased their activity. And now Uncle Rick was out at Grafton Stake, searching for Devlin. Viv shivered.

When would it end?

Regular as clockwork, Helen called the search and rescue team for updates each hour. And every time, she'd hang up the phone with a careful, neutral expression before turning towards them — and Viv knew.

Nothing yet.

With each call, the disappointment blossomed anew. Worry strangled Viv further, suffocating clear thought. She smoked several cigarettes, jittery from the nicotine and the fear, smoke streaming up from her like a stalled train. The hours eked by like a funeral procession, each one darker with still no news. By nightfall, Viv was a mess. The others weren't any better: Cat had smoked the remaining cigarettes, and alternately snapped at people or began crying. Of the two, Viv preferred the anger. Crying meant that Cat had given up hope. In contrast, Joel had retreated further and further into himself over the day. The furrow between his eyes, the dark circles beneath, grew both deeper and darker.

Helen remained a quiet version of her normally cheerful self: Calm and reassuring, her words designed to keep morale up and despair at bay. Every hour, after each call, she would hang up and offer the empty update.

"No news yet but it's still early."

"More volunteers have joined the search."

"Let's not jump to conclusions."

The last words, uttered over an unwanted dinner hardly touched within the noisy environs of Honey's Diner, were grim and a little tired. Viv studied Helen for a moment, and her heart sank. It seemed that the older woman was losing hope, too.

Helen got the call as they walked back to the Har' Luck 'otel.

"Whiteaker here."

Viv could hear faint strains of some speaking. Joel and Cat watched Helen, hope and concern warring on their faces.

Helen paused in mid-stride, phone still clutched to her ear. Her face paled, turning her skin almost gray in the dim light of the streetlamp. A streak of alarm rushed across her face. "What?"

Viv paused. The pit of her stomach dropped further. Whatever the news, it wasn't good.

"Are you sure?" Helen confirmed. Her lips tightened when the other voice responded. The older woman's eyes darted to Viv, then she fixed her gaze on the ground in front of her. "I see."

A moment passed as the caller continued. Then Helen spoke. "And still no news about Devlin?"

The answer was short and clear from even where Viv stood: No.

Viv tilted her head, confused. If they weren't talking about Devlin, what had they been talking about?

"Okay, will do." Helen sighed into the phone. "Please, please keep me updated. Yeah. Yeah, I got it. Okay. Talk to you later."

Helen hung up the phone. Her shoulders sank and her head hung down. Viv watched the woman take several deep breaths with growing concern. *What news had Helen received?*

Finally, Helen raised her head. "Joel and Cat, could you excuse Viv and I for a moment?"

Joel was startled; Cat, worried. "Uh, s-sure," Joel said. "We'll go back to the motel, I guess."

"Thank you." It was clear Helen wouldn't speak until they left.

Viv watched the others leave, then turned to Helen. "What's w-wrong?" Her voice cracked on the second word. She trembled in the cold air, wrapping her jacket tighter around herself. The garment did nothing about the chill within her chest.

"I'm afraid I have some bad news." Viv heard Helen's voice as though the woman spoke through a tunnel, distant and muted. "Your uncle has gone missing."

## CHAPTER TWENTY FIVE

V iv shook her head. "Sorry?" This wasn't happening.

It couldn't.

Not Uncle Rick.

*He's all I have left.*

Helen stepped forward, her hands up and her manner gentle, as if approaching a wild animal. "The search and rescue team lost contact with your uncle around mid-afternoon. They haven't heard from him since," she explained in a soft voice. "They are searching for both him and Devlin. They will call us as soon as they find him. Them," she corrected herself.

Viv didn't answer.

She stared at Helen without seeing the other woman. Her mind reeled and wrestled and tumbled around the knowledge and Viv frowned, concentrating. Suddenly, a wave of heat and grief and fury broke inside her chest. She knew.

*They have him.*

The ghosts of Grafton Stake.

They had driven away Zane, damaged Morgan, and stolen Devlin.

And now had her uncle.

*Oh, god, they have him.*

Viv gasped and choked at the sudden rise of bile in her throat. She turned from Helen and tried to vomit. Nothing much emerged, and Viv stared at the ground, bent double with her hands braced on her knees. Tears slipped down her face and splashed onto the pavement below.

After a moment, Viv struggled upright. Helen started forward, trying to help.

Viv flinched. Helen paused, concern etched on her face.

"Vivienne, how can I help?"

Viv thought of the ghosts, the damage they had wrought over the last few weeks. In the face of those creatures, what could Helen do? What could she do? She shook her head. "You can't." More tears slipped down her face.

*I'm going to lose him. Just like Mom.*

Helen paused for a moment, as if uncertain what to say. Then she stepped forward. "Let's get you back to the motel."

Viv hardly heard Helen.

Two thoughts chased each other throughout her mind like twin koi in a pond, despair and grief circling and circling and circling.

*They have him.*

*I'm going to lose him, too.*

Helen ushered Viv into the motel room she shared with Cat, dropping her keys on the table just inside the front door. The clatter roused Viv from her fog for a brief moment, and she flinched. Cat was clearly worried about Viv, and opened her mouth to speak but closed it when Helen shook her head.

Viv stood in the middle of the room, uncertain of what to do, her mind and heart in turmoil. She stared at Helen's keys on the table. Something about them bothered her.

"Vivienne?"

Vivienne turned to Cat. "Yes?"

Cat spoke again. "Maybe a shower? If that would help?"

Viv turned back to the keys on the small table. Most of them were silver coated brass connected by carabiner used by rock climbing enthusiasts. They glinted in the faint lamplight within the motel room.

"Sure," Viv answered in an absent tone.

In stiff and slow motions, Viv turned to the bathroom. She was relieved to be able to shut and lock the door behind her, to get away from the prying, worried, helpful, pitying, suffocating gazes of Helen and Cat. Viv stripped off her shirt, then paused as she caught sight of herself in the mirror. The symbol on her chest ached whenever she moved and she saw that the edges were angry, red with infection. The bright color contrasted the pale skin of her chest, and was lined in a blistered, scaly yellow as parts of the wound tried to scab over. *It's gotten worse,* Viv realized. *So much worse.*

Viv studied the motif scrawled across her chest, the single line of the key spine that ran between her breasts, ending at the forked tines of the old-fashioned key scratched into her flesh. She thought of Helen's keys on the table outside the bathroom, across the room. Plain, worn. Utilitarian. A memory surfaced: Viv remembered the keys at the museum. The chatelaine, Leonard had called it. The ornate silver ring with floral filigree and several chains that extended to different keys. The very keys that secured the rooms within the Fortress.

A sudden, deep cold settled over Viv and she *knew*.

Finally, she understood.

*GIVE THEM TO ME.* The demand rattled against the back of her skull.

*They want the* keys.

*They want to be free.*

*They must believe the keys will free them.*

Her dreams about being trapped in a tight, dark, and cold space, the footsteps that faded away until they disappeared and didn't return, washed over her and left chills in their wake. Viv traced the key shape scarred into her chest. She shuddered, and felt foolish that she hadn't figured it out earlier.

*What if I return the keys? Would they give Uncle Rick and Devlin back?*

*Or is it too late?*

She redressed in a hurry, her impatient fingers fumbling with the buttons of her flannel shirt. Leaving the bathroom, Viv found Helen and Cat in the midst of a low-voiced conversation. They paused as Viv entered the room, and Cat examined Viv for a moment, then glanced away, her gaze stricken.

"How are you feeling, Viv?" Helen asked. She studied Viv as if she could divine the answers.

Viv shrugged, not meeting the older woman's eyes. She nursed the beginnings of a plan within her and Helen was astute. She could pick up on clues Viv hadn't meant to share. "I think I want to lie down."

Cat moved up and off the bed, the motion distracting Viv. "Then it's my turn," Cat said with false cheer. The bathroom door closed with a firm thud behind her.

Helen spoke in a sharp voice. "Viv, where did you get that scratch?"

Viv peered down at her chest. Her flannel shirt was open at the throat. She could see the angry edges of the key head above the fabric. She glanced back up at Helen. "Tree branch," she lied.

Helen seemed skeptical. "Do you need first aid?"

Viv shook her head. "It's just a scratch."

Helen's pleated with concern and worry but she didn't press. Viv watched her rise up from her perch on the lone chair in the motel room and head to the door. "I'm going to check on Joel but I'll be right back. Will you be okay, being alone for a few minutes?"

Viv nodded in response. She ignored the keys on the small table, the ones Helen hadn't picked up on her way out the door.

Helen seemed reluctant to leave. "I'll be right back."

After Helen left, Viv moved quickly. She chose her thickest jacket and jammed her feet into the now-worn work boots. In a small knapsack, she packed a headlamp, a first aid kit, a pocket knife, and her wallet. She picked up Helen's keys, clenching them in her fist to mute the jangle of the brass together. Viv peered out the door to the cabin she shared with Cat, scanning the dark. She didn't see Helen.

Viv stepped outside—

And almost fainted.

An older man with an ice bucket stood a few feet away, puzzled and a little wary.

Her heart a fierce drum beat in her head, Viv nodded to the man and moved on. She ducked out the circle of light cast by the lamps and made her way to the bus in the parking lot, staying crouched low and out of the sporadic pools of light that shone down from the streetlamps.

"Viv."

Viv tripped in fright, dropping the keys on the ground. The metallic clatter jarred against her ears and she breathed out in quick bursts as she struggled upright. Once steady, she glanced behind her.

Joel stood beneath the porchlight of a nearby cabin, his hands loose at his sides. "Where are you going?"

Viv peered behind him but saw no one else. Helen and Cat were still inside, and she heaved a sigh of relief. Then she refocused on Joel. "I'm getting my uncle back, Joel."

Joel cursed, then ran a hand through his hair. "Viv, no—"

"Don't get in my way." Viv had never before heard herself use that tone. Implacable. Tinged with threat.

"Viv, it's dangerous." Joel stepped forward. "Let me come."

"I said I'm—" Viv stuttered to a stop. "What?" Confused, she took a step back.

"I know you're doing this, one way or another." Joel took another step, one hand out in supplication. "Let me help you."

Viv shook her head. *Why? Why did he want to help?* "I don't understand."

Another step. "You don't have to do this alone."

Viv stared at him, her heart in her throat. Something like hope fluttered through her but she shook it off. Good things, good people, didn't happen to her. Or if they did, they didn't stay. She knew that. Then she remembered Joel's cousin, the one who had committed grand theft auto for a mere Kia. How Joel had tried to extricate him from the terrible decision. How she had envied that unknown cousin for having Joel at his side. She shook her head, already regretting the words that poured out of her. "I'm not your cousin, Joel. I don't need you to rescue me."

Joel winced at her words, and Viv felt a smear of shame coat her insides. Her cheeks heated. *I shouldn't have said that. Even if it's true.*

"Fuck. I know that," Joel muttered. "This—" he waved a hand between them "—is not about *that*. I just don't want you to go looking for Devlin and Rick alone. Grafton is *dangerous*."

Viv stared at him, considering. Would it be so bad? To have a friend with her? She had been fighting everything on her own for a long time. She was so *tired* of it all.

She made her decision. "I'm driving."

Joel sighed in relief, then nodded. He jogged over.

At the bus, she scrabbled with the keys, finally getting the right one in the door lock. Viv hauled herself into the seat, tossing the knapsack behind her as Joel climbed into the passenger seat. She put the keys into the ignition and the bus started up, a rumble that seemed too loud to Viv. She leaned forward and peered at the gas gauge. Two-thirds full. She could make the drive to Grafton

Stake on that, no problem. She gripped the steering wheel with white knuckles; she felt too small to drive a vehicle this large but she had to make do. Viv cast a quick glance at the parking lot.

Still no sign of Helen or Cat.

Viv put the bus in reverse. "We're making a quick stop," she told Joel.

Then she would get her uncle back.

## CHAPTER TWENTY SIX

"D on't smash the glass!" Joel hissed.

Viv glared at him, the tire iron in her hand suspended in midair. They crouched before the back entrance, a locked door with a wide window panel embedded in it, to the Hard Luck Historical Museum. "How else are we going to get inside?"

"Move over." Joel pulled a multitool and then a second thin length of metal out of his pocket. "*Move*, Viv," he repeated.

She stepped aside. Joel knelt down, and Viv watched him insert two slender shafts of metal into the keyhole of the doorknob. He twisted the shards in practiced motions while staring at the ground, his brow furrowed in concentration. He was picking the lock, she realized.

"Where did you learn this?"

"Internet." Joel grinned up to her, and after a few minutes, his wrists turned in a sharp motion. A click echoed in the darkness around them, and the doorknob turned. Joel pushed open the door. "After you."

No alarms screeched when she stepped inside. Viv walked a few steps forward, then paused. The mess within overwhelmed her. Even in the darkness, she could tell there was so much *stuff*. The smell of rust and old paper rose up to greet her. Boxes of newspapers, books, and photographs. Farming equipment, saws, gold mining pans — all of the disparate items cluttered the walkways on the floor and choked the shelves that lined the perimeter of the room. Viv squinted, trying to see in the faint light cast by the streetlamps outside the museum. A brief moment of despair shook her resolve.

How would she find anything in this mess?

"What are we looking for?" Joel's voice was quiet.

"The silver chatelaine." Viv cleared her throat. "The keys to Grafton Stake."

Viv moved from the back room into the front. She heard Joel begin to search the back room in her wake. She could hear him ruffle through papers and nudged boxes aside. Viv continued forward. She refused to turn on a flashlight, not wanting to draw attention from anyone passing outside. The clutter in this room was more manageable, confined to the shelves and not scattered everywhere. She stalked the edges of the room, searching for the chatelaine.

*There*.

She found it.

The ornate silver ring still lay on the black velvet tray that Leonard had brought out earlier that week. Resting on a shelf, the keys spread out in several directions like a metal spider. Viv stepped forward and grasped the old keys with a gentle hand. A crackle of static shocked her and she jolted in place. When nothing else happened, she tucked the keys into her pocket and retraced her steps out of the museum.

"I found them."

Joel peered up from a pile of maps. Streetlamps across the road illuminated half of his face. "Yeah?"

Viv took a deep breath. "Yes. Let's go."

Once Joel was outside, she paused to relock the door.

Viv walked the bus in quick steps, glancing around for observers. She saw none, and hoisted herself into the driver's seat. Joel joined her on the other side of the vehicle. She started the engine, then eased from the alleyway she had parked in. Seeing no one on the street beyond, she pulled onto the road and made her way to the turn-off to Grafton Stake.

Viv drove fast, pushing the bus as hard as it could go. The vehicle was larger than anything she had driven and surprisingly top heavy; she had swerved too hard on a couple of corners. Out of the corner of her eye, she watched Joel white knuckle the grab bar above the passenger seat twice during the drive.

The darkness from the night enclosed her. The thick forests that lined either side of the road, limned in the headlights, contrasted against the darkness and made it seem deeper, fuller, alive. A living creature with no eyes and too many limbs. Viv gripped the wide wheel with tense knuckles and taut fingers.

*Will this even work? How can I even give keys to a ghost, let alone several? What if I don't get there in time?*

What if Uncle Rick were already dead?

Viv shook her head, ignoring the tears that cascaded down her face. She had a foolhardy plan, yes, one she wasn't sure would quite work, but she had to try *something*. Viv couldn't wait nearby and watch her uncle and Devlin die, doing nothing.

So she continued on into the darkness, staring out at the night with her aching hands locked around the steering wheel and her breath tearing deep gusts from her lungs, in and out. In and out. And again.

Close to a junction that led to Grafton Stake, Viv saw a truck incoming in the opposite lane. In her headlights, she saw that the dark pick-up truck had a search and rescue logo blazoned on the driver's side, with large flood lights mounted atop the carriage. As the truck passed, her heart sank in her chest. The search and rescue team were still out at Grafton Stake, continuing the search for Uncle Rick and Devlin. If she wanted to deliver the chatelaine to the ghosts, she would have to avoid the team members. She exchanged a worried glance with Joel.

"Don't worry." Joel stared into her eyes. "We'll find a way to avoid them."

Viv turned right at the junction and drove up the gravel road that led to the parking lot. She slowed, then stopped along the side of the road, flicking off the headlights. She killed the engine and eased out of the bus, knapsack in hand. The night had a cold wind that bit at her face, and Viv pulled up the hood of her thick jacket. She glanced over at Joel. "Ready?"

He gave a single nod. He wore Devlin's jacket, Viv saw. It had been left behind in the bus.

Walking up to the parking lot and beyond, they skirted the edges and crouched low to avoid notice. She saw a trio of people conferring besides an SUV, headlamps illuminating a map stretched between them. Viv quickly ducked between cars, crashing into Joel in her haste. He steadied her while they peered around the bumper of a truck. The basecamp, where she woke up only yesterday morning, was flooded with lights and more of the search and rescue team. A ring of people stood around the firepit; some sipped coffee while others talked.

Snatches of the conversation rose up.

"...still haven't found the boy." One of the men spoke in a hushed voice.

A woman sighed. "Yeah, we're worried. He's been out here too long."

"We might still find Rick." A new man offered. Viv could hear the doubt in his voice from where she crouched behind the girls tent.

The fire popped and Viv flinched at the sudden sound. The woman spoke again. "Rick was — is — an expert in wilderness and forestry skills. He's missing because something got him or he's injured, not because he got lost."

"Like the ghosts and goblins of Grafton Stake?" The first man jeered. He chuckled at his own wit.

"No. Like a cougar." The woman's voice was abrupt. Viv could tell she wasn't amused.

The conversation around the firepit ceased.

Viv moved on. Whatever the other woman thought, Viv knew better: The ghosts of Grafton Stake *did* have her uncle and Devlin. She fingered the chatelaine in her jacket pocket. But how to give this to the ghosts?

"Where are we headed?" Joel breathed out the words.

Viv studied the grounds for a moment. Then, "Homestead house first."

Casting a quick glance to see if anyone watched, Viv stole up the path that led to the homestead. The search and rescue team hadn't bothered to install lights in the homestead or the Fortress, and had ignored the barns entirely. Viv crept up the steps and across the porch. The front door was unlocked. Joel followed her inside. "I'll check the first floor," he offered.

Viv murmured her agreement and headed for the stairs. The house was empty and somehow colder within than outside. Viv pulled out her headlamp and set the beam on the lowest setting. She swept the second floor, aiming the focused, single shard of light at the floor. She peered into rooms, searching for something: a sign, a presence, *anything* that would tell her what to do. Viv grasped the chatelaine with tight fingers inside her coat pocket. She hoped she was right.

She couldn't afford to be wrong.

Viv forced herself to pull down the stairs that led to the attic. Her heart hammered against her ribs and blood rushed in her ears. Adrenaline flooded her body in waves, first in the deepest cold and then in blistering heat. She stepped up the ladder, took a deep breath, and rose into the attic to search.

Nothing.

Breath whooshed out of her. Relief coursed through her but then dread began to mount. *If they weren't here*, she reasoned, *they had to be in the Fortress.* She shuddered, then steeled her spine. *Let's go. Rick and Devlin need you.*

Viv eased down the stepladder and folded it into the ceiling, back into the position. As she made her way down the stairs, blue-white flickers grabbed at the edges of her vision like static on a television. She paused on the steps, took a deep breath, and looked.

A row of eyes, mid-air, studied Viv where she stood. They glowed, white and luminescent and pulsing in the darkness, different sizes but all with a similar almond shape. No faces, she realized in numb horror. Only eyes. One by one, they gave slow blinks or opened wide or scowled. Viv swallowed hard. She took one step, then another. And another. Halfway down the stairs, she tripped on nothing and stumbled against the banister. Her ribcage slammed against the hardwood and she heard a crack. Viv gasped at the sudden pain; she saw bright stars in her vision, even in the darkness. Gripping the rail, she pulled herself up and darted out of the homestead, with the glowing eyes following her until she had passed the threshold of the front door. Viv darted down the steps, and turned to look back at the homestead.

The eyes had vanished.

"Viv. Viv!" Joel appeared next to her. "What's wrong?"

She took a few deep breaths. "I saw them," she gasped. Air sawed in and out of her, and her ribs protested each movement. Viv shuddered, trying to calm herself. She had to continue. She needed to find the ghosts, to deliver the chatelaine. And hope that her gambit would work. After a few more breaths, Viv straightened. "Let's check the Fortress."

On her way to the Fortress, Viv could see new members of the search and rescue team had clustered around the fire pit. They spoke in urgent tones, a worried hum that carved into the darkness like the roots of a tree. She couldn't hear the precise words they said but she saw that one of them held and spoke into a satellite phone, concern etched into her face by the faint light of the fire. Viv wondered if the caller was Helen, notifying the search and rescue team of Viv's escape and arrival at the basecamp.

Viv broke out into a jog in the darkness.

"Hey!" A man shouted from the firepit. "Who's out there?"

Viv ran faster, a hand hovering over her aching ribs. She couldn't let the team find her, not before she finished what she had started.

"I'm over here!" Joel's voice rang out behind her. "I came out to look for my friend."

*He's distracting them*, Viv realized. She cast a quick glance behind her and saw Joel surrounded by the search and rescue team members, the lights from lanterns and flashlights bouncing across the trees. *He's drawing attention away from me. He's giving me a chance to do this.* Relief chased through her, gratitude swift on its heels.

She picked up the pace, her footfalls light and rapid against the muddy earth beneath her.

The door to the Fortress was unlocked. Viv pushed into the dark, then closed the door behind her before flicking on the headlamp. The mere possibility of Helen's likely phone call, the sacrifice of Joel's surrender to the search and rescue team outside — these events felt like a ticking clock on a bomb to Viv. And she was running out of time. She raced up the staircase to the top floor, where the medical operating theatres were. Her ribs protested each and every footfall but she ignored the pain as best as she could. She scanned each room on the third floor with perfunctory sweeps of the headlamp, seeking any sign of her uncle or Devlin or *something*.

Anything that would tell her what to do with the chatelaine clutched in her pocket.

She needed to finish this.

## CHAPTER TWENTY SEVEN

The third floor yielded no sign of Rick or Devlin so Viv moved on to the second floor, taking care to clutch the staircase banister to avoid falling again. She walked down the hallway in quick motions and peered into the small rooms. Looking into the last room, she paused as she heard a sound.

Footsteps. From above, on the third floor.

A sudden cold crept down Viv's spine. She stilled in the doorway of the last cell, waiting. The footsteps continued across the floorboards, then paused. They started again.

Someone walked down the stairs.

Viv couldn't make herself move. Her mind shrieked at her to flee, to run, to escape. But to no avail.

The footsteps ceased.

After a moment, Viv peered into the darkness, looking for... something. She took a step forward, then another.

Still nothing.

Viv frowned. She eased forward, and the pain in her ribs redoubled as the adrenaline wore off. She stopped at the staircase landing and peered down the steps.

A woman dressed in an old fashioned, bone white gown stood at the bottom of the stairs. Black blood stained the hem of her gown and dripped down the bodice. She grinned up the stairs at Viv; more black stained her lips and sharp teeth. Her arms rose up as if to welcome Viv with an embrace.

*The woman in the window.*

Viv gasped. She plunged her hand into the pocket of her jacket, and grasped the chatelaine. She pulled the ornate ring out, the keys spilling out behind like a metallic waterfall. Viv held the chatelaine up. "Is this what you w-want?" Her voice cracked on the last word, her heart in her throat.

The woman hissed, her black teeth bared in a grimace and her black eyes slitted. She started up the steps and Viv stepped back. *Oh no, oh no, oh no. This isn't good.*

Viv held the chatelaine up higher, as if to ward off the spectral woman. She didn't know what else to do.

To her surprise, it worked.

The woman hissed again but fell back and away from the bottom of the staircase.

Viv stepped forward.

The woman crept back.

Viv came down the staircase in careful movements, clutching the banister in one hand and the chatelaine raised high in the other. The woman stepped further and further away, as though they were enjoined in a bizarre dance. At the bottom of the stairs, Viv stopped and glared at the woman.

She jerked the chatelaine and the keys on the long chains bounced off her arm. "You wanted this and I brought it. Now I want them back. My uncle and Devlin."

The woman stared back at Viv, her eyes black holes that were narrowed in malevolent glints. Her mouth cracked open, a deep abyss that split her face. Then she screamed, the sound an unholy noise that felt like a baseball bat applied to Viv's ears. Viv gasped at the pain, almost doubled over. She managed to keep the chatelaine held high but after a moment, she could feel warm fluid gather and then trickle out of her right ear. Her heart sounded an irregular drumbeat in her head and Viv gasped for air, her breath sawing in and out.

The woman continued to scream — and then vanished.

Viv glanced up, surprise and relief swirling within her. She peered down the grand front room of the floor, the headlamp catching the blue and white patterns of the delft porcelain tiles. The darkness of the large room pressed in on her, tried to swallow her up. Viv swept the light across the room, searching for the specter.

But the woman had disappeared.

*Why didn't she want the chatelaine? I don't understand.*

Viv continued forward, leaving the Fortress behind as she eased down the front steps. Blood trickled out of her right ear and she reached up to wipe it away. She winced when her ribs ached anew. She sighed. That hadn't gone as planned. Not that she had a plan but if she did, that wouldn't have been it. The woman seemed afraid and angry at the sight of the chatelaine.

*So now what?*

Viv took a deep breath, trying to calm her nerves. She stilled; her breath stuttered out of her body like air being let out of a balloon.

The boy in the pajamas stood several feet away, on the newly made trail the crew had created over the last several weeks. He grinned at Viv, his sharp and jagged teeth evident even in the distance. He beckoned at Viv, his gesture at once impatient and imploring.

Viv didn't move.

The boy beckoned again, his grin wider, more grotesque.

Viv held up the chatelaine.

The boy nodded. After a moment, he beckoned again. His eyes narrowed to slits and he pointed up the hill. He spoke and somehow Viv heard.

*The graveyard. Take them to the graveyard. Help us before* she *finds you again.*

The key etched into her chest flared in burning pain, as if a punctuation.

Viv froze. *Help us? She?*

The boy vanished.

Viv flinched in surprise. She started forward in a slow walk, then picked up speed as she found herself on the trail. She discovered that her ribs wouldn't permit a jog but she moved as quickly as she could, one hand bracing her ribs, the chatelaine clutched in the other. The keys bounced off her arm with her jerky gait. She breathed as deeply as she could but stars lanced through her vision. She was lightheaded, either from the injuries or the fear. Likely both. The dark forest surrounded her, a poisoned womb with black branches and reaching roots. Viv stumbled again and again on the trail.

*What did the boy mean by* she?

Then the ghosts appeared.

As Viv stepped off the trail to scramble up the hillside to the graveyard, the woman in the window reappeared in front her. Her face a furious mask of malevolence, she screamed and screamed at Viv. Fresh blood seeped from Viv's right ear, and she sobbed at the pressure the horrid screams against her ears. Her eyes squeezed shut, Viv held the chatelaine up, in front of her.

*This is who the boy meant. She's their captor. A Grafton.*

The screams lessened but didn't stop.

Viv squinted and took a step forward. The woman in the window swirled around her, the screams a cyclone of fury and rage. Viv continued.

Another sound, the drag of a heavy weight across a floor, trailed behind Viv. She peered behind her. Bile rose in her throat: The woman without her legs dragged herself behind Viv in rapid, jerky motions, a trail of slugs and snails behind her. Viv flashed the chatelaine at her but the woman kept crawling, her baleful gaze locked onto Viv.

*Take them to the graveyard.*

Viv took advantage of the moment to scramble up the hill. She cleared several feet but she tripped and fell face first into the sodden grass, made black by night. She screamed through gritted teeth at the new pain in her ankle. Viv didn't have to look: She knew the woman in the window had caught up with her.

Viv braced herself with her good leg, then hauled her body off the ground. She gripped the chatelaine and set off up the hill again.

She would finish this.

As she crawled and struggled up the hill, her ribs and her ankle bleating in pain, her ear dripping a gush of blood, Viv saw that more and more of them appeared. The ghosts spilled out the ground like trees reaching for the sky, all of them injured or abused in some way.

One man with dark hair and pale skin had a large incision down the center of his chest, his ribs stretched open to reveal his heart and lungs. Twin boys clutched each other's hands, staring at Viv in fright and she saw handprints wrapped around their shoulders, the bruises dark against the spectral white of their skin. An elderly woman with a broken hip listed from side to side as she made her way towards the graveyard in slow and awkward motions. Another woman, her midsection stained in blood and her fingers a broken jangle as she pointed to the graveyard.

There were angry and broken ghosts everywhere Viv could see. She held the chatelaine high and struggled up the hill. After a moment, Viv realized that the ghosts surrounded her but didn't touch her.

Only the woman in the window had attacked her, Viv realized. *She wants them to stay. She won't let them leave.*

Nausea crept up her throat and Viv swallowed hard.

The woman in the window appeared in front of Viv. Her surprised scream was cut short as the woman lunged past the chatelaine to bite her on the neck. The ghost reached around her back and gouged her flesh, the long talons leaving behind a burning sensation. She shoved Viv, tripped her, screamed at her.

Still, Viv pressed on.

Still, the other ghosts watched in silence.

She had to finish this.

*I can't lose Rick, too.*

She sobbed in relief when she saw the obelisk. Finally, she was at the grave-yard.

Falling to the ground, she began to dig in the dirt with her bare hands. The woman in the window — the Grafton matriarch — converged on her. Pain flared everywhere and she couldn't hear her thoughts, the spectral screams deafening. She dug and dug, her nails breaking off in jagged tears, one hand still clenched around the ornate ring of the chatelaine so tightly that the edges of the floral motif cut into the flesh of her palm. Blood mixed in with sweat and dirt, and her hands slipped in the sod and the grass.

She dug down into the ground, the soil a damp clay past the sod. She ripped through the soil with both hands. Another scratch, deep and bloody, lanced across her left side. Viv choked out a scream, then dug another inch. Tears streamed down her face. She hoped that this would save her uncle. She couldn't lose him, too. She kept digging and hardly flinched when the ghost kicked her bad ankle.

Finally, she couldn't reach any further into the soil: She had dug as far as she could reach. Viv unwrapped the chatelaine from her wrist and peeled the chains off her arm, smearing blood and sweat further along her skin.

She dropped the chatelaine into the ground.

And began to bury it.

With the first layer of dirt, the screams from the woman in the window less-ened as if someone had closed a door. Another layer of soil and sod, and Viv felt fewer fists pummel her side. She kept adding more and more dirt, burying the chatelaine as quickly as she could. The screams, the assault — those sensations reduced further and further with every layer of blood and sweat soaked soil. Viv cried in relief as the noise subsided. The fluid still pulsed from her ear, dripping down her neck.

The ghosts wavered, then dimmed as though someone turned down a dial. The woman in the window emitted another scream, rage and despair and frus-tration in a dying wail.

When the last inch of dirt lay over the submerged chatelaine, the ghosts disappeared.

Viv crumpled onto the ground over the erstwhile grave and rested her forehead against the disturbed sod. She gasped for air. Everything, everywhere along her body, hurt. She knew that she needed to get up and go look for her uncle and for Devlin. That's why she came out here. To find them.

*I need to get up.*

Then she passed out.

## CHAPTER TWENTY EIGHT

Viv woke up on the way to the hospital.

She tried to open her eyes but had to squint: The light was too bright. Pain flared, first in her eyes and then, she realized, all along her body. She laid flat on her back on some surface, and when she tried to shift, to see if that would alleviate the pain, Viv felt the restraints on her arms and chest.

*She was trapped. No. No, no, no.*

She heaved herself up off the gurney, forcing her eyes open against the bright light. She felt firm hands restrain her and push her torso back onto the gurney.

Her ankle and ribs screamed in protest; tears rushed to her eyes. Through the blur, she saw concerned faces lined either side of her, their EMT uniforms identical. An IV line draped from the ceiling and plugged into the crook of her left elbow. "Vivienne, you are in an ambulance. You are on your way to the hospital and you need to remain calm," the EMT on her left said.

Viv ignored her. She remembered something. "My uncle. Rick. Did you find him?"

The woman leaned forward. "Vivienne, can you repeat that?"

Viv moaned as a familiar flush of heat ran through her system. She recognized this feeling: They had given her a sedative. She wouldn't be conscious for long. "My uncle," she managed. "Did they find him?"

"Yes." The young woman nodded. "They found Rick and the young man, Devlin."

Relief crested over Viv like a wave and for a moment, she didn't feel any pain. She did it. Rick was safe. Devlin was safe.

For the second time that night, she passed out.

Viv next woke in the hospital.

She knew where she was before she opened her eyes: The beeping of the machinery. The steady and frequent footsteps of medical staff walking through hallways. The faint aroma of flowers and the robust, astringent scent of soap. Viv remembered these sensations from the times her mother was in the hospital, near the end. Hospitals never changed. She opened her eyes. She lay on a bed, an IV line still attached to her arm, covered in thick blankets. Viv could feel bandages across her body: Ribs, back, and ankle.

Uncle Rick napped in a chair next to the bed.

She studied him: Dark circles carved under his eyes and he had an unusual pallor for a healthy man who spent most of his time outdoors. His forehead sported a bandage that led up to his hairline. Viv scanned him. Flannel over a t-shirt with worn Carhartts and boots. She didn't see any other injuries.

"Hey, kiddo, how are you doing?"

The question brought her eyes back to his face. Uncle Rick smiled at her, worried but happy.

"Okay." Her voice was scratchy, weak. "You're okay? Where's Devlin?"

"I'm okay. Devlin's safe. He's already out of the hospital." Uncle Rick shook his head. "I'm glad you're awake. You had me worried."

"Sorry." Viv wasn't sorry. She did what she had to save Rick and Devlin. But she knew what adults wanted to hear.

"You need anything? Water?"

Viv coughed. "You need to check with the nurse before you give me fluid." She remembered the protocol from her mother's last days in the hospital.

"I can do that," Rick nodded. "I'll give it a minute, though."

Viv glanced at her uncle, puzzled. There was something he wasn't telling her. "What is it?"

Rick sighed. "You have a lot of unexplained injuries, kiddo. The social workers have already been by. They want to know who did this to you." Rick waved at the hospital bed. Sadness and anger and wariness fought across his face, and he shifted from one foot to the other.

Viv studied her uncle's face. "You saw them, didn't you?"

Rick met her gaze. His eyes were wide and troubled. Then he gave a slow nod.

Relief flooded Viv. "I'm not crazy," she said. "You saw them, too. I'm not crazy," she muttered the last words almost to herself.

"I did see them...but..." Rick seemed to struggle to find words. "What the hell? I mean, what *was* that?"

"Ghosts," Viv said.

When she didn't say anything else, Rick waved his hand, gesturing for more. "And?"

"Angry ghosts."

Uncle Rick rolled his eyes. "Viv."

"I don't know much more than that." Her throat was irritated. She tried to clear her throat twice. "Things had been weird at Grafton Stake for *weeks*. Tools were broken, stuff went missing. We found the graveyard and then started seeing them, everywhere. I think they were trying to tell us all along what they wanted but..." Viv shrugged. "It's hard to figure that out. It's not like they gave clear instructions. I only discovered that they wanted the keys to the Fortress yesterday afternoon."

"Did you tell Helen?" Rick asked. "What did she say?"

"No." Viv shook her head. "I don't think she saw them. Or if she did, she didn't tell us."

Rick seemed to think this over. "The girl who went home? Morgan? Did they get to her?"

Viv nodded. "Yes. The woman in the window. She somehow possessed Morgan."

Rick shuddered. "Awful," he muttered. "What *did* they want?"

"They wanted the chatelaine."

"The what now?" Rick was confused.

"They wanted the keys used to lock them into the cells within the Fortress," Viv explained. "I think... I *hope* the keys set them free."

"What did you do with the keys?"

"I buried them. In the graveyard, next to the obelisk. As soon as I buried them, they disappeared."

"Did that free them?" he asked. "Or just contain them?"

Viv shrugged. "I honestly don't know. I just wanted to find you. I thought if I gave them the keys, they would give you back."

Rick smiled, a tender look in his eyes. "You did good, kiddo." A pause. "Wait, where did you get the keys?"

Viv winced. "I stole them from the museum."

"Viv." Her uncle sighed.

"Well, I needed them and it worked. I won't apologize." Viv paused, then continued. "I don't think I damaged the building." She didn't mention Joel. She didn't want to cause him trouble, especially after what he had done for her.

Rick waved a hand. "We'll check with Leonard."

Fatigue stole over Viv and she laid back on the hospital bed. "What happened to you out there?"

Rick rubbed the back of his neck. He seemed almost embarrassed. "Honestly? I'm not sure." He shook his head, a flush high on his cheekbones. "I lost some time, I think. One minute I was searching for the young man, Devlin. And the next? I woke up with blood in my eyes, surrounded by EMTs."

Viv shivered. "Where did they find you?"

"A mile past the graveyard." Rick shrugged, then winced. His hand went up to touch the bandage on his forehead. "I'm fine, all things considered."

Viv nodded. The fatigue grew stronger, like a whirlpool gaining momentum. The pain in her ribs ebbed with every heartbeat; her ankle twinged, as if in response. She laid her head on the pillow, her eyes shuttered. She had done it. Rick was safe. Devlin was safe. And Rick believed her. He understood. She smiled to herself.

"Hey, kiddo." Her uncle's voice called through the fatigue. She opened her eyes.

Uncle Rick smiled at her, warmth in his eyes. "Thank you." His voice was gruff with emotion. "You did good."

The social worker, an older man crowned in grey hair named David, wasn't happy with her answers. He had shown up a few hours after her conversation with Rick. After asking her uncle to leave the room, David went over a full accounting of Viv's injuries: Two cracked ribs, a badly sprained ankle, bites along her arms and neck, deep lacerations, several bruises, and a mild concussion. But he made no mention of a scar traced in the shape of an old fashioned key and Viv wondered if it had disappeared. She would not miss it.

After this litany, he proceeded to ask Viv how she came by the injuries. She kept her lies short. Embroidering the truth too much always led to needless complications.

"Why did you drive out to Grafton Stake?" David asked, pen poised over a notepad.

"To find my uncle."

"There was an entire search and rescue team seeking him," David replied, a furrow between his brows. "Why did you feel that you need to join them?"

Viv stared at David. "He's my uncle," she replied in a flat voice.

David seemed taken aback. He made a note before continuing. "How did you receive your injuries? They are extensive." The last words were sympathetic.

"I don't remember."

The man's brows flew up. "Excuse me?"

"I don't remember," Viv repeated.

David paused before speaking. "To be clear: You don't remember how you got your injuries?"

"Correct." Viv stared into his eyes, daring him to contradict her.

David cleared his throat. "Forgive me but that's difficult to believe."

"I don't remember how I became injured." Viv was adamant.

David tried a few different angles of inquiry but Viv shut each of them down. She wasn't about to disclose to this stranger that she had been attacked by a *ghost*.

Finally, David gave up, frustration clear on his face. He tucked his pen into the spiral edge of his notepad with an irritated huff. "You know, I can't help you if you won't tell me the truth."

Viv examined the man and felt a wave of sympathy. He seemed like a nice enough man who cared. He was only trying to do his job. "Don't worry about me," she told him. "I'm going to be just fine."

Helen visited her next.

"Vivienne," she greeted from the doorway. "Are you up for a visitor?"

Viv nodded. "Sure."

Helen stepped into the room. Uncle Rick rose from his chair and stepped forward to shake hands with the woman. "Helen, always good to see you."

"Likewise, Rick." Helen motioned to the bandage on his head. "You going to be alright there?"

"This? Oh, yeah, I'll be fine." Rick gave a forced chuckle. "The search and rescue team won't let me live down though. They're convinced I wandered into an overhang, knocked myself out." Rick and Viv had agreed not to tell anyone about the ghosts.

Helen laughed. "They'll move on eventually."

"Not soon enough," Rick grumbled.

Helen turned to Viv. "How are you feeling?"

Viv shrugged, then winced when her ribs protested at the movement. "Better."

"Are you sure?" Viv heard the humor in Helen's voice.

"Not really." Viv gave a small smile.

Helen turned serious. "I have to tell you: It was foolhardy to go after your uncle and Devlin. And you and Joel took the bus without permission."

"It was my idea. Joel didn't do anything, he just rode with me," Viv hurried to explain. "I'm sorry for taking the bus. Really, I am. I was... worried."

Uncle Rick stepped forward, hands on his hips. "Look, Helen, could you consider cutting the kid a break? She was under duress — and her life hasn't been a picnic for the last few years."

Helen sighed. "I know. That's why I'm not saying anything to the police."

Relief whooshed out of Viv. "Thank you. So much. I'm really sorry, truly."

"I'm not an ogre. I get why you did it," Helen replied. "But you took a dangerous chance. You could have injured yourself or Joel, crashed the bus, hit someone else." She shook her head. "You have got to be more careful in the future."

"I will." Viv made eye contact with the older woman. "Helen, I promise."

Helen gave a slow nod. "And the injuries? What happened?"

Viv avoided her uncle's gaze and focused on Helen. "I don't remember." Her voice was steady, low.

Helen studied her for a moment in clear disbelief. "I'm going to ignore that." She shook her head. "So when do you get out of the hospital?"

"Tomorrow." A thought occurred to Viv. "The project? It's cancelled, right?"

Helen shook her head. "Paused, actually. Our portion is mostly done, anyways, so the BLM is going to hire a different crew to finish the renovation in about a month or so."

"Oh." Viv was surprised people still wanted to go to Grafton Stake, given the horrid history of the location. Even with the ghosts free from their captor, it wasn't a happy place. "That's good, I guess."

Helen stepped forward and Viv finally noticed an envelope in the other woman's hand. "Aside from checking in on you, I also wanted to give you this." Helen laid the sealed envelope on the hospital tray.

Viv looked up at Helen. "What is it?"

Helen rubbed the back of her neck, her gaze fixed on the floor. "The project was disrupted and paused before you could complete your required service. That's not your fault and I don't want you held responsible for that. So I wrote a letter to your judge and explained the circumstances, asking that he consider your service fulfilled." Helen nodded at the envelope on the tray. "That is your copy. I've already emailed my letter to the judge's office."

Shock rippled through Viv. "You did what?"

Rick extended his hand to Helen again. "Helen, thank you. That's a marvelous and kind thing to do."

Helen accepted the proffered shake, her eyes on Viv. "Not a problem. Vivienne, you worked hard and I hope you move onto a bright future." She paused and a wry smile carved into her face. "Just stop stealing people's vehicles."

"I can do that." Viv shook her head in disbelief. "Seriously? Thank you. So much."

Helen nodded again. "No problem." Her voice was gruff. "Take care, Viv."

Viv smiled. "You, too, Helen."

Uncle Rick came to stand by her bedside as the other woman left the hospital room. "Good news, huh?"

Viv nodded. "Yes." Her jaw cracked on the yawn that followed.

"You look beat. You should rest, especially if you want to leave tomorrow."

Viv gave a half smile to her uncle. She reached out and clasped his large, warm, and callused hand in her own. She squeezed.

He squeezed back. "I know, kiddo. You, too."

# EPILOGUE

She took a deep breath despite the cacophony of scents that assailed her.

"Vivienne?"

She studied Alice with the unibrow. "Yes?"

"That's what you wish to share today?" Doubt edged the other woman's words.

"Yes." Viv's tone was firm.

A guffaw erupted from her left. Jake or Jackson shook his head. "A ghost story?" He snorted. "You told us a goddamn ghost story."

"Jake." Alice interrupted the young man in a gentle tone. *So that's his name.* Alice turned to Viv. "Thank you for sharing your truth, Vivienne." Viv heard an echo of irony under the words.

"You're very welcome." *Two could play that game.*

"I think that's all for tonight," Alice said. She stood. "Please stay for refreshments if you can. Otherwise, I'll see you all in a week."

The group dispersed and Viv stood. She folded her chair, and placed it on the nearby rack, nestling it against the others. She swung by the refreshments table, and wrapped a few sandwiches and cookies in napkins, tucking them into her backpack. She didn't turn down free food, not since she had moved out of her father's house and had started supporting herself. She nodded a farewell to some of the group members that hadn't yet irritated her and left.

Outside, she lit her sole cigarette for the day on the sidewalk and waited for her ride.

In the months since she had buried the chatelaine at the graveyard at Grafton Stake, Viv had finished high school online and got a job at a thrift shop. She would start classes at the community college in a few months. Uncle Rick had even co-signed on her apartment in Portland.

She was ready for her future.

She still dreamed about Grafton Stake. The ghosts, the incidents, that night as she fought up the hillside and into the graveyard to bury the chatelaine. She still didn't know if the very keys that had denied the ghosts their freedom during their lives had set them free in the afterlife. She only hoped. Viv wanted to believe that there could be justice for the dead.

Her phone buzzed. *Still on for our date?*

Joel was persistent. She found it endearing but would never tell him that. At least not yet. Viv texted back. *It's coffee, not a date.*

*It's coffee AND a date.*

Viv smiled to herself. *I'll have coffee with you, yes.*

A horn honked. "Get in, loser. It's raining."

Viv ground out her cigarette. She smirked at Cat in the driver's seat and settled into the passenger side, closing the door. They shared the apartment, the very one Rick had co-signed on. Surprisingly, they made good roommates. Or maybe it was more accurate to say that they hadn't killed each other yet.

Cat merged into traffic after issuing another honk, followed by a rude gesture at the motorist beside them. Viv swallowed back a grin.

They were on their way home.

# DISCUSSION PROMPTS FOR BOOK CLUBS

1. What was your favorite element of *False Haven*? And your least favorite element?

2. Which character was your favorite? And who did you least like?

3. *False Haven* comes with a playlist. Which songs most resonated with you? Which songs would you add or remove?

4. Did you find the author's writing style easy to read or hard to read? How long did it take you to get into the book?

5. Did the author use any literary devices, techniques, or styles to enhance their writing, and to what effect? Discuss the author's use of symbols, metaphors, or imagery to convey the story.

6. How did the author use the setting, characters, and atmosphere of the book to enhance the story?

7. The history of medical institutions and their care or lack thereof of vulnerable populations is a fraught topic. Why do you think the author chose this setting for *False Haven*? Is the author is trying to say something through this story?

8. Were you satisfied with the outcome of the novel? Why or why not?

# AUTHOR'S NOTE

The history of medical institutions and their care — or lack thereof — of vulnerable populations is a fraught subject. The inhumanity of these places documented throughout the centuries is horrid and heartbreaking, and the choice to situate *False Haven* in a setting drawn from these experiences is not to sensationalize the subject matter but to acknowledge the truth: These places existed. They caused tremendous harm. Many vulnerable people died in disturbing ways in these places.

Grafton Stake is not a real place. While all of the scenes in this novel are fantastical (this is fiction, after all), some of them draw inspiration from historical events and locations. In fact, *False Haven* was inspired by two very real locations: Starvation Heights and Northwestern State Hospital, both in Washington State. And when we learn about these historical abuses, it's not difficult to imagine a story in which the ghostly survivors of such horrendous injustices are furious, scared, and wish to be free from a hell they were forced into.

If you're interested in learning more about this subject, here are a few recommended reads.

- Brownstone, Sydney. July 16, 2023. "The Lost Patients of Washington's abandoned psychiatric hospital." *The Seattle Times*. **Link**.

- Horn, Stacy. 2008. *Damnation Island: Poor, Sick, Mad, and Criminal in 19th-Century New York*. Publisher: Algonquin Books.

- Olsen, Gregg. 2005. *Starvation Heights: A True Story of Murder and Malice in the Woods of the Pacific Northwest*. Publisher: Crown.

## ACKNOWLEDGEMENTS

My deepest gratitude goes to the fantastic cover artist, Paper & Sage Designs; my wonderful editor; and my beta readers. You all helped transform this project into something special and I'm thrilled I was able to work with you. Thank you for sharing the gift of your skill and talent with me.

My friends and family have long championed me. Their unwavering belief, support, humor, and kindness has helped me in innumerable ways, especially when I went through the hardest years of my life. I wish everyone in this world were as lucky in their community as I am in mine.

A heartfelt thank you goes out to Rachel. You've read everything I've sent your way, even the earliest, shittiest drafts, and your incredible insight, superb GIF reactions to our meme exchanges, and stalwart support have been a blessing. Thank you for everything.

Lastly, I deeply appreciate my readers. I became a writer to share the joy that comes from an excellent story and I'm grateful that I get to this work. Thank you for your support through your purchases and reviews. It means the world to me.

# About the Author

Rebecca Rook designs tabletop games, manages a little free library dedicated to sequential art and comics, writes young adult fiction, and lives in the Pacific Northwest with two wonderful dogs. A 2021-2022 Hugo House Fellow in Seattle, WA, she also attended the 2021 Tin House YA Fiction Workshop in Portland, OR. Prior to this, she completed the wonderful Yearlong Workshop for Young Adult and Middle Grade Fiction at Hugo House. The author of the award-winning novel, *The Penance of Valentine Cash*, she writes young adult fiction in the fantasy, thriller, and horror genres.

**Learn more here: https://byrebeccarook.com/**

Instagram:

Sign up for her email newsletter, The Rookery, to stay up to date with new releases, giveaways, and more!

# ALSO BY REBECCA ROOK

*The Penance of Valentine Cash:* **Order Now!**

## *Coming Soon*

*A Strange Affinity* (Available March 2024). **Pre-order today**!
*City of Graves* (Available June 2024). **Pre-order today**!

# REVIEWS OF THE PENANCE OF VALENTINE CASH

"Author Rebecca Rook has crafted an atmospheric and immersive fantasy novel that was a truly captivating experience from beginning to end. I adored the slick and intelligent blend of mythology and contemporary themes, creating a narrative that captures contemporary YA readers but also feels suitably grand in its proportions as it resonates with the struggles and triumphs of the human condition. Valentine's journey is both fantastical and deeply relatable, exploring themes of redemption, identity, and the interconnectedness of lives through emotively penned narrative moments and some really excellent speech and thought presentation. Thanks to the confidence and delicacy of the author's narrative structure, this novel goes beyond the simplicity of a modern retelling to produce a poignant reflection on the consequences of one's choices and the transformative nature of redemption, all in a format that is easily digestible and still action-packed for its target YA crowd. Overall, I would not hesitate to recommend The Penance of Valentine Cash for fantasy fans everywhere, and I cannot wait to see what more this talented author has to offer." — Five Star Review from *Reader's Favorite*

"Good God was this book utterly amazing! I honestly picked it up on a whim, and I cannot express just how delighted I am that I did so, because I loved it so so much! The story of an up-and-coming musician forced to complete a series of harrowing tasks to earn a return to life, The Penance of Valentine Cash is the Americana urban fantasy I didn't know I needed until I read it. Despite the clear inspiration from The Twelve Labors of Hercules, this book draws from an eclectic mix of American folklore for its fantasy elements, which is an angle that I surprisingly don't see too much of these days! Not to mention it's backed up with fantastic characters, with the titular Valentine Cash being an absolute standout. Her grappling with not only the supernatural challenges she has to undertake, but also with the weight of her actions and whether or not she really deserves a second chance is the core of the story, and it makes the magic feel so much more real! And shout out to Six, who is the best personification of an American highway I've ever seen in fiction. All in all, an utterly enchanting novel, and one that I heartily recommend!" — *NetGalley Reviewer*

"This debut author knows how to write books! Incredible storytelling, the characters were so well developed. I even shed some tears. I read this in less than a day. It flowed so beautifully. Very very good." — *Goodreads Reviewer*

"Such a great story and loved the characters, especially Six. I was rooting for her more and more as the story went on... definitely worth the read." — *Goodreads Reviewer*

"This book was WOW!... The adventure, the fear, the courage and self doubts that Valentine experienced...the unlikely relationships she made while on penance...made her a legend in my eyes... and also very human. I had cheered for her, feared for, wept with her and my heart breaks for her and with her." — *Goodreads Reviewer*

**Click here to order your copy today!**

## Coming Soon: A Strange Affinity

**In the Wild West, magic is real.**

When two strangers arrive in her small town along the Oregon Trail, Gloriana Rue learns that she has the magical ability, called an Affinity, to manipulate metal. Even more shocking, her late mother was a renowned magical scholar but had abandoned the world of Affinities. Desperate to know more about this secret past, Glory agrees to attend an academy for magicians to find answers.

Soon immersed in train robberies, a magical education, and adventure, Glory begins to find her footing in this dangerous new world. Until she stumbles upon a disturbing discovery: A killer is hunting magicians throughout the American West — and he's getting closer to her new home. Glory must glean the truth hidden in her mother's long held secrets to save her community before it's too late.

*A Strange Affinity* is a young adult fantasy novel set in an alternate nineteenth century American Wild West. Fans of *Vengeance Road* by Erin Bowman, *Revenge and the Wild* by Michelle Modesto, and *Upright Women Wanted* by Sarah Gailey will love this novel about found family, adventure, and magic.

Don't miss this magical tale where
*True Grit* meets *A Deadly Education*!

Available March 26, 2024.
**Pre-order today!**

# EXCERPT: A STRANGE AFFINITY

## Chapter One

Death and a blackbird were her only companions on the quiet plain.

A weather-worn, wrought metal fence encircled the town's lone cemetery, guarding the dead from the living who resided in nearby Agate Creek. Glory stood before the patchy dirt that covered her father's grave. Five months of a cold winter combined with a late start to spring hadn't done much to disguise the ground into which her father was welcomed last September.

Next to his grave lay the healing sod that marked her sister's plot. Both had simple grey stone slabs etched with the right names and dates, more permanent than many of the wooden markers throughout the cemetery. Lily's had a floral motif on her headstone, bluebells and forget-me-nots. Glory's father had insisted on it. In contrast, her father's headstone was plain. Her mother was absent, having died just after Lily had been born. She had been buried in another town.

*Lily would like the bluebells*, Glory thought.

Her blackbird companion fluttered to a different headstone, distracting Glory. She knew Mrs. Buntwell expected her to return to the general store soon, but Glory didn't move. Instead, she glanced around. Young maple trees hugged the metal fence along the north and east side of the cemetery. No wind cooled the sunshine that shimmered down upon her.

She watched as a procession of mourners and a small wagon with a closed pine casket made its way along the carved dirt road. Glory didn't recognize any of the tired faces, made further haggard by grief. Judging by the dated church clothes and the dilapidated shoes on some members of the procession, Glory suspected that another wagon train bound for the Oregon Trail must have stopped in Agate Creek, which rested near the halfway point on the journey, to bury their dead before moving on.

Glory turned to leave. She had done enough grieving to know that she preferred privacy for her tears. She didn't want to intrude on another's grief.

*Funerals should not occur on sunny days.*

Her blackbird companion had long since left, and the procession was at the final bend of the road that led to the cemetery. She could hear the creaking of the small, uncovered wagon that carried the casket. Glory stepped through the gates and as she did, something caught the corner of her eye: Two men stood near the graves of her father and sister. She stopped and stared. Tailored clothes, new boots, well-groomed blonde hair, and similar enough in build and appearance to be family. Glory watched them for a bit longer, and then turned away.

*Visitors*, she thought. *No business of mine.*

***

The walk from the cemetery into town was longer than most people liked to travel by foot. Many chose to ride or to drive a carriage out here. But Glory welcomed the exertion in exchange for the quiet. Late spring had softened the flat prairie, and the well-trod roads were lined with wildflowers and weeds. In full daylight, the flat lands stretched out from the town and the cemetery as far as one could see. No hills and few trees broke the visual monotony. During the summer, the haze of hot days across the prairies made her feel as though life were an illusion that would wink out at any moment. The snowbound winter days were just as bad, the land carpeted with white and grey and dark. Glory liked spring best. Fresh buds and new greens created bright and irregular textures that she trusted better than any other season. It seemed bumpy, rocky, *real*.

A small town situated off an Oregon Trail route, gossip was that Agate Creek would not remain small for much longer: The arrival of the railroad companies just over a year ago, coupled with the recent discovery of a tin mine located to the southwest, made the town attractive to merchants, miners, and even the families who'd had to abandon the arduous journey to Oregon. Some of the main streets in town were cobbled now, and it seemed to Glory like new buildings grew overnight.

Soon enough, Glory arrived at the outskirts of town. She walked down the wooden planks that fronted the new businesses. These shopfronts had fresh paint not yet faded by the combination of wind, sun, and dust. A gaily painted sign in the window of an otherwise empty shop, garnished with bright blues and yellows, prompted her to stop. Glory stopped to read:

"Healing, Herbs, and Health: Receive Guidance from a Magician with a True Affinity for the Healing Arts. Proprietor: Monsieur Cuthorpe. Grand Opening Soon."

A new magician in town? Intrigued, Glory peered into the window but only saw empty shelves that lined both sides of the narrow shop. A counter stood at the back of the shop and dozens of crates and trunks were stacked on the floor. Nothing stood out as striking or unusual. It seemed so...uneventful. Rather like her Mrs. Buntwell's general store, or perhaps a pharmacy. This *was the magician's shop*? Glory leaned back, disappointed.

"Good afternoon, Miss Gloriana."

A deep voice interrupted her thoughts. Glory groaned inwardly. Just her luck to have the pastor of the Agate Creek Church catch her peering into a magician's shop. She turned to face him.

"Good afternoon, Pastor Brooks." Glory gave a half-hearted smile – and braced herself for the forthcoming lecture.

"I hope you have better endeavors to occupy your time, Gloriana." Despite his youth, or because of it, the dark haired and unmarried pastor had narrow-minded views about women's roles in the world, the proper behavior for the citizens of Agate Creek, and the recent legality of magic in the United States and all affiliated Territories. Glory disagreed with Pastor Brooks on the first two issues, and thought he lacked a sense of adventure with regards to the latter.

"I'm simply curious," Glory replied. "Isn't it exciting, to have a new magician in town?" Glory knew that she stirred the hornet's nest and was promptly rewarded when Pastor Brooks furrowed his brow.

"Exciting?" he echoed, doubt and an edge of anger clear in his voice. Pastor Brooks shook his head. "Regardless of our nation's regrettable decision to make magic legal, magic remains forbidden by God." He smiled but the warmth didn't reach his eyes. "I hope you agree."

Glory smiled with her teeth. "But I thought magicians were born with their abilities?" She furrowed her brow in pretense, as if puzzled. "Those who are born with magic can't help having it, right?"

Now it was Pastor Brook's turn to sneer. "That remains a matter of debate. It still is against God's word, and His law transcends that of man."

*What an ass.* Fortunately, she was interrupted before she could respond aloud.

"Pastor Brooks and Miss Gloriana! What a delight to see you both this afternoon." The syrupy sweet trill came from a young matron who was popular in the Ladies Circle within the church; Glory only knew her from afar and had seen enough that she was reluctant to know more. As the young woman swayed up to them, and the town clock tower struck on a new hour, Glory seized her chance. With a few further pleasant noises and an entreaty to see her next Sunday from Pastor Brooks, Glory escaped down the wooden walkway.

Glory shook her head to herself. She couldn't stand the devout young man. He had arrived a year earlier upon the prior pastor's death from a rattlesnake bite. Brooks had endeared himself to the more conservative families in town, and of course, none of these illustrious lineages had a magician within their ranks. Glory thought that these same families would likely disown a member, or hush up the manifestation of an Affinity, despite the United States government having made magic legal twenty years ago.

*Too concerned about propriety and appearances.*

A twinge of disappointed pinged through Glory. Though magic had been legal in her lifetime, and the right to practice magic protected, Glory had never met anyone with an Affinity. She had only heard that those with magic often applied their skills with one eye on the social temperature of the surrounding neighborhood. Religious tolerance for magical practices varied greatly, and many pastors, priests, and church elders frowned upon it. Often called the devil's work – *Even in 1886*, Glory thought, rolling her eyes – magic still had the stench of the unfamiliar and the dangerous for many. Most magicians felt safer in the cities, as some were driven out of the smaller towns and more rural areas.

Glory continued down the wooden esplanade and thought more about the new magician. *Maybe something interesting will finally happen in this town.*

Available March 12, 2024.
**Pre-order today!**